Praise for the John Linwood Grant's
A Persistence of Geraniums

"The stories in John Linwood Grant's *A Persistence of Geraniums* would not have been out of place in the pages of Pearson's magazine, alongside those of E.F. Benson. Indeed, it's easy to picture Benson reading Grant's stories approvingly. Grant skillfully evokes the sensibility of Edwardian Britain in a series of supernatural tales distinguished both by their elegance and by their wit."

—John Langan, author of *The Fisherman*

"In the stories collected here, Grant has managed to create one of the most interesting and exciting characters to come along in some time: the enigmatic assassin, Mr. Dry. Possessed of great criminal and murderous ability, Mr. Dry is a power unto himself, moving like an unstoppable force of nature against evil and, sometimes, justice. These stories present a writer who has a strong narrative voice, a keen mind and a masterful ability to create characters that stay with the reader long after the book is finished. Brilliant and exciting, my only regret upon reading these stories is that I cannot hire Mr. Dry to remove Mr. Grant so that I could steal these tales for my own."

—Sam Gafford, author of *Whitechapel* and *The Dreamer in Fire*

"Each of the stories in this collection is utterly steeped in that bygone era, both in terms of setting and style. It's one thing to believably transport readers through space and time to immerse them in a vividly realized historical environment. It's a whole 'nother thing to be able to meaningfully evoke the tone and language of the writers from that period, all while still retaining a viably modern sensibility and enough of a unique voice to rise above mere facsimile. Through seven tales of mystery, murder, madness, and mysticism (plus a couple conversational interludes), Grant does exactly that."

—Ginger Nuts of Horror

To understand more fully events hidden from the POV character, Catherine Weatherhead, in this story, please read the companion novel, *The Prostitute's Price*, by Alan M. Clark, also available from IFD Publishing.

The Assassin's Coin

a novel by John Linwood Grant

IFD Publishing

P.O. Box 40776, Eugene, Oregon 97404 U.S.A.
www.ifdpublishing.com

The Assassin's Coin
Copyright © 2018 by John Linwood Grant

Cover art, Copyright © 2017 Alan M. Clark
Interior illustrations, Copyright © 2018 Alan M. Clark

ISBN: 978-0-9996656-2-6
Printed in the United States of America

Thanks to my partner Sarah, who may have been driven insane by my late career choice, Sam Gafford, whose excellent 'Whitechapel' reminded me this sort of thing could be done, James Bojaciuk who first believed in 'Tales of the Last Edwardian,' Elizabeth Engstrom for her valuable comments, and of course Alan M Clark, who initiated this entire project and introduced me to the real Mary Jane Kelly.

AUTHOR'S NOTE

I have no illusions about violent crime, no morbid fascination with the terrible things which have been done to innocent people throughout the centuries. Nor do I confuse fact with fiction. In my series of linked stories, 'Tale of the Last Edwardian', I explore many dark and strange areas, but the subject in this novel was the hardest to enter. There is no twisted romance, no cunning or esoteric mystery, about the person often referred to as Jack the Ripper. That person killed women who could not defend themselves and who did not deserve their violent ends.

I was also resident in West Yorkshire during the activities of the man who the press called 'The Yorkshire Ripper', and experienced directly the impact on the people around me. Once more women walked in fear, and once more, there was no aspect of the affair which held exciting mystery. It was grim, and unpleasant.

But this book is fiction, however tightly historically based. It only came into existence because of Alan M Clark's extraordinarily detailed and sympathetic series on the women who were murdered in Whitechapel during 1888. I could not have written it without knowing that we shared an equal distaste for the Whitechapel Murderer as a figure. And in keeping with Alan's approach, I quite deliberately chose to see the events of the period from the viewpoint of a strong female protagonist, Catherine Weatherhead.

As for the other major figure in this book, Mr Edwin Dry, you must choose how you see him. Other readers have pointed out, from examining his previous excursions, that he is not even an anti-hero, with some charismatic trait which endears you. He is, and knows he is, merely Mr Dry.

The Deptford Assassin.

This is Catherine's story, and that of women finding ways to survive—her cousin Clarissa, old Mrs Hollis, the resourceful Mrs Bessovitch and others.

It is also, in part, Mr Dry's story.

Nothing in this book belongs to Jack the Ripper, and if you take anything away, I hope that it will be Catherine's determination, and Edwin Dry's judgement on the weak and warped man who did such harm.

—John Linwood Grant
Yorkshire, UK

WEST HAMPSTEAD

↑ MUSWELL HILL ↑ HORNSEY

ISLINGTON

CLERKENWELL
SMITHFIELD
HOLBORN

BLACKFRIARS

KNIGHTSBRIDGE

WESTMINSTER

VAUXHALL

CHELSEA EMBANKMENT

LONDON AND

↑
-N-

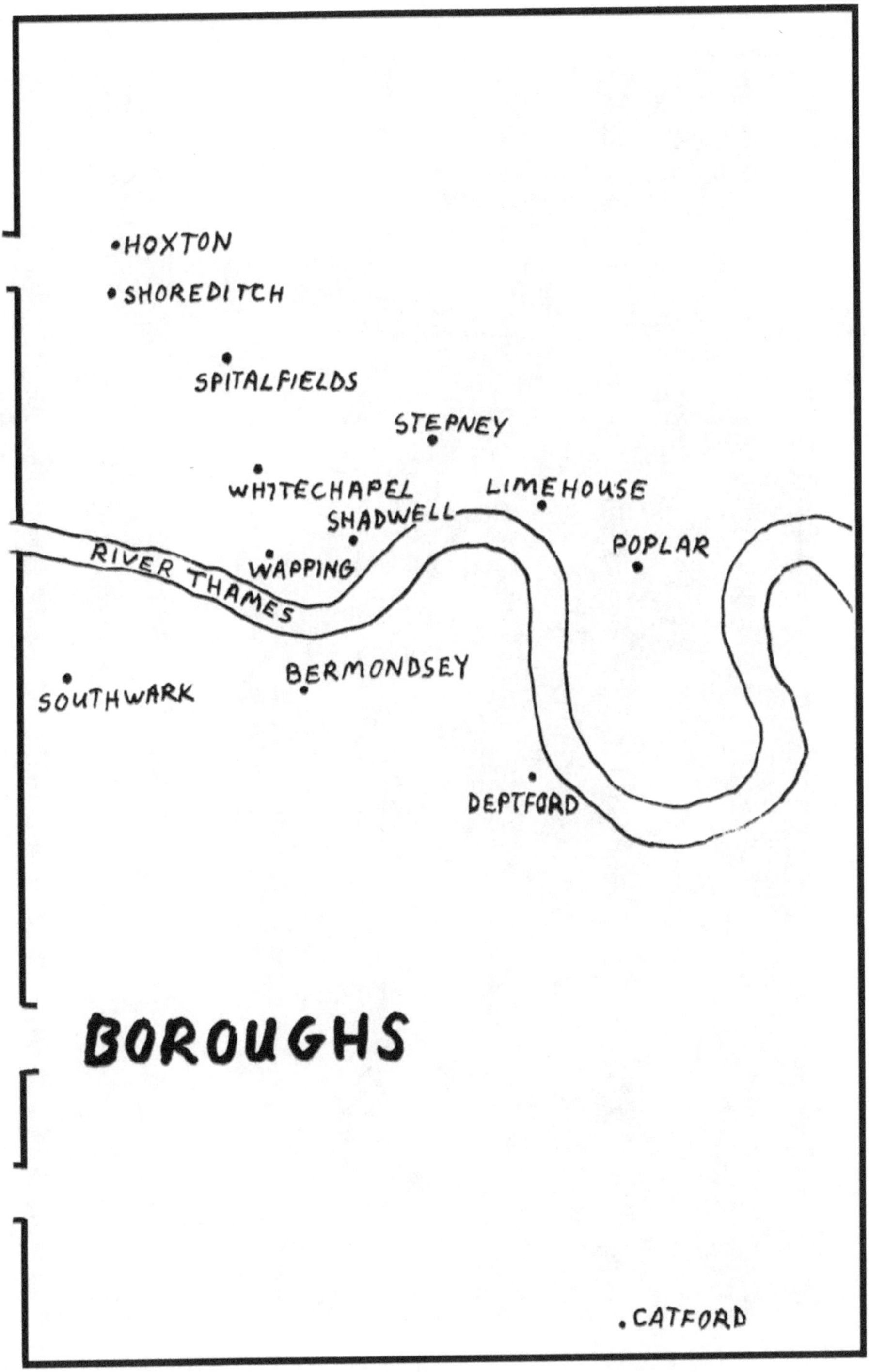
HOXTON
SHOREDITCH
SPITALFIELDS
STEPNEY
WHITECHAPEL
LIMEHOUSE
SHADWELL
POPLAR
WAPPING
RIVER THAMES
BERMONDSEY
SOUTHWARK
DEPTFORD
BOROUGHS
CATFORD

The Assassin's Coin

a novel by John Linwood Grant

I FD
Publishing

Eugene, Oregon

PROLOGUE

Keighley, West Yorkshire, January 1876

The girl turns, whimpers.

The attic room is hot and airless, and a sheet, damp with sweat, clings to her legs. It twists around bone-thin ankles and long feet which might be cleaner; it confines her.

She twists onto her back. Her eyes are the shining grey of the ice on Redcar Tarn, high above the town, and they are wide open. The girl, however, is asleep—or beneath sleep, her mind wandering through phantasy and fever. The Night Mare presses on her chest.

She should be seeing the plaster which flakes on the ceiling, the patch where a rotting roof joist shows through. Instead, she is elsewhere...

Another room nearby, a plain enough room with solid, old-fashioned furniture. Dark furniture, crouching against brown walls—dressers, side-cupboards, and crooked, over-stuffed chairs.

And in the centre of that other place, a man's hands tighten.

The hiss of the woman's breath is gaslight and regret, forced through a windpipe that will soon have no purpose.

Again the man's hands tighten.

The legs of the woman spasm and jerk under a plain grey dress, their movement mirrored in a girl's bedroom, not so far away. And then they stop. Two bodies relax.

In the small attic, grey eyes close and true sleep comes at last. The girl presses her face into her pillow, and draws in deep, slow breaths.

But now the woman's eyes—hazel-brown—are wide open. They will stay that way until rough thumbs close them.

This night will be remembered...

The Assassin's Coin
PART ONE

CHAPTER ONE

Islington, September 1886

His hands are not large, though they have an unusual span and the fingers are most dexterous. He knows each sinew, each vein, even the slight resistance to torsion at the base of one thumb. That is being addressed. The nails are pared clean at every opportunity. He knows that you do not let your tools, your instruments, fall into disrepair.

His hands are the cornerstone of his trade, and what they might hold is largely irrelevant. Wire, blade or gun; a boatman's hook or a carpet needle. The requirements change with every commission. If necessary, his hands can do the work themselves, without further assistance.

And it is work. It is his only claim on the city.

From spattered fluids on brothel sheets to the brandy which drools from a politician's lips; from the fine walks of St James's Park to the Southwark stews—it does not matter to him where they live, or how they comport themselves. Vice does not make a target, nor Virtue a shield. Let bishops debate whilst the workman does his job.

London town must provide...

The way down to the cellars was poorly lit, the steps old and heavily scrubbed. Madame Rostov moved as quickly as she could, aware of the urgency, but nevertheless she halted at the foot of the stairs, unsure. The air held a smell that was visceral, crouching like a beast in its own right between the low ceiling and the stone-flagged floor. All was clutter, and only two small windows let in a glimmer of daylight. One of the pale muslin blinds was speckled with blood.

The woman with the cleaver seemed oblivious to her arrival. The blade slammed down, the fat of the woman's arms shook with the impact, and some slippery piece of flesh was tossed onto a tray more bloody than the window blind.

Madame Rostov coughed. "I need..."

The woman in the cellar turned with remarkable speed for her bulk, cleaver in hand.

"Who are you, then?"

"Mr Carlton returned early, to pick up...papers, maybe? I was told I needed to..."

Understanding softened the lines on the woman's face. She put the cleaver down on the block, and wiped her hands on a stained apron.

"Keep out of the way? Sorry, madam. Can I make you a cup of tea?" She looked almost apologetically at the chopping boards, trays and pans behind her. "The master is perticular about his cuts, and the butchers round here can't tell a Barnsley chop from a short rib. Has me at it, the master does, to put their mess right."

"You must be Mrs Greath, the cook."

"I am so. I heard we was having a visitor, one of them spiritualist ladies. I suppose that—"

"Madame Rostov."

"Pleasure, I'm sure." The cook wiped her hands, and went to place a kettle on the range in the corner. "Not that I hold with it, especial, but the master—he's always railing against such things. No wonder the mistress wanted you down here. You'd think we had them Paris postcards in the house, to see his face when the mistress gets out her pamphlets."

Madame Rostov looked around. Underneath it all, there was an order of sorts. Mrs Greath might be accounted a creative rather than a traditional cook.

"Don't mind the mess on the blind," the woman said. "I had an accidental with some liver, getting the stringy bits out for the cat."

"Yes, I see."

In the house above, a door slammed.

"There," said Mrs Greath. "He's off again, and the coast's clear. I'll bring the tea up. Maid's day off." She winked. "She'd tell the master what had been going on, as soon as scratch her surface, she would."

Elspeth Carlton, thin and breathy, was already on the stairs. "So sorry, Madame. My husband has certain views—"

"Mrs Greath tells me."

"Do come up to the parlour."

"Tea's on its way," the cook called after them.

The large parlour was no brighter than the cellar kitchen, but it smelled of lilac water, and the blinds were clean. The gloomy paint was broken up by a mismatched selection of photographs in silver frames, and an excess of white lace doilies and silhouette portraits. A table and four seats had been prepared in the centre of the room; a small harmonium stood ready by the empty fireplace.

"An intimate sitting," said Mrs Carlton. "My cousin Grace, and a Miss Cobb from the next street. They are on their way."

Madame Rostov inclined her head, a tangle of black hair almost hiding her eyes.

"They are believers," added the hostess.

Small talk accompanied some excellent almond biscuits and a cup of tea which seemed to bear the tang of raw liver. A faltering discussion on Blavatsky's *The Secret Doctrine*, which Mrs Carlton clearly had not read, was relieved by the arrival of the others.

"We have an hour and half, at least," said the hostess as she let them in.

Madame Rostov was grateful that Mr Carlton's disapproval meant for a short session, fitted in before he arrived home for an early dinner. Miss Cobb, a squint-eyed woman in an expensive dress, sat at the harmonium and sought to raise what she called "sympathetic vibrations." What the indifferent playing might be sympathetic with, Madame Rostov forbore to say.

And then they were to table, the spiritualist opposite her

host, the others eager on either side.

"Does someone—something—always come, madame?" asked Grace Carlton, a mouse voice in a mouse body, as thin as her cousin.

"No. But I feel that you three ladies, you understand the ways of the Aether. I am being hopeful." There was a touch of the East European in her voice, as if despite her proficiency, English might not be her first language.

In the half-light through the blinds, Madame Rostov threw back her head and began to speak, a low mutter which clearly conveyed nothing to the others. The harmonium creaked, making Mrs Carlton jump.

"Will you come to us? There are those here who would have word of the Beyond."

"We are supplicants," added Elspeth Carlton. "Only guide us to—"

Madame Rostov cleared her throat before the woman could continue. "A dear one is near," she said. "He—no, she—flutters on the edge of this place, anxious to move on. A mother, old with care…she waits."

Grace Carlton gripped her sister's hand. The room darkened, though it might have been the passing of an omnibus outside.

"My mother, Elspeth's aunt, yes. Is she here?"

"She waits. A name…Meg?"

The three women craned forward, gripping each other.

"Aunt Margaret." Mrs Carlton's breathy voice was almost a whisper. "Uncle Edgar called her Meg."

Miss Cobb's squint intensified. "But surely your aunt died five years ago, Elspeth."

"She waits," repeated Madame Rostov. "There is a task undone."

"Can we speak to her?"

The spiritualist turned her head slightly, towards Miss Cobb.

"Five years, yes. Her earthly voice is gone—only her will remains. And those who should remember her…"

Grace Carlton gave a small shriek. "We haven't been to the grave this year, or left flowers for her. Oh, Elspeth, we forgot!"

Her cousin paled. "That must be it. The 'work undone.'"

"Those who have passed must be remembered." Madame Rostov lowered her chin to the dark silk which covered her breast. "Remembered. Ah, now that you understand, she has gone."

"I shall take a vase to Aunt Margaret's grave tomorrow." Mrs Carlton said, decisive.

The four of them sat in silence for some minutes. After an awkward cough, Miss Cobb spoke up.

"Madame Rostov, are there others who might come to us today?"

A keen observer might have seen a twitch of irritation at the corner of the spiritualist's mouth. Beneath the unruly black hair, sharp blue eyes regarded the woman with less than charity.

"I will ask," she said. "But if the vibrations are no longer right, do not expect too much."

Her eyes closed; her head came forward. Madame Rostov's breathing slowed—long, deep intakes and a wait before her hair fluttered with the exhalation.

"A man."

The women waited.

"Grandfather, perhaps," said Mrs Carlton, when nothing else was forthcoming. "He was—"

The spiritualist gave a shudder, half-rising from her seat.

"A man, and water…"

She could see no one in the parlour, nothing around her, only another place, which had nothing of fanciful Aetheric planes about it.

"A man…a dreadful man with dark intentions…"

The bathroom is spacious, tiled in the Italian manner and dominated by a claw-foot bath of great proportion, dwarfing the slim figure of the occupant.

"Who in God's name are you?" asks the man in the bath, his

hair slick with soap, his left eye half-closed. He places one hand over his half-erect member, the other on the side of the bath, preparing to lift himself.

The visitor steps into the room. Small, careful steps. The air is full of steam, the tiles slippery. He is not a tall man, nor is he as slim as the bather, though his dark suit is well cut. A black felt bowler shades his eyes, incongruous in these surroundings.

"My name is Edwin Dry." An even, neutral tone.

"But what are you doing here? Get out at once, man!" There is a shrill note in the bather's voice.

"I fear, Mr Tether, that you are no longer required."

A small revolver appears in Mr Dry's left hand, which is very steady. He draws a length of soft cotton material from beneath his jacket.

"You're not one of my clients."

"No, I am not. Hold out your arms, Mr Tether."

"I'll do no such thing."

"Then I will have to shoot you in the head, which would be an annoying development. Annoying, but nothing more. Plans can be changed."

Tether trembles, the water slopping from side to side. After a moment, he holds his arms out.

"Why…why are you doing this?"

Mr Dry comes forward, the revolver aimed still at the bather's forehead.

"You are a solicitor, Mr Tether. You are paid to undertake certain tasks, according to your talents. Your work for a Silas Smith, of Chelsea, has become troublesome. And so, you are no longer required."

"But…" Tether watches as the other man works deftly, wrapping the material around Tether's forearms one-handed, binding them gently but firmly together. "Are you to take me somewhere? What is to happen to me?"

Mr Dry pauses, tugging the material a little tighter until he is satisfied. The revolver disappears. He takes off his jacket, and removes his cufflinks, placing them side by side on a washstand. He rolls up his sleeves.

"What happens to us all."

The solicitor does not have time to cry out as Mr Dry grabs his ankles and tugs, sliding Tether down so that his head goes under the water. It is at that point that he tries to scream, but the water is already in his lungs. With his arms bound, the man can only writhe and kick; the grip on his ankles is relentless. Bathwater splashes the tiles once, for a second and then a third time, until Tether is motionless. His face, wide-eyed, open-mouthed, is a mask beneath the water. His erection has passed, and will never return.

Mr Dry bends forward and unwinds the length of cotton, which has left no mark on the man's forearms. He takes a towel and mops the tiles, making sure to leave no boot-print as he works away from the bath. The cotton goes into an oiled canvas bag at his waist; the towel into the laundry basket, beneath others. At the last he retrieves his cufflinks and his jacket.

"Good afternoon, Mr Tether."

The solicitor does not reply.

Madame Rostov stood up, ending the séance abruptly. She pushed aside twitters of curiosity and concern, refused all offers of refreshment.

"A mischievous spirit," she managed to say to the powdered faces around her. "Pay it no heed. But I can do no more today."

Making her apologies, she left the Carltons' house in a rustle of silk, almost forgetting to grab the battered case with which she had arrived.

Away from the house, still unsteady, she checked that she was unobserved and turned into a quiet side street. There, under the shade of a plane tree, she bound back her hair, placed a simple grey bonnet over it, and found a long, light jacket from her case, obscuring much of the black silk that typified Madame Rostov the medium.

Catherine Weatherhead strode more evenly back into the late afternoon traffic, though her heart pounded. Each man she saw, on the pavement, on the omnibus, in shop doorways, was a neat, bowler-hatted figure with murder in his hands.

"It is not true. It is not true," she muttered as she crossed the river, seeking diversion in the sight of the great sluggish Thames.

But she did not believe herself.

CHAPTER TWO

Southwark, September 1886

Some women survived.

They survived despite everything set against them—disease, the injustices of society, and the casual ease with which a body could trip and fall under an omnibus or a carrier's horse. They avoided the blows of a man's grimy fist, the scratch of another woman's claws, and the lawyers of the rapacious rich; they remained strangers to the poorhouse or the prison.

To Catherine, Mrs Bessovitch was one of those women.

Swathed in perpetual mourning, she used black lace and brocade to dissuade gentlemen callers, and sharp glances to see off the few who nevertheless persisted. She flaunted tragic memories of her husband, and when it was useful she shed onion tears for his loss, years long gone, in some distant naval conflict. Only her closest confidantes (and her lodger) knew that Mr Aaron Bessovitch had leaned too far over the rail of the Dover to Calais packet ship whilst inebriated. Tragic, possibly, but not of great value to the Empire.

Catherine looked on her landlady as a safe harbour, and thanked God (with whom she was not overly familiar) for guiding her to Gilda Bessovitch's lodgings in Southwark.

"Madame Rostov, she was success?"

Mrs Bessovitch clattered at the sink, her accent thicker than usual. Catherine knew that she was concerned.

"I...yes, it all went well. At first." She sat down at the kitchen table.

"These ladies, they had doubts about you?"

"It isn't that. I'd done the usual work—picked up details on them from the local shops as myself, gossiped a little. You know."

That part had gone smoothly. It had been easy to check the local cemetery and see that Margaret Carlton's grave was untended. For backup, she had a rumour about the family's time before they came to Islington, and a tale from a garrulous greengrocer. Catherine knew how to read people, without needing her unreliable gift. The Aether did not need to stir itself to satisfy most séance goers.

"So…what is matter?" The landlady peered at a smudged glass, wiping it with her cloth.

"Something…something that reminded me of the past, that is all. It's nothing."

"Da. Nothing, that is always frightening."

They shared a smile.

"I'll tell you some time, Mrs B. For the moment, I should rest."

"No dinner?"

"Later, if I may."

Catherine trudged up the stairs, her feet sore. Her imposture as Madame Rostov, the psychic from somewhere vague in Eastern Europe, involved far too much walking. Hansoms were expensive, on the little she had made so far, and she had always to make sure she wasn't observed in her transition between roles. She had learned far more than she wanted about the streets of London in her first six months. More comfortable boots would have to be her next major purchase.

Her bedroom on the first floor was too tidy. Mrs Bessovitch's work, but she could hardly complain. The rent was modest, nor were there any other lodgers at the moment, which made it a peaceful place.

"Is my home," the landlady said when Catherine asked about this. "If I wish company, I let my rooms. You are company. So…"

In the ancient, creaking wardrobe hung Mrs Bessovitch's cast-offs, ideal for Madame Rostov. Furs—not grand, even slightly moth-eaten, but with the right look for the part.

Old-fashioned clothes, easily tacked (by the landlady) to approximate Catherine's taller, leaner figure.

Madame Rostov had been her landlady's idea, in a sense. Catherine, after her first winter in the capitol, needed shelter. Her savings were low, and previous lodgings had been unsafe, plagued by drunken fights. Then she had seen a notice in the paper. Quiet room available. Single lady only.

She walked to the address in Southwark on a raw March morning, and presented herself. With her black hair in disarray and her face scrubbed red by the wind, Mrs Bessovitch approved.

"You look like good Russian woman," she said as she made them a pot of tea. "I will like you."

"The room is still available?"

"Da. A young woman, she comes but she is pretty. She smiles too much. I do not think she knows life."

"And me?"

"You are not so pretty."

The blunt comment took Catherine by surprise, and she laughed, spilling her tea.

"You see?" said Mrs Bessovitch. "You understand."

When the landlady discovered that Catherine was earning her money, such as it was, as a medium offering herself for sittings and séances, she considered the matter seriously. Questions of spiritualism and psychic matters seemed to be of no interest to her, but she confessed a long love of performance, and the theatre.

"Who is this Miss Weatherhead? She is nobody." She reached into a sideboard drawer, eventually pulling out a sheaf of ancient theatre handbills. "The Flying Farinis. The Great Tai-Kin. Maskelyne the Magician." She waved the handbills at her lodger. "And here is young woman, no one knows her."

"Perhaps I should be Madame Bessovitch, the Russian Mind-Reading Miracle?"

Her landlady frowned. "Name is too long. Bad for spelling, also."

After some days, they settled on Madame Rostov. Catherine was introduced simply as the new lodger to some of Mrs Bessovitch's European friends. Polish women who worked on the markets, other widows whose time was spent laundering or on street barrows. A rabbi from St Petersburg, and a number of small children who seemed to belong to everyone. Some were Jewish, some were Orthodox, which Catherine didn't quite understand. Her landlady didn't make any obvious religious observance.

Catherine learned quickly, picking up useful words, comments on faraway lands—enough to pass casual muster and to know when she was out of her depth. A friend of Mrs Bessovitch had, for a small fee, provided various papers establishing Rostov's credentials, including a forged recommendation from a genuine minor member of the Polish nobility, now deceased.

"It's still easy to be caught out," Catherine admitted one night. "If they ask too much…"

"You have troubled past," said Mrs Bessovitch.

The comment had startled Catherine, until she realised Madame Rostov was the person under discussion.

"Yes," she managed to say, aping a faint Russian accent. "One that I do not care to discuss."

Which was true for both of her lives.

Sleep did not come, not in the wave of exhaustion for which she had hoped. It brushed her, caressed her, but would not stay. Each time she was on the verge of nodding off, she slid into a blur of unwanted visions. Some were nonsense, but of the two particular scenes which came again and again, she saw a man drowning—and a woman being strangled. The former was the session in Islington, turning itself over inside her head again and again; the latter was something she had hoped to bury, to lose sight of forever.

Islington had uncovered it once more.

At three in the morning she got out of bed and paced

around the room for a while, but that was no help. She went downstairs.

The landlady was at the kitchen table, a pan of milk on the stove.

"I hear you walk up there, I think maybe warm drink."

There was a small bottle of brandy on the table, waiting.

"I didn't mean to disturb you," said Catherine.

"Is no matter."

She sat down opposite Mrs Bessovitch, the stone slabs of the kitchen floor a welcome coolness for the soles of her feet. The woman cocked her head, staring.

"Is yesterday, da? When you sit for these people. This 'nothing' you speak of."

"I saw...a death, I think. Images of one, I mean, during the sitting."

"A death. Tch, this is not so much." She stood up and went to fuss with the pan and two large stoneware mugs. Bringing them over, she added a generous shot of spirits to both. "My grandfather, he was shot by Prussians. My father, was a tavern fight. Drunk." She shrugged. "Two of my sisters, they die of cholera, and last month, you remember my friend Yentl Przkowski? She fall on stairs, break her neck."

"That's...dreadful."

"Is what we are. My other sister, she has six children, all healthy, one a doctor. So, I say Tch, we accept it."

"It's not that." Catherine let the brandy ease her. "I 'saw' a murder being committed, as if I stood there in the room."

"Death to come?" Mrs Bessovitch looked more interested. "Now you are, what is word, fortune-teller...clairvoyant! That is it. You know them, these people in picture your head makes?"

"No, not at all. Nor could I tell where this dreadful thing took place, nothing beyond the immediate surrounds. It could have occurred years ago, it could be yet to happen. How can I know? It...shook me."

She described the scene in the bathroom, slowly at first, but the details came back more easily than she had expected. It was as clear to her as if the bathwater was swilling around her feet. She omitted only the names she had heard. Tether. Silas Smith. Edwin Dry.

More brandy found its way into the milk.

"I am not spiritual woman," said Mrs Bessovitch when the story was complete. "Not hearing ghosts or such things. Maybe this is from head of one of your ladies, at sitting?"

"Possibly."

"Katerina, whatever is gift you have, you should trust. You are true cake. Madame Rostov is, what we say, icing. Decoration for ladies and their purses."

Catherine nodded. "I suppose so."

"Anna Bessovitch is like stone, she has no thoughts to give away. So with me, you must listen with your ears. These others, I think their heads are soft, like sponge."

They laughed together.

"I'll try and sleep now."

"Good. I get brandy to myself. And you forget man with hat. What is your tomorrow?"

Catherine winced.

"Family," she said.

Mrs Bessovitch knew enough to need no elaboration.

CHAPTER THREE

Stepney, September 1886

The house where Catherine's cousins lodged had once been as respectable as that of Mrs Bessovitch's, but here the mortar was crumbling, the roof tiles in disorder. The roof itself sagged, making the top floor uninhabitable, and bold red brick had long since blackened. Cramped between other tenement houses in a similar condition, it never failed to depress her by its very nature.

She knocked on the ill-hung front door, and waited. Already she was being noted by passers-by, and she imagined them trying to fit her into a suitable category—tradeswoman or dolly-mop, regular or stranger. The looks were not friendly.

Clarissa Weatherhead answered the door at last.

"Catherine? I did not expect you."

The woman's face was narrow and care-worn. Pale skin clung to high cheekbones and wrinkled around thin lips which never quite closed, making her seem far older than her forty or so years.

"Don't let me disturb you. I merely thought I'd enquire—"

"Come in. She's no better." Clarissa glanced upwards as she ushered the younger woman into a narrow hallway. "She sleeps more today, which is something."

"Might I see her?"

Clarissa smoothed down her patched sewing smock. "If you must."

They climbed the dimly-lit stairs with caution. Catherine could smell the damp, and see faint blooms on the wallpaper where mould was finding its own residence. In places the paper had been scrubbed with some form of bleaching agent, which only served to expose the sad state of the plasterwork beneath.

There were two shabby rooms on this floor, barely habitable. Whilst four people shared the bedroom to the right, the other had only one occupant, the dying matriarch of this branch of the Weatherhead family. Whether this arrangement was out of respect, or fear of disease spreading to the others, Catherine did not know. As Clarissa herself was hardly healthy, she inclined towards the latter.

Levinia Weatherhead lay in relative comfort under the only coverlet in the house, pillows stuffed with rags and off-cuts to prop up her head. Fine grey hair spread in tangles on the patched pillow-cases, and her nightgown, a memory of better days, was in disarray, exposing one shrunken breast. Clarissa hurried forward and re-arranged her mother-in-law's clothes, drawing the coverlet higher.

"Who is there?" A weak, querulous voice from the bed.

"Mama, it's Cousin Catherine, come to see you."

"Joshua's girl?"

Closed eyelids flickered, but did not open. Catherine sat on the edge of the bed, ignoring the tang of sweat and stale urine. She began to smooth out her aunt's hair, but Clarissa stopped her.

"It sets her off," she warned. "The coughing."

Catherine drew back her hand.

"How are you, Aunt Levinia? Comfortable, I hope?"

"I must…have words with Joshua's girl. Before…"

Clarissa leaned closer, cold-faced.

"Before what, Mama?"

But the old lady was asleep again, her breathing ragged. The air was cold, the window-pane cracked. There was no fire in the small hearth.

"I had some good fortune the other day," said Catherine as they went back downstairs. "Mrs Merson wished to be rid of some trifles from her jewellery—paste and the like. I had no use for them, so I sold them to a costumier." She reached into her purse, and brought out three half crowns. "Coal is so expensive now, and with the children, and Aunt Levinia's chest..."

"We manage."

Catherine bit back a retort. "I feel so guilty," she said, "And I'm kept so busy, I can rarely call on the old dear. Please, to assuage my conscience."

Clarissa took the coins, feigning reluctance. "Well, as you say, it is the devil to get good coal. The cheap stuff spits so."

It was a charade all the more painful because both knew the truth of it. Any coal was a stretch for her cousins.

Her entry fee paid, Catherine accepted the offer of a cup of tea, to be taken whilst her cousin continued at her labours, sewing and mending for those who could afford it. Workmen's overalls and aprons were heaped in one corner of the small front room—a bounty from a local factory, Clarissa explained.

"All to be patched by Thursday—at a fair rate, as well. There may be more to follow, God willing."

"That sounds promising."

False smiles flashed between them. They exchanged news, such as they wished to share. The weather had been mild; cheese was not of the quality it had once been. The children, Benjamin and Maisie, were in good health. As was Clarissa's sister-in-law Jennie, who lived with them.

"And how is your Mrs Merson?" asked Clarissa.

Non-existent, Catherine wanted to admit. *Part of our usual game.*

For months she had constructed the pretence that she was companion to Amelia Merson, a widow from Streatham with adequate means. It was a story which gave her both an excuse to visit her relations as little as possible, and a convenient explanation as to how she could offer small but regular amounts towards her aunt's care. Towards the family's care. Most importantly, it allowed her to conceal her work as Madame Rostov from her family—here in London and back in Yorkshire.

"Oh, you can guess," said Catherine. "Temperamental, as

the elderly can be. Why, only the other day…"

An invented tale of marmalade and missing spoons followed, raising the occasional nod from the woman sewing. Her fingers were nimble, but the tips were red and cracked from the work, and occasionally she paused for a hollow cough.

Had Catherine liked her relative at all, she might have felt more pity. The woman had married Catherine's blood-cousin Charles, but Catherine doubted she would ever have become friends with this lean and waspish soul, even if Charles had lived.

The photograph was on the mantelpiece, as always. A plain man, made more interesting by his naval uniform. A little old for a lieutenant, a place-holder rather than a climber. As an officer aboard HMS Penelope, on Harwich guard-duty, he had provided for his family and engendered moderate respect. And though Charles had been eighteen years Catherine's senior, she remembered the young man who played hoops with her when she was a child. The young man who had slipped her toffees during occasional visits to Keighley, despite her father's disapproval. He had seemed more handsome back then.

"I shall never forgive any of them," said Clarissa, following the direction of her cousin's gaze. "Caille, the business partners, the lawyers."

Spoiled rations had killed Lieutenant Weatherhead the year before. War and the perils of the sea had spared him; the shoddy practices of a victualling company had ended him. One of the many companies of Frederick Caille, a name which was spat out at Brantridge Street.

"Not a shilling, not a penny did we see. Not even an expression of regret."

Catherine, who had heard the tale many times, nodded vaguely, her eyes still on the photograph. His half-pension barely fed and clothed the surviving family. The buckled silver frame, the only thing of value in the house, would be the last thing Clarissa would sell. Catherine gave her that—Clarissa retained some genuine affection for her dead husband. Or defiance in the face of the family's misfortune. It might also have been defiance.

She finished her cup of tea, placing it noisily back on the saucer. She needed to get away from this place.

"I am so very sorry—you know I am."

"Charles was fond of you," said Clarissa, but the words were tight, ungenerous, from those lips.

"And I of him…of you all." She added the second part, the lie, because it was what she had learned to do. "I fear I need to get back to my own work."

The other woman titled her head, eyes narrow. "She has nothing to leave you, you know."

They stared at each other, and then the older woman lowered her head.

"That was wrong of me," she said.

Silence paced the cluttered parlour, inspecting the cobwebs, until Catherine shuffled her feet.

"I could stay and sew with you for a while, if that would help."

"We both know that you're no seamstress." The shadow of a smile came with the words. Clarissa stood up, and they walked to the front door.

"Will you write to me if there is any change—in Aunt Levinia?"

"I shall, if I have time. At the post office, as usual?"

"Mrs Merson prefers it this way." Better that than the Weatherheads find out where she really lived, and what she did for those half crowns.

Catherine did not look back to see if her cousin remained at her door, watching. The morning was gone, and so was most of the money from her purse. There would be donations after tomorrow's sitting, if it went according to plan.

If. There were ways to assist the spirits, and it would do no harm to check her homework.

She found an omnibus heading south of the river, and after a short walk, bought a sixpenny bunch of roses from a flower-seller near St John's. Sad, late blooms, but they would serve.

Rain was coming, and the comet-shaped weathervane spun on the spire, high above the streets. Inside the musty church, three or four women were seeing to floral arrangements. The mid-week changeover, an ideal time for talk. It was her second, carefully planned visit.

"Hello, dear," said a woman by the font. "Nice to see you back."

Catherine held out her own floral donation and made over-kind comments about some of the others. There was a hierarchy here, and a set of rules more closely adhered to than those of a palace. Modesty, and open ears. She accepted a few menial tasks, as befitting a relative newcomer, and listened as closely as she could.

Confounding her drab initial appearance, the short, round Mrs Glebe, in her second-hand clothes, was a mischievous woman. Her eyes were sharp, and her smile gave her face its own attraction. She was a fine source of local gossip, and had no fear of listing the various peculiarities of her neighbours.

One of those neighbours was a "too good for her own cat" spinster who had engaged Madame Rostov to sit the following evening. Miss Bournelle had bunions, a rebellious cook and a niece in India. By offering to fetch a fresh pail of water, and by assisting with certain minor arrangements of stems, Catherine soon had Miss Bournelle's details fixed, with one or two corrections on what she had heard during her last visit.

These details were the meat and drink of the jobbing medium, unless she or he were too proud to have a little earthly assistance. The name of the niece's milliner in London; an unfortunate incident with a dog-trap some years ago, and more of Miss Bournelle's medical history than might be had from a personal physician, were all offered gratis by Mrs Glebe over an hour's work in the church.

"She 'as one o' them mediums coming t'morrow," Mrs Glebe confided. "A Roosian, or somethink like."

"Really?" Catherine snipped a dying rosebud from its stem.

"'Struth. Mind you, many o' them's no better than swindlers. Tell you any old tale, they will, 'bout Uncle Alf meaning to leave 'is will in the sideboard, but being mistook of 'isself, like."

Catherine laughed.

"I'm sure you're right, Mrs Glebe. Let us hope that dear Miss Bournelle has more sense than to fall for any old nonsense."

Counting her time well-spent, she made her apologies and quit St John's to face the bluster of rain outside. A September shower, not yet cold enough to trouble, and an easy walk back to Mrs Bessovitch's. Yet as she faced the grey pall of rain, her good humour failed her.

Aunt Levinia would die soon. Clarissa and Jennie would lose the force which had driven them for the last year and a half; poor Benjamin and Maisie would be stripped of another face they knew.

She slowed, the rain soaking her coat, and her mind in conflict.

To flee the North, having managed to escape expectations there, only to end up with ties here in London, seemed unfair, unjust. It was her own fault, in part. She had looked up her cousins when she first arrived, not knowing the precise details of their circumstances, only that Charles was dead. It had been intended as a politeness, and no more.

That first sight of the decrepit house on Brantridge Street, an address which meant nothing to her beforehand, had told her much. Matters had not improved when she stepped inside and learned how low this branch of the family had sunk, for it was then that affectionate memories of Charles had trapped her...

A bicyclist swerved across her path, swore, and then apologised as he careened on down the street. Southwark reared around her, churches and tenements challenging the pewter sky. There would be blood-pudding at the lodgings. Dumplings sour with turned milk and caraway; cabbage stewed in butter.

There was no conflict in knowing that you were hungry.

CHAPTER FOUR

Southwark, September 1886

Catherine was relieved that the séance at Miss Bournelle's offered no surprises, no gruesome visions. She played her part as the medium by filtering snippets of what she had heard on the streets and in the church, clamping on to the small slips and betrayals of the old lady's face, the nervous twitch of fingers on hearing a particular piece of information. It was easy enough, with some background, to steer a session in the right direction.

"Your niece reaches for you across the ocean…she has the finest bonnet, trimmed with blue Madras silk, which she so wants to send you…"

Because Catherine had heard that Miss Bournelle loved blue silk, and if a bonnet did ever arrive from India, the entire concept could be put down to Madame Rostov's insights. If it turned out to be red, then there must have been "disturbances" in the Aether. But she had seen into their souls and their desires, obviously. Safe enough ground.

She fielded an enquiry about a dead relative, picking up from the questions put to her by Miss Bournelle and an elderly sister that this relative had not had an easy life. The usual talk of a soul at rest, peace at last, served to meet that one.

During the two hours Catherine spent there, from the first wheeze of a harmonium to the patter of applause for her at the end, she kept herself closed, making no real attempt to use her gift. Islington had disturbed her. She concentrated on performing, and her approach worked well enough.

She left Miss Bournelle's not long after four in the afternoon, and still posing as Madame Rostov, treated herself to half an hour in a nearby ABC teashop. In the busy establishment, her poise and her loose, raven-tinted hair drew attention. The waitresses considered her with respect, and gentlemen touched their hats to her. Settled into a suitable corner-seat, she made a show of placing a book of Russian romantic poetry (barely readable) on the table, and chose to enjoy herself.

It was unfortunate that Madame Rostov took tea with lemon, but Catherine didn't let this spoil the moment. She even ordered cake. Miss Bournelle's had yielded one pound and seventeen shillings, and a recommendation to a Miss Chambers, who apparently dwelled in far fancier circles of society. A week's wages, if she were careful. From this she had to maintain her appearance and standing as a medium—and pay out the occasional gratuity to garrulous parlour maids and other servants or tradespeople. Of the remainder, some had to be put aside for the Weatherheads. All went down in her pocketbook at the end of each week. Part of her was still, reluctantly, a merchant's daughter.

Prices in the capitol were steep compared to her home town, and she had to rely on donations at the end of each sitting. Such donations were not always forthcoming—and there was always the tiresome game of pretending not to require anything.

Catherine had "seen" things since she first bled. There had been, with one terrible exception, little sense to the visions. One month it might be women sewing in a house she did not know; the next, nothing—or the sight of a dead bullock being dragged from the canal. What she saw was unpredictable, never under her control. At first it had seemed normal. She had assumed other people were the same—until children of her own age pulled away, older ones mocked her, and her father began taking his belt to her for talking "nonsense."

Keighley taught her not to mention what she saw.

As she slid unhappily into her twenties, serving in one of her father's shops, cooking and cleaning at home, she grew restive. Rebellious, he called it. Her initial idea had been to capitalise on her unreliable talent as an extra source of income, one which she could keep from her parents. Discreet sittings in nearby Bradford or Leeds, possibly, under the guise of a night out with friends.

For weeks she worked her way through borrowed spiritualist literature—her home town was awash with pamphlets and screeds, testimonials to miraculous voices from beyond the grave. Or "Beyond the Veil," as many preferred. She asked questions of those who attended spiritualist groups and chapels, and those who sat awaiting word from planchette or slate.

When much of the literature turned out to be sentimental tosh, fit to be dismissed out of hand, yet even the newspapers reported flights of fancy as genuine cases of ghostly visitation, she came to an unexpected conclusion. If the majority of spiritualists were deluded, mistaken or fraudulent, if not all three, then why miss out on the game?

She had dared a far larger thought. This could surely be done not for pin money, but for higher stakes.

A summer of scheming had tempted her; another autumn of family strife had decided her. Her beloved grandfather had died the year before, and there was nothing in Keighley which was bearable, let alone of any promise. There was only betrayal—and subjugation.

The clink of tea-cups; fragile laughter from another table in the tea-house. Catherine smiled, shaking free of her thoughts. She sipped her tea, and had the pleasant conceit of coming here again one day, and hearing someone say "Why, is that not Madame Rostov herself over there!"

She was working her way up carefully, seeking out better clients as she went. Already her name was being passed round middle-class women who sought, she suspected, release from long boring afternoons. A chance to avoid "good works" and to titillate themselves. A scare or two in the process did no harm, if properly managed.

There were other clients, though, more difficult ones. They mourned lost relatives and friends, and were desperate to make contact with those who had passed on. When she sensed genuine grief, she changed her act. Sometimes she would say, with regret, that she could find no trace of the departed. That not everything Beyond the Veil was open to scrutiny. If delivered in appropriate tones, it usually served.

If not, there were those rare sympathetic—or unguarded— moments when she truly touched the Aether, whatever that was. It was as good a word as any for the cloud of voices and images which brushed her in those moments when her mind opened and she "saw." Occasionally her visions seemed to have relevance to those gathered around the table, but she knew that most were fooling themselves, finding only what they wanted to find.

It was always about the audience's expectations, not her own. At one sitting she had uttered words which meant nothing to anyone there, prompted by the image of a confused child in a crimson dress. Rather than being disappointed, the participants had taken it as a sign of something rare and strange, enhancing her reputation for a few weeks.

All that truly mattered to Catherine was that here was a route to influence and a steady income. In the villages and small towns of her childhood, she had been Mardy Cath, the girl they taunted for her moods and daft thoughts.

In London, she was whatever she chose.

The end of that same week brought a letter. Not to her lodgings, but to the Southwark post office where Catherine collected such mail as there was for either of her personas.

The envelope at the post office was cream and of quality, as was the brief letter inside. She read it twice on a bench outside. "Would Madame Rostov consent to take afternoon tea on Sunday, and to discuss the fascinating subject of spiritualism? A small but attentive audience eagerly awaits such an opportunity."

It was signed by Charlotte Chambers, Miss, and the reply address was a well-to-do neighbourhood near the Chelsea Embankment. The session with Miss Bournelle had borne fruit, and sooner than Catherine expected.

Catherine hurried home, penned her assent, and had it posted within the hour.

Her elation did not last. As night clutched at the lodgings, so she began to drift back to the vision from Islington. Mrs B was out, playing cards with friends, and Catherine was left to toy with needle and thread over the kitchen table. A fur collar was coming loose from one of Madam Rostov's coats. Slightly impoverished was an acceptable look, but down-at-heel was not. Clarissa would have made a better job of it, but Clarissa would have wondered at such a garment being in her cousin's possession.

Without Mrs B's presence, the kitchen was an empty snail shell found in a garden, a reminder only that its true occupant was gone. The Dutch plates on the dresser had no purpose; the pots and pans were too idle. Even the fire which burned in the small range seemed to give no heat. Taking one of her landlady's aprons from behind the door, Catherine put it on. It smelled of cooking fat and caraway seed, of Mrs Bessovitch. Solid, comforting things.

Attacking the sewing, she jabbed herself twice, pinpricks of blood. The thread broke at a crucial moment, and she came close to sewing part of one sleeve to the collar. The hide beneath the fur was stiff and old, a *memento mori* for all small, furred creatures.

Death in all things. She knew what was bothering her. Her mind kept flickering back to Grace Carlton's parlour, and that unwanted, unexpected vision.

The stranger steps into the room. Small, careful steps. The air is full of steam, the tiles slippery. He is not a tall man, nor is he as slim as the bather, though his dark suit is well cut. A black felt bowler shades his eyes, incongruous in these surroundings...

So specific, down to the smallest detail—the gleam on the killer's boots, the careful replacement of his cuff-links...she would not think of it.

Nothing else had come to her since, not the glimmer of such a scene. But that was how it had been before, cut clear as glass; brutal and direct. She tried to tell herself that she was ten years older, and her own woman now.

The sound of the front door opening was a blessed one. She dropped her work and rushed to fill the kettle. Tea for both of them, and perhaps a slice of seed-cake, even though it was late.

"Did you have a pleasant—" Catherine stopped at the sight of her landlady's face as she entered the kitchen. The usual worldly-wise smile was missing.

Mrs Bessovitch placed her large bag down on the sideboard, and drew out a newspaper, laying it next to her bag.

"I have been with many people, Katerina. We play whist, we chatter. Like many birds, we chatter. We discuss what is to become of this fine country; what has become of our old countries." She frowned. "And there is Sadie Gerstein. You know her?"

Catherine shook her head. "You might have mentioned her once or twice. I'm not sure."

"Ah. She cooks for good family, maybe talks too much."

"Has something happened to her?"

The landlady glanced at the sewing, saw that the kettle was on the hob. She hung her outdoor coat on the back of the kitchen door.

"Sadie Gerstein, I say she cooks for good family—in Islington." She handed her lodger the newspaper. "This she had with her."

The Gazette, from the week before, was folded over to page three. "A Tragic Accident" was the main headline there. Catherine read the article beneath, already sure of what she would find.

> We regret to report the loss of a promising young legal mind. On the evening of 3rd September, shortly after ten o'clock, Alfred Turner, manservant to Mr Philip Tether, solicitor, returned from an errand on his master's

behalf to find the house silent. Ascertaining that Mr Tether was not in his bedchamber, Turner was shocked to find his master lying in his bath, deceased.

Thomas Merchant, a doctor resident four doors away, was summoned, but it appeared that death had occurred some hour or more previous to the discovery. An inquest is to be held, but we are reliably informed that the police are satisfied as to the accidental nature of this sad event.

Dr Merchant confides to our reporter that he found no signs of foul play. He conjectured that Mr Tether had fallen asleep during his ablutions, or had suffered some minor fit, and, confused, had failed to prevent his own demise, which came about by drowning. The doctor further warned of the practice of hot baths after the ingestion of alcohol…

She put the newspaper down slowly.

"The address…this is the street behind Mrs Carlton's house. The séance was held that same night, virtually next door."

Next door.

Exactly as it had happened ten years ago in Keighley—a murder, and Catherine open to every sensation. If a man screams ten miles away, you are none the wiser. If he screams on the other side of a brick wall, then you cannot mistake it. For the second time in her life she had been yards from violent death…

"Da." Mrs Bessovitch patted Catherine on the shoulder, and eased her into a chair. "You did see this, like you are camera. It is not dream, or ghost, or thing in other ladies' heads."

"It is worse," said Catherine.

"How so, worse?"

"I know his name. I know who killed this solicitor, Tether."

The kettle hissed on the range; the old house settled around them. It should have been comforting. It was not. The older woman began to tidy away the sewing things, tutting at a loose stitch, avoiding the obvious question.

At last Catherine looked up, and when she spoke, it was close to a whisper.

"Dry. His name is Edwin Dry."

CHAPTER FIVE

Chelsea Embankment, September 1886

Madame Rostov, ice-eyed and haloed by loose black tresses, sat at one end of the long oak table. Her fingers glinted with rings, not ostentatious but curious—dark red enamel on silver for the most part. They had that quality of another place, and might have been seen on hands of painted icons—Greek, Russian, or passed down through some Serbian family of limited wealth but much history. Her lips held the same shade as the enamel—port wine and garnet, not the modern reds.

Her sitters were of a different world. Young and in the latest fashions, sipping sherry and smiling knowing smiles. They seemed slender and bird-like in comparison.

"It is *such* a pleasure," said Charlotte Chambers, heart-faced and open of manner. Loose, straw-coloured ringlets made her seem girl and woman at the same time.

"Oh, indeed." Amelia Baring-Smith, a slim blonde in the same green taffeta as her friend, giggled. "Most of your profession, Madame Rostov, seem so—"

"Plain." Lady Seldon said the word without hesitation or obvious offence, as she might remark on a length of cloth at a haberdashery.

Catherine was at a loss as to how to respond. This was a grander house, and Lady Seldon a far more important figure in society, than she was used to. A liveried butler had welcomed her; a housekeeper in grey silk had shown her into the drawing room. It occurred to her within minutes that she might have made a mistake taking up this invitation.

"But we are entranced by the idea of hearing from beyond the Veil," added Lady Seldon. She brushed back a dark tress which had escaped one of her ornate hair-combs. "Lottie has herself toyed with the board and planchette—"

"And we saw that Indian man on the stage, remember, Lucy?" Miss Chambers leaned forward, elbows on the table like a schoolgirl. "With his levitation, and his 'electric grip.'"

"We did," agreed Lady Seldon. "Mirrors and wires, Harry says."

The three young women were clearly close. They made in-jokes, and finished each other's sentences like sisters. The speed of the invitation meant that her usual research had been rushed. Charlotte—Lottie—Chambers was the daughter of a banker, and by all accounts likeable enough, courted by several young men who saw more than marital partnerships in their futures. Amelia Baring-Smith was a complete unknown.

As she watched them chatter, Catherine considered the third woman to be the most likely to cause problems. She gave Lady Seldon only three or four years on the other women; there was a sharp intelligence there.

"I meet them, of course, these people." Catherine put on a dismissive tone. "They entertain, which is enough for some." Passing entertainment would probably be enough for these three, she thought, but to be lumped amongst the frauds and mountebanks would not suit Madame Rostov. She needed better than that to prosper.

"Miss Bournelle speaks highly of you, Madame Rostov." Lottie contemplated her empty sherry glass. "And a girl always trusts her nanny."

That was something Catherine had missed, nor had Miss Bournelle confided it to her. So the old lady had been Charlotte Chambers's nanny. A very useful connection.

Amelia Baring-Smith giggled again. "My nanny was on the gin most of the time."

Lady Seldon frowned. "I don't think Madame Rostov will be staying long with that sort of talk, Amelia."

Catherine considered it time for Madame Rostov to take centre stage. She turned the conversation to an entirely imaginary occurrence at a séance that had also never happened. Stitching together various stories she had read, and altering a few names, she soon had the three women thrilling to a tale of communications from the dead.

"And this is what you do, Madame?" Lottie handed round a plate of tiny almond biscuits. "You communicate with those who have passed on?"

Catherine offered an expression which she hoped was one of thoughtful consideration, and not hasty invention. "I do not know, Miss Chambers. The nature of that which travels the Aether is beyond me. The departed, possibly; the hopes and wishes of many minds in communion…who can say?"

"The Devil?" suggested Amelia. "I've heard some scorching sermons on the subject of consorting with spirits. The Witch of Endor, and suchlike."

"I am not whispered to by daemons, Miss Baring-Smith, if that is what you imply."

"Oh, no, Madame, I didn't mean…"

In the awkward silence that followed, Catherine stared at her hands, pale fingers pressed against the dark, polished oak. The rings she had borrowed from Mrs Bessovitch glinted in the soft light from outside. What had whispered to her in Keighley, and then in Islington? Who sent such visions, without apparent purpose? She doubted God, and was reasonably sure that the Devil too was a construct of church and chapel. Evil was done by man's hand, and drawn from man's mind.

Lady Seldon coughed. "Amelia is excitable—she reads too much."

"Well really, Lucy!" Amelia reddened. "They're Lottie's books I borrow, after all. Especially those shocking French ones"

All three laughed, and Catherine smiled, not sure of her place.

"Literature is a gift," she said, "As is imagination." She found that she was unsettled—two of the women here at least were much of an age with her, and Lady Seldon could not be thirty. "I am not so old that I do not understand amusement," she added quickly. "If I am too...formal, forgive me."

In the look which Lady Seldon gave her, an intelligence passed between them. Another woman playing a role, then, one way or another.

"We will not ask you to 'perform' for us today, Madame Rostov." Her tone was decisive, but not unfriendly. "It has been a pleasure to meet you, and Lottie was quite right to seek your acquaintance. Would you consider a small sitting, say, next week? The four of us."

She had passed a test, it seemed.

"With pleasure" said Catherine. "I am at your disposal, Lady Seldon."

~⚜~

She was trembling as she waited for the omnibus, hair pinned, and covered with a plain, drab shawl; another shawl hid the fur trim of her coat. Foolish, foolish—and fortunate. She should never have taken up such an invitation without time to study those who would be there. These were not middle-class mourners or bored women trapped at home, but people of more influence, more knowledge about the world. It was conceivable that they had met Polish and Russian nobility, and highly likely that they were far more widely read than Catherine.

As she stepped on the omnibus, a man jostled her—a well-dressed man of moderate stature, with a black felt hat pulled low. She gasped, and then pretended she had come close to losing her footing. The irritated face she glimpsed bore no similarity to that in her Islington vision.

I am not whispered to by daemons.

It was Sunday, and she wished for rest, for sleep, but there was only time to return to her lodgings and change. Out came the dull dress that made her Mrs Merson's dowdy companion, and borrowed rings were slipped into their box. She wiped her lips clean of any adornment, tied her hair into a tight bun, and set out for her cousins, bound by a thread of duty which felt more like a chain with every day. Five shillings she could spare, which would be presented as a contribution towards Aunt Levinia's medicines. Why she and Clarissa had to keep this charade was beyond her. She nodded at Mrs B's talk of lamb cutlets for dinner, and was out of the door again.

This was not a day of rest, whatever the pulpit might demand. Some still worked; others paraded with their sweethearts or paid fawning court to their enemies in tearoom and tavern. The process was much the same. Evening services would begin soon, and churchgoers lined the parks, showing off how proud they were of being so modest and Christian. Across the river, the beggars increased in number the closer she came to Stepney. The blind and the limbless on one side of the street, the palliards with their artfully applied "wounds" and woeful falsehoods on the other.

She knew deception when she saw it. The bent, straw-haired man by the closed butcher's shop—she had seen him changing his clothes in an alley not five hundred yards away, putting torn fustian on over a clean shirt and experimenting with his limp. With a good act, he would make more than a factory worker, and drink it down as quickly as one of them. Two prim, tightly-buttoned women passed him as she watched, tossing coin into his cap. She could shout after them, and explain that the man was a fraud, but what was Madame Rostov?

The sight depressed her, and as she approached the Weatherhead's, she felt the weight of lies on her. Lady Seldon's had been exhausting. Now here she was at Clarissa's door, ready for another round.

It was a relief to have the door answered by Jennie Weatherhead, the same age as Clarissa but with a friendly, honest appeal.

"Why, dear Cathy!" said Jennie, smiling.

They embraced, a reminder that they were blood. Jennie had taken her brother's death badly. The last of the family money had been lost in court fees, and the spirit had left the family. The move away from Harwich, to cheaper lodgings in

London, had stripped Jennie of much of her life. Promised jobs never materialised; Clarissa's health did not improve. It had been a mistake. Laundry and mending was all that was left to them.

"You look well," said Catherine. She did not; she looked drawn and tired, despite her greeting smile.

"Mama has been asking for you."

Catherine paused in the hall. It was an oddly direct thing from Jennie, before they had even exchanged news and pleasantries.

"She is worse." Jennie bit at her lip. "We intended to write to you today."

"The doctors—"

"Have pronounced, Cathy. There is little hope."

In the parlour, Clarissa looked up from her patching a long gingham dress in an old-fashioned cut.

"You've heard?" No warmth, no welcome.

"Yes. I have some money for medicine. I thought—"

"Keep it. Mama won't need it."

Jennie looked shocked at the bitterness in her sister-in-law's voice. "Clarissa! Catherine only seeks to help—you are too harsh."

"I know." Clarissa let the dress fall to the floor. "I know. Everyone seeks to help, but what good does it do, any of it?" She looked to the discoloured wallpaper. "I had my nice little house in Harwich, with flowers at the door. The vicar's wife would call, as if I were her equal, and there would be fresh scones, brought in by a maid..."

"I remember, dear." Jennie sighed.

"That was a home. And all we entertain these days is 'Joshua's child.'" Clarissa spoke in mimicry of the invalid in the room above, her eyes now on Catherine. "Your father should have helped us. He has wealth aplenty, enough to buy this house and raze it to the ground."

"Oh, he does," said Catherine, a red heat coming to her cheeks. "Write to him this day, and be welcome. Let him list the whys and wherefores of how it would not be reet to assist thee." Anger stripped her talk back to the open sewers of Keighley. "Of how we mek our own way, of the perils of charity. Aye, have to it, cousin, and read the sermon he sends instead of coin!"

Panting, she stared the two women down, even as she knew that Jennie deserved better.

"I meant—" began Clarissa.

"You meant what you said." She took a deep breath, seeking to find some composure, to return to herself. "You try your hand with that lying prater of a man. I'd not ask a penny of him, nor take one, neither—not if I was lying like Aunt Levinia in his very front parlour."

The sudden heat was spent. Jennie stood astonished; Clarissa Weatherhead put her long face in her hands and wept. Unable to risk another word, Catherine went upstairs on her own. Where were the children, Benjamin and Maisie? Waiting at some laundry, probably, for mending work to bring back to the house. Or hoping to cadge half-bars of soap, a collar that no one would miss. She would leave them a gift, what change she had—Clarissa could not refuse that.

The smell of the old lady's room was worse than before, the tang of incontinence and something else beneath the lavender water. There was a small fire this time, but Catherine thought she smelled fever. Her aunt's lined face was too pink, her eyes too bright.

"I heard you," she said, struggling to prop herself higher in the bed.

"I'm sorry, Aunt Levinia. My temper."

"The only thing you got from him, God be praised." Levinia wiped discoloured spittle from her lips. "You have your grandfather's sharp mind, and sense of duty. You have his iron in your jaw, and in your eyes. Be thankful."

And with that at least, Catherine agreed.

"You wanted to see me, aunt."

"I did. Time is short—I have weeks left, maybe less." She

waved aside a murmur of denial. "Time is short, I said, and you are the only one to whom I can talk."

"What is it you wanted to say?"

"I want revenge. Frederick Caille caused my son's death, and then laughed at us in court. I was there to see him smirk to his fine and noble friends..." The old woman paused, strained for breath. After a brief coughing fit, she continued. "He brought us to our knees, and lower, yet it meant nothing to him. I doubt he remembers our names. I want the man who killed my son to suffer."

Catherine had often heard it said that one should humour the dying. She didn't subscribe to the belief. What was the value of false hope?

"Aunt Levinia, it cannot be done," she said. "If it could, some other would have done it long before. I hear he has no shortage of enemies and detractors, as he has his allies and lickspittles."

"Reach under my bed. There is something for you there."

Next to the chamberpot sat a large pasteboard box, which Catherine pulled out. It felt as damp as the house, its lid held down with faded blue ribbon.

"I have kept everything," said Levinia. "That which was said of Caille in the papers and the courts. What little I found out, before and after. One day it may be of use—now it is yours."

The wind through the cracked window was an echo of her aunt's laboured breathing. Levinia's eyes had closed, but Catherine felt her still awake.

"Someone might spread calumny, or expose more of his false dealings, I suppose," she said after a minute or so had passed. "They might seek further ways to besmirch his name."

It was possible, though it was a task beyond one in her position. There were people like Lady Seldon, and maybe others, if Madame Rostov was fortunate enough to get closer to them. Should she rise in renown, and be courted...there were surely spider-webs of gossip and influence in those fine drawing rooms, and each wealthy man had some consort to whisper in his ear. Would that make any difference to a man of Caille's standing?

"I charge you, Catherine Weatherhead, to hold this in your mind. If opportunity comes, if Caille's black armour cracks…" The old woman's voice was stronger, steadier, than before. "The grave has not been dug that can hold me, if you deny me this one last hope. I want ruin to come to Frederick Caille, for him to sink to the level he has driven the Weatherheads. Swear."

"No," said Catherine. "I will not swear."

She was astonished to see a weak smile form on her aunt's lips.

"Iron in the jaw, and in the eyes," said Levinia. "You see, that is why I have you alone left to me. Clarissa, Jennie—they would have sworn, and lied, to please me. And it is how I know that you will remember my charge."

"I did not say that," Catherine protested.

"I know. But you will take the box."

Catherine lacked the energy to argue. There would be her cousins to placate downstairs, and then the long journey back to her lodgings in Southwark. The lamb cutlets would be cold. And on Monday, she must find sources which told her more about those three young women of Chelsea, before she sat with them.

"I will call again in the week, Aunt Levinia, if that suits you?"

The old woman coughed, and lay back to rest. She did not answer.

CHAPTER SIX

Chelsea Embankment, October 1886

The first few sittings for Miss Chambers and her friends did not pay, not directly. These were women who bought everything on their accounts at various stylish stores. They carried money when issuing forth to the theatre, or some other performance, but even then they rarely had to open their purses. That was the function of men—to order another bottle of champagne, to offer purchase of a bauble on display in a shop window. Catherine would not have called the women spoiled, exactly. They knew the worth of things, and they knew especially the worth of someone else footing the bill. It placed her in an awkward position, as little able to ask as they were likely to think of offering.

At the same time she was burdened with her aunt's words, and could not help but wonder if she might find out more about Caille through such circles. She was determined not to let the old woman's phantasies of revenge become her niece's obsession, but she could at least be observant. Even banking magnates and wealthy industrialists must make mistakes.

Her own income was still an issue, and so two or three times a week she offered her services to the Mrs Carltons and Miss Bournelles of middle-class London. The lower the status of her sitters, the more they understood that she, too, needed to eat. It was ironic that those who worked hardest would cover her fees willingly, but had the least money available to do so.

Miss Bournelle was content that her dear Lottie was being well served, though the former nanny might have been surprised at the nature of the sittings, which involved more gossip and discussion of literature than it did psychic enquiry.

Catherine, who had been a precocious girl and an avid reader, had heard of few of the books which Miss Chambers held in esteem. Miss Chambers, on the other hand, would have never read *The Rearing of Chicken for Profit*, or the *Creed of the Congregational Church*, not that Madame Rostov could admit to those. Catherine's grandfather had been generous with his books and a man of eclectic tastes, but those tastes had not often run to fiction.

In such fields as spiritualist enquiry, theosophy and similar areas, however, Catherine held her own. Her months of candle-lit reading in her room had not been wasted. She had also devoured those works debunking various mediums and clairvoyants. Each sceptic who penned his exposure of deception added to her own knowledge of how to deceive—and how not to be caught. A recent article concerning dubious practice by Madame Blavatsky had warned her away from posing as a physical medium—the methods were tedious, requiring much training, and could still be detected by a researcher or sceptic with a good nose. Wires, extendable rods and trumpets were not for her.

Catherine's line came from lean hill farmers, men and women able to wrestle down a truculent ram or raise a dry-stone wall, who did their own slaughtering and walked a dozen miles in a morning. Some of that lived on in her, in a strong face and a figure which would never be called dainty. It amused her that even Lady Seldon thought her older than the others, a convenience when she was posing as Madame Rostov.

"You will understand, Madame," Lady Seldon would say, as one wiser head to another. There was potential there, she was sure. She feared, however, that she would have to start dropping hints about the expense of hansom cabs, or tut-tutting at the price of good sherry. She was not a charitable concern.

It was that or "borrow" the occasional silver spoon from Lady Seldon's cutlery drawer.

Early in the month, conscious of her light purse, she

undertook to sit for a Mr Arthur Brompton of Wandsworth. One of Arthur Brompton's sons had died in the Sudan, and she might have rejected the opportunity, but for chance. Elsie Brown, a Keighley neighbour and friend, had two brothers in the South Staffordshires. Both had been on the Nile Expedition the year before, and their welfare had been a regular topic in the Brown household, to the point of tedium. Catherine gauged that she had absorbed enough to produce relevant "colour," should it be required.

She had scant information otherwise. Brompton was, it appeared, a widower, described as mild and pleasant by one of his neighbours (posing as a flower-seller for a few hours gained her this, and a similar character sketch from a local policeman). His maid was sadly recent in her post, and untalkative.

It would have to do.

Number Six Harbut Road, not far from the Wandsworth and Clapham Infirmary, was a pleasant terraced house, well-kept inside and out. The dour maid let Madame Rostov in, taking her outdoor coat and conducting her to a small dining room. Brompton sat there already, in one of only two straight-back chairs at a bare pine table. He rose, and smiled.

"I appreciate your willingness to indulge me, Madame Rostov." A soft voice, London but educated, from beneath a broad moustache which almost concealed his mouth.

"There are no other sitters?" She hesitated in the doorway.

"My maid will be at hand, and the daily is somewhere about, if you fear impropriety?"

His round face had a sort of grave innocence to it, and she shook her head. "It is not a difficulty."

He offered her coffee in a delicate china cup, patterned with sad blue willows, and stood by the bay window, looking out. And he talked, as if they had known each other for many months. He told of his wife, who died suddenly of the influenza two years before, and their relative content throughout their marriage. He told of his surviving son, who worked in France as a junior architect; of his dead son, the eldest, who he had loved. He recited his boy's campaign, and his death by accident at the hands of terrified Anglo-Egyptian regulars.

"Gerald crossed a picket-line without thought, and failed to hear a challenge. The sand and dust had damaged his hearing, you see, Madame—"

"I should not have come." Catherine made to rise. "I cannot help you, sir."

Brown eyes fixed her, brown eyes and a drooping moustache.

"You do not have...the gift? They said—"

"For this, I do not think so."

The small set seemed frozen—Brompton half-turned from the light, his hands entwined; Catherine standing, with one hand on the table.

"I have been fooled so many times," he said. "They say that my boy will speak through them, that he will comfort me. They talk in vague military tones, and whisper that he is near. But he is not."

She sat down again.

"I do not know what will come, Mr Brompton. I do not control...what I see or hear. If there is nothing, or if it makes no sense, you will be grieved."

So much acting, for so long, that she had forgotten what she should feel. There was a sense of unremitting sorrow in the room. It flowed from this small man—a barrow-boy could have read it.

"Will you try?"

No, she meant to say. And in a word, she would condemn him to more searching, to tricksters and black-clad women with clickers and strings hid beneath their skirts, with stolen snippets just like herself...

"Yes."

He sighed with obvious relief, and sat opposite her, holding out his hands.

"That is not necessary."

His moustache twitched, either with humour or disapproval. She ran her fingers through her tangled hair, spreading it on her shoulders. The room was a cabinet, containing only them.

It was Catherine who sat for Arthur Brompton, not Madame Rostov. She closed her eyes, and fed all that Brompton had said to herself, each word, like the mantras of the Eastern thinkers. She remembered Elsie Brown and her brothers, until her tongue was dry with sand, her lips thick for lack of water. Men had died, far away. Gerald Brompton had died, far away…

And she knew him, taller than his father, less full of face. The uniform, down to polished buttons, and a vile-looking, unkempt beast at his side. A camel, though she had never seen one in life, only pictures in a children's book. He had Arthur Brompton's eyes, too sad and soft, and the rifle in his arms was wrong—he was not meant to kill. He missed his home, and his father…

"He should never have gone," she said, almost a whisper. "Only a boy, a gentle soul…"

Brompton was silent. She let the Aether, the terrible flux of minds, thoughts and emotions, take hold of her, lead her through images of young men spilling their blood, their intestines, into the disinterested sand—some trapped in borrowed uniforms, some choking their last in the Arab *jellaba*. White skin burned red, and black skin scarred with anger. All children. All sons to a stricken father…

Was what she saw being drawn from the man before her? From others who had known Gerald Brompton, or from the living brother, so far away? She struggled, screwing her eyes so tight shut it hurt. There was no soul, no voice from beyond, only the wash of sorrow and imagery.

It faded.

"He is dead." The palms of her hands were wet, and she had broken a nail gripping the edge of the table. "He was alive, and he loved you, as you did him. He has passed on beyond our cares." She almost believed the words. "I have nothing else."

When she looked, Brompton seemed radiant, even the moustache failing to hide his smile.

"Thank you, Madame Rostov."

"I have given you little enough."

"You did not lie. You did not lie, which is all I asked of the others, but they could not oblige."

She sat back, drained. "Do you have brandy, Mr Brompton?"

He poured them a glass each, and they sat, watching a blackbird on the tree outside the window. Neither spoke until the bird, startled by a passing cart, flapped off to the south.

"Would five pounds be suitable recompense for your time, Madame?"

She meant to refuse, but thought of the Weatherheads. "It would be more than generous, sir."

"I have no reason not to be." He counted out the notes from a pocket-book, and held them out. "Please take them."

They parted on the doorstep, the man with a lightness to his step; the woman with thoughts she did not like to face.

That night in her room she opened the box from Aunt Levinia. Her attention was not on the task, and she flicked through ragged clippings without great interest. She read of Frederick Caille, noting his many holdings here and abroad, his position on so many boards and committees. She went through scraps she had already seen more than once, scraps which laid out the utter pointlessness of common citizens taking men like Caille to court.

It was depressing. One law in the land, but only truly effective if you owned the land, it seemed.

There was a wife, and a young son. Was she as wicked as the husband? If not, how could she bear to be with such a man? Catherine could almost answer that, she thought. Comfort, wanting for nothing, and access to the finest of the capital's entertainments. Influence beyond that which most woman achieved.

There were, no doubt, many reasons why Mrs Caille might lay herself down next to wickedness.

CHAPTER SEVEN

Southwark, October 1886

He walks in shadow, and shadow serves him. He thinks nothing of thieves and thugees, of miscreants and murderers. He thinks of purpose. His collar is starched, and his cuffs are white as sepulchres; his black bowler is not jaunty, or angled to a fashion—it is proper. A half hunter watch is seated in his waistcoat, its chain the only visible mark of many and varied devices.

It is a tavern, as it so often is. He slips into a quiet corner, a glass of porter placed before him. He will not drink it. His guest is not far behind—a thick-necked man, overweight, whose collar is stained with sweat. The settle by the window creaks as the man sits down.

"They say you are good. That you know your business."

Mr Dry does not answer.

"I have a job, and it needs discretion."

A woman shrieks near the bar, discordant laughter. The Smithfield men are in, a scant half hour before the cleavers begin their work.

The large man is uncomfortable. His suit is of quality, his whiskers waxed back. He appears out of place in the Crown and Sceptre public house.

"You want the details, then," he mutters. "Yes, I suppose that's next. I have an inheritance due, from my brother, who won't see out the year. His heart. But he has a brat, and as his sole uncle, I would have to be his guardian."

"And?" Mr Dry moves his glass a half inch to one side, considering the dimensions of the small, copper-topped table. The large man looks annoyed.

"I can't wait, do you see? I have debts, and matters to manage.

Others are pressing me. So, should there be an accident—with the boy, I mean—I would be my brother's legatee. I could put my affairs in order. These others who make demands, they will realise that I have expectations. They will wait."

"How old is the boy?" The voice is soft, but certain.

The large man scowls. "Thirteen years old."

"Then I cannot help you."

"You have a conscience?" The man laughs. "You are a killer, a man for hire. Since when did such as you pick and choose? The boy swims daily; he walks alone through woods which are known as haunts of beggars and dross. He has no mother to watch him. Can you make nothing of this?"

Mr Dry has eyes which are dark and pale, according to what you choose. They take in the bustling tavern—the butcher's apprentice with his arm around a judy; the fishwife who slips her hand into men's pockets. There is meat on the air. The morning markets will blossom soon, and all manner of things will be well.

"The young, like dogs, have little say in what they receive." He touches his forefingers together. "And I do not kill dogs. I am rather fond of them."

"An inconvenient hound should be put down." The large man is sweating, angry. "I've gone this far—paid handsomely to track you down. Now I've said too much about myself to leave the matter there. You'll do it."

"I will not."

The quiet, neutral tone seems to infuriate the other even more.

"Then I'll have word of this put round, and damn your choices. The Tradesman, indeed! That's what they called you, but you're a milksop and a taunt, less use than any lascar from the docks!"

He rises, and storms through the gathered patrons, pushing his way to the narrow streets outside. He obviously feels that his information has failed him, and the meeting has been a waste of time. There will be others, without scruples, who will assist him.

Dawn grows faint to the east, a blotch of rose on a charcoal sky. He takes a side-street heading out of Smithfield.

"Our business is not concluded."

The large man pauses, uncertain. The man he left behind in the Crown and Sceptre could not have got ahead of him, but he is there, by a rusting iron gate in the wall.

"You've changed your mind?"

"I have not."

"Then to Hell with you." The large man turns to leave the way he came, yet Dry is before him again, a slender knife in one hand. They are alone on the street.

"I...I didn't mean what I said. It was...bluster, truly. I'll say nothing, of course."

"I consider your word unreliable," says Mr Dry.

At ten minutes past five in the morning, approximately two hundred yards from Smithfield Market, Constable Samuel Markham discovers an obstruction on his beat, one which yields to his bulls-eye lantern to become a body. A corpulent man in his forties, whose throat and wrists bear the marks of a blade—three long, well-placed slashes, no more.

Constable Markham can see how deep the flesh has been cut, through artery, windpipe and gullet, down to bone. Despite his evident wish to vomit, the constable tries to do his duty, examining the wounds. The throat must have been first, for no one in the area recalls a cry for help.

The constable will conclude that the assailant must surely have been as large and powerful as the victim. The cobbles run with blood which has not had time to coagulate; the body is warm. When colleagues arrive, he tells them they seek a tall, muscular man with blood on his clothes.

A police van arrives to remove the body, and high above, gulls scream their annoyance. But there will be other carcasses...

Catherine gasped, almost screamed at a tightness which burned through her calf muscles. The candle was long down to a puddle of wax on the night-stand, the curtains grey squares of growing day. She had dreamed. She had dreamed of him, Edwin Dry, and woken with such pain in her legs, spiking up to her spine. Sitting on the edge of the bed, she massaged the muscles until the discomfort abated.

"Night cramps, nothing more." She drew the curtains back. On the streets, a faint mist mingled with smoke from early hearths. The hands of her clock showed a quarter of six.

The man in the vision in Islington had killed again. If she dared to find a newspaper, if she dared to look, she knew that there would be a report—"Man killed by unknown assailant in Smithfield."

Not unknown to her.

She gulped water from a carafe, stretching her toes, letting the last of the cramps subside. When she was fifteen years old, when she grew maddened by the taunt "Mardy Cath" from a gang of local children she had hired a man. That was how she saw it. Slow Charlie, a forge-worker who had his eye on her. His own mind was little better than a child's, though behind the steelworks she pulled on a cock larger than she could have imagined. When she wiped her hands and her dress clean of his spendings, she had him in her debt.

The leader of the gang was a spindly fourteen year old who brushed floors at the ironworks which employed Slow Charlie. He discovered that week that he was not to make fun of Catherine Weatherhead. That he and his friends were to give her a wide berth. The boy's arm never did set quite right.

There were obviously more malevolent creatures than Slow Charlie available for hire in London. But what was the significance of that to her? Why did she see Edwin Dry? A question which kept intruding. She would drive it back for a day or so, and then it would return.

She could only pick at her breakfast kippers. Mrs Bessovitch saw the hovering fork, the lingered-over cup of tea.

"You have bad night."

Catherine smiled. "I had the cramps."

"In the…" Mrs B rubbed her abdomen, a generous curve beneath her apron. "Or lower, where you are a woman?"

"No, just my legs. I need some exercise. A gentle stroll."

She forced down the second kipper, tried to give her

landlady a reassuring smile, and set out for the river.

The Thames smelled better in autumn, freshened by the breeze which carried away the stink of night-soil and sour mud. Sunday's promenaders had gone. The roads by the river-front were busy with brewery drays and coal-wagons; omnibuses nosed their way through, announcing "peerless" washing powders and Liptons Teas. The scene was normal, tangible. On the way she passed the church where her flower arrangements had brought her useful talk. She should probably go back there at some point, to keep her face known and the gossip flowing.

Office workers slipped passed her, the occasional apology if they brushed her arm. Too many dark felt bowler hats. This commonest of symbols began to startle her, make her glance beneath in fear she would see *that* face. Smooth shaven, slightly rounded; the hair dark brown and neatly cut.

In her second vision there had been glasses, possibly tinted. Circles set over circles. What colour were his eyes? She thought them a pale blue, but couldn't hold the vision. Or, more likely, some part of her did not want to see that clearly. It was a face you remembered and yet forgot. Not a single distinguishing mark.

But why had she seen a murder far from where she slept? That had never happened to her before. Nor could she understand why visions of the same killer had come to her a second time...

Gulls wheeled above, said to be the sign of storm approaching at sea. More likely they were regulars, come up river for London's waste and sewage. It reminded her of Brantridge Street and the squalid tenements there. She couldn't face her cousins when she felt like this. Later in the week, it might be easier. As for Aunt Levinia—a dying woman could scheme and hope, and if that brought some small satisfaction, what was there to say?

Catherine despised Frederick Caille for causing Charles's death, but also because she understood at least something of what he was, a detail which eluded her cousins. Her own father could have been such as Caille, given opportunity.

She herself had hurt people, physically and emotionally. And in abandoning her father, she had left behind a weak and subservient mother. But she had never killed, or caused a death to occur. She had wished for a few such occurrences, certainly...

"Help a soldier, miss? Queen and Country."

She had hardly noticed the man, tucked into an alcove between two office buildings. A torn red tunic, stained dress trousers over the remaining leg. He held out an empty cocoa tin.

"I were with Wolseley, Gawd bless him, at Amoaful."

"I don't know those."

"Ashantee, miss. 'Struth, they did fight so, them blacks. Soldiers of their King, they were."

A clerk pushed past her, and she shared a choice Yorkshire expression with his pin striped backside.

"You were in Africa, then? Is that where you lost your leg?"

"Didn't lose it, miss. It were took, sliced like rare beef by a 'Shantee spear."

He had dirt in his whiskers and under them, yet there was something about him which appealed. She reached into her bag, and found her purse. A sixpence made its acquaintance with the otherwise empty cocoa tin.

"Gawd bless you."

"I don't think he's even heard of me."

"I'll ask when I sees him," said the man in the alcove.

"You do that, sir. And whilst you are there, be so kind as to ask him why I am plagued by Edwin Dry."

"He don't sound like no Ashantee."

"No. I don't know what he is."

The stiffness in her legs had gone, and at least she had two of them. Lady Seldon would want her later in the week; there might be a sitting in Catford on the Friday evening. She bid farewell to the soldier, and turned south, back to her lodgings.

Hard work would clear both family and killers from her head.

Two unremarkable séances in Vauxhall swelled her coffers a little. Accepting that she could at least pay lip service to her aunt's obsession, she bought a notebook, and sat up late, the pasteboard box open on the bed. This time, as an exercise, she noted down every mention of Mrs Caille in the clippings. She could not say why, except that she had become curious. Lady Seldon's husband was mentioned briefly in one paper, beneath the spots of mould which had begun to confuse the text. Lord Seldon had spoken of a wish that families in another case against Caille might be recompensed, a wish shared by some others in Parliament, but not those in power. Did the Seldons know the Cailles personally? She could find nothing on that.

The banker's interests were too wide, his influence too pervasive. If she drew anything from what she read, it was that he bought and sold both men and women as he pleased.

"Nothing can be done, Aunt Levinia."

Spoken to the wardrobe in Catherine's room, of course.

CHAPTER EIGHT

Chelsea Embankment, October 1886

The watchman takes his rounds with heavy step. The eel in his belly was none too fresh when it entered that night's pie; the woman who served the pie was none too kind in her views on her husband's prospects. The two war inside him, and instead of turning right, by the passage to the vault, he turns left towards the privy meant for bank staff only. As he strains for relief, he neither sees nor hears the cracksman at the far end of the building that night. A bad eel and a sharp tongue save him from the lead-filled cosh.

A man lives.

The civil servant's mistress has jilted him, gone with a cavalry man to play hogmagundy before the Regiment sails. Whitehall is a place of gas and shadows, and the civil servant's eyes are thick with misery. He dips his pen and signs an end to one Mr Orlesky, being held at Her Majesty's displeasure. As Left might have been Right, the man who should have been marked to dance for the hangman is a Mr Orlenski, but Her Majesty's servant is too tired to notice.

A man dies.

These are the vagaries which Edwin Dry observes. They are why he prepares each venture in detail, yet has always alternatives in mind. Small things without intention come to pass, and great plans slip out of one's hands, like fat eels that once held so much promise. Not by logic and conscious effort, but by the contents of a pastry crust, or the blotting of a single word.

Such things cannot be predicted.

All eels are grey in the dark.

Catherine attended a late supper at Lady Seldon's on the Thursday of the week after Vauxhall. A light meal of game pie, a syllabub and cheese went smoothly, but as the evening progressed, she began to realise that she should earn her invitation.

They did not ask, but that was not the way these people lived. All was done by vague suggestion, and by a system of mutual obligation which was, at times, hard to penetrate. Nor was language direct. A maid who was considered "lively" or "so bright" could as easily anticipate dismissal as advancement. Favour waxed and waned easily.

Catherine sought to play safe. She provided vague imagery of foreign lands at a short sitting, and afterwards intrigued her small audience by recalling snippets from spiritualist literature, concerning the phenomenon known as automatic writing. She had determined Amelia Baring-Smith to be the most impressionable of the three, and she directed a number of enquiring looks in that direction as she spoke, drawing the girl in.

Under Catherine's direction, each of them sat with paper and pencil, whilst Madame Rostov asked if there were souls upon the Aether who wished to communicate. Eyes closed, the three let their pencils wander across the table, with occasional supportive murmurs from the medium.

The results were a mixture of nonsense and scribbles, with barely any distinguishable words, but Madame Rostov pronounced that Amelia's paper might hold some blurred meaning.

"Is that not the word 'Berlin,' below the half-circle?" she suggested, and after a few minutes she had them inclined to agree.

"I had an uncle at the Embassy there!" cried Amelia. "Uncle Freddie. He's in Budapest now, but still…I must write and tell him. Perhaps he has unfinished business in Germany."

Her object achieved, for almost an hour she sat and nodded, saying little, as Lottie Chambers read from her new acquisition, a book entitled *The Strange Case of Dr Jekyll and Mr Hyde*. Catherine knew only that the author had published some sort of pirate tale a few years before, and was somewhat mystified by Lottie's attempts to explain Stevenson's latest.

"And he takes this potion, this serum, but it no longer works, or something along those lines. So he kills himself, except that I don't think he does." Lottie beamed. "It is what Papa calls a metaphorical death—that side of him has to die, but the brutal, terrible Mr Hyde may survive."

"It sounds rather lurid," said Amelia Baring-Smith. "Are you sure it is worth the time, Lottie?"

"I enjoyed it. What if we all have two sides to us? I might take a draught, and—"

"Become a quiet, sensible young woman," finished Lady Seldon, provoking laughter all round. "What do you think, Madame Rostov? Are we all more than one person?"

The irony of the question did not escape Catherine.

"We are many persons," she said in a grave voice. "I have not read this Stevenson, but perhaps he asks, which part of what is within us will we let dominate? Do we let our monsters out?"

More sherry flowed, and Lady Seldon lit a slender cigarette.

"I know some who do," she said. "Harry considers old Salisbury a positive monster, living in his privileged past. Harry has moments where I think he should have been born a factory worker, causing agitation, not a marquess."

It seemed an opening that Catherine could use, if they did not think her speaking above her station.

"But then he might have to work in one of Mr Frederick Caille's factories. I would not envy him that."

The other women looked at her.

"It was something I read. In the newspapers." added Catherine. For a moment it seemed she had overstepped the boundaries. "Where there had been many accidents, and people hurt."

The two younger women looked to Lady Seldon, who drew on her cigarette and then nodded.

"No, that is not a fate any of us would wish on friends or

relatives. Not the decent ones, anyway."

Charlotte and Amelia relaxed.

"I saw Evelyn last month," said Lottie. "I was *allowed* to see her, I should say. Her husband's an absolute horror. I could see him as Mr Hyde."

"Evelyn Caille?" Amelia sighed. "That poor woman."

"To have to share a name with that ghastly man. Intolerable. More scandal over his South African mines, and talk of a Spanish *condesa*, would you believe?"

"He all but bankrolls several peers." Lady Seldon pulled a face. "What have you heard of him, Madame Rostov?"

Catherine considered what she should and should not know.

"That he is a banker, an industrialist. Many do not seem to like him, but he has much power."

"That is the nub of it." She stubbed out her cigarette. "Do you think we should sit again tonight, Madame?"

Surely she had paid her dues? It was almost midnight.

"I would prefer not to, my lady. I am tired."

"More sherry, then. My husband's *oloroso* is far too expensive for his boorish friends."

Catherine was aware that she was little more than a diversion, an act to enliven the evenings of these young women, and yet she liked them, in their way. They were less shallow than they had at first seemed.

"This Mrs Caille…" She pretended to test out the name as she took a glass of sherry from Miss Chambers. "She is badly served?"

"Oh, indeed. They live apart," said Lottie. "You'd think she was under house-arrest, the way she's treated."

"There are no children?"

"A young boy, Beresford, trapped under his father's wing. She's hardly allowed to see him."

The spiritualist wrapped an unused deck of cards in soft black silk, and slid them into her bag.

"That is sad. And she is a good woman?"

"Absolutely! Married off young, like Lucy here—"

"Have a care," said Lady Seldon. "We should not gossip too much, or we will bore Madame Rostov."

The moment's familiarity passed. These were women of position, and where Madame Rostov fell on the spectrum between hired entertainer and honoured guest would never quite be certain.

Conversation shifted to the fashion in hats, and half an hour later, Lottie Chambers showed the spiritualist out.

"Do you think that next time, Madame, there might be word for me?"

"There are disturbances on every Plane," said Catherine, feeling inventive. "They interfere, but they will not last. I am sure that more is to come."

Lottie seemed thrilled at the words. It was clear, even after only a few sittings, that the young women of this circle wanted something a touch more visceral and exciting than organ music and soothing messages.

"Marvellous," she said. "Shall I have Merrins find a hansom for you?"

"I shall walk, thank you."

She slipped into the streets of the Chelsea Embankment an hour before midnight, leaving Lady Seldon and her friends to more *oloroso* and a round of cards. Unobserved, she pinned her hair down, turned the hood of her cloak and slipped her rings into an inside pocket. She checked her small change, and walked back into the gaslight. A hansom trotted by, and she gestured.

"Where to, lady?" The cabbie tipped his felt hat.

"Southwark St Saviour."

And home. She had much to consider.

The Chambers family's town-house was an imposing red-brick building no great distance along the Embankment from Lady Seldon's, on Cheyne Gardens. On Saturday morning she presented her card, as Madame Rostov, to a limping butler, and was shown immediately into a high-ceilinged room which still bore the marks of the nursery—a child's easel in the corner, a faded map of the Empire, and wallpaper with soft forget-me-nots. Miss Bournelle must have ruled here once. Charlotte Chambers and a girl of ten or eleven years sat side by side on an old divan, peering through an illustrated book.

"Madame Rostov, what a pleasure." Lottie sounded genuinely pleased. "May I introduce you to my sister, Jemmy."

The girl, small and with the same pale blonde hair as Lottie, stood up and curtseyed.

"It's Jemima, actually," she said, scowling at her older sister. "Most pleased to meet you, Madame."

Catherine tipped her head politely. "You are also a lover of books, Miss Jemima?"

"She is worse than I am. Go show Mama the drawings of the heron and the crane, Jemmy, there's a good girl."

"If I must." Jemima's skipping exit managed to display both insolence and reluctance. Lottie smiled fondly after her.

"A man will pay when he catches her," she said. "I hope."

Whether by common practice or by some hidden signal, a maid came in with a tray of tea-things, including scones and butter.

"A wasp has been in the jam, miss," said the maid. "I can send out for more."

It was agreed that jam was not required, and they sat on the divan, tea cups in hand.

"You are kind to see me," said Catherine.

Lottie looked surprised. "I think you an intelligent woman, Madame. Papa would not have me at casinos, or late card games, nor does he approve of many theatrical productions. Am I to sit alone and read until parcelled off to a son of one of his friends?"

"I do not—"

"If I did not have Lucy and Amelia, and our afternoons, our evenings, I would be mad." The words were emphatic. She leaned closer. "I am a suffragist, not that my parents know. I shall teach Jemmy accordingly, though she hardly needs it."

The subject—and the conspiratorial tone—were unexpected. Catherine had a limited grasp of politics. She smiled, nodded, and attended to her tea, hoping that this would suffice.

Lottie laughed. "But you are here for your own purposes, I'm sure. How can I help you, Madame?"

Here was the test. If she had judged Charlotte Chambers correctly, if she had understood aright the way she had talked the other evening…

"You spoke of a Mrs Caille."

Eyebrows raised slightly. "Evelyn? I don't know that she has any interest in spiritualism, or tilting tables and the like. I do not see her often these days."

Catherine hesitated. How was she to put this? She had thought it over each night since the name of Caille had come up. Of course these people knew each other, and so eventually most names would arise in casual conversation. It was no different from Keighley high street, in many ways. The wives gathered, glancing into each others' shopping baskets, seeing who had ironed their pinafore and who bore a bruise from a drink-sodden husband. They spoke of this girl who had spread her legs once too often, of that woman who no longer ordered anything but the cheapest cuts…it was the way.

She could ignore Charlotte Chambers's passing mention of acquaintance with Evelyn Caille at the Seldon's, knowing it would most likely lead her nowhere, or…

"I sense a grief about this good lady. A heavy cloud that weighs upon her. She wished, perhaps, to marry a Jekyll, but was misled?"

Lottie seemed pleased at the literary allusion. "Oh, quite so. Caille—the brute—is a man of ideas. But each idea is squeezed for profit, not for progress. Harry Seldon loathes him; even Papa keeps his distance."

"Yet this man has great influence."

"Bought, all bought, Madame." Lottie broke a scone in

half, then placed it back on the plate. "Not that I know that much, you understand. Though I have very good hearing. It's surprising what people will say when they think you are out of ear-shot. No, you would do well to keep clear of Mr Caille."

"I shall do so, Miss Chambers. And yet, his wife...still I have the sensation that there should be some comfort for her. I cannot say why this touches me."

"Oh, I see." Lottie considered this for a moment. "Is there a sentiment you wish me to convey to her?"

Catherine pretended awkwardness. "I do not know... without having seen her in person, you understand? It can be difficult to be sure what is required. Possibly there is a message for her, from Beyond."

"Oh." The young woman's interest was undoubtedly engaged. "I suppose..."

"Yes?"

"Lucy—Lady Seldon—*might* arrange for you to meet Evelyn. She has more influence than I."

"If it would cause you trouble..."

"A challenge. I like challenges. You see, Madame, Mrs Caille is practically confined to her place at Muswell Hill, a rather dismal old house. Caille does not wish his wife in society."

"But how can he stop her?" It was a stupid question. There would be ways, for a man of Caille's wealth and influence.

"She loves her son very much," said Lottie, sighing. "And Caille holds that over her. He will have an heir in his own image, if he has his way. A dreadful thought, really." It was one which seemed to stiffen her resolve. "I shall speak to Lucy this weekend. We will find some pretext for you to see Evelyn, and trust that you can bring her some kinder words than she usually hears. I doubt Caille knows enough of spiritual matters to question a minor diversion for her."

A shriek from the hall outside marked the return of Jemima Chambers, clutching her book. The girl's fingers were smeared with jam, and she careened across the polished floor of the old nursery looking unabashed.

Catherine smiled, expressed her appreciation, and bade the two sisters farewell.

The air outside was crisp, the sky less grey than usual. The red brick of Cheyne Walk glowed warmer in a shaft of rare sunshine.

As a merchant's daughter from a Yorkshire town, she would hardly have stood much higher in London society than the tradesmen who called at the back of these houses.

As Madame Rostov, new doors appeared to be opening for her.

CHAPTER NINE

Stepney, October 1886

Levinia Weatherhead's health continued to deteriorate, and Clarissa's moods grew worse. Each of Catherine's visits to Stepney was fraught with misunderstandings and hopeless silences.

"The doctor says she will leave us all the sooner if we try to move her to the infirmary. A colleague of his kindly came out from the London Hospital…he pronounced that there is no help except a comfortable end. The tubes and passages of her lungs are blocked; her heart cannot force her breath, and now she may have the grippe. She eats little in her fever."

"I will sit with her a while," said Catherine. Clarissa herself was coughing intermittently, a condition of long-standing. The sweating sickness would put her at risk as well.

"Good. I have mending to do, lest we do not meet the rent."

"I could—"

"Make us more beholden to you than we are already." She turned away. "I begin to mutter like Mama, and wish Frederick Caille in a cell while I can still rejoice in it."

Catherine was torn between annoyance and pity. "Have you thought of moving to Yorkshire? I know that it is not your own native county, but there are other folk there—neighbours, friends of the Two Gentlemen."

This had long been the family term for the two brothers, Joseph—Catherine's grandfather—and Charles—grandfather and namesake to Clarissa's late husband. Farmers together on the wilder moors above Keighley, who had thought two foot of snow no more than a spattering, yet who could cry at a lamb lost to crows.

"There is nothing up there for us." The words were sharp, final.

Nor was there anything in the room upstairs except the shallow gasps of an old woman. Catherine sat for two hours, reading a borrowed copy of Stevenson, but took none of it in. She left two sovereigns by Levinia's bed, and let herself out. Those would have to be earned back quickly—unlike her aunt, Catherine had a fine appetite.

An omnibus saw her down Whitechapel Road and as far as the Tower. Work had started on the new bridge, and she could see barges all around, plying to and fro from the site of two reinforced piers which were to be set into the Thames. They said in the papers that this Tower Bridge might cost near a million pounds, a sum which made no sense to her. Caille would understand it, easily.

She walked to London Bridge via Botolph wharf, where Mrs Bessovitch regularly took advantage of those crates which were damaged as they were swung from ships' holds. Oranges, and other fruit such as limes and sometimes figs, could be had there for a pittance if it were done quietly, in the shadow of the creaking and almost decrepit wharf buildings.

She was fortunate. A sleepy-eyed black sailor, his head wrapped in a silk scarf, sold her a handful of Sicily oranges for tuppence, adding a bag of sweet sultanas. They would have cost him nothing. She cut an orange with her pocket-knife, and sucked on it as she crossed the bridge to Southwark—this haul would get her an extra chop from her landlady, at least.

⚔

Madame Rostov conducted a vexing session with two local women, and made mistakes. Catherine's intelligence on the women failed her. In seeking to recover her sitters' confidence, she let her mind wander and open, which brought blurred images of an endless leaden sea, great waves beneath a twisted sky. By useful coincidence (for Catherine did not think it had true meaning) one of the women had been married to a sailor, lost in the Baltic. The sitters pronounced themselves satisfied, but only to the tune of a shilling each.

Walking home, she settled in her bed with backache and a distinct feeling of being hard done by…

The mirror is large, a shard of the true world bound in a simple ebony frame. It needs neither gilt nor adornments. It shows a room like any other, in which stands a man of no particular interest. He might be clerk to a shipping office, or secretary to some branch manager of a modest bank. His form is that of Everyman, in essence. The thought pleases him.

He considers his reflection, long enough to adjust his collar a fraction and be sure that his jacket sits perfectly square upon his adequate shoulders. He is not Everyman, of course. He is a journeyman, and journeymen should always be presentable. To be otherwise reflects badly on the trade.

A journeyman must not be prey to appetite—of any kind. He will dine on a small pork chop, with potatoes and peas. A little cheese to follow, matured and with the faint crunch of salt. He will set out without hunger. And without malice or anger.

Those who must hate would not understand.

No death.

In the half-light of the Southwark dawn, Catherine clutched her blanket to her.

No death had occurred, and yet still he came to her, entered her dreams.

Was this how it was to be?

A visit to the post office revealed another cream envelope waiting for her. Inside this one was simply Lady Seldon's embossed card; on the back of the card, a neatly written couple of lines.

'Evelyn—I would consider it a favour if you were to receive Madame Rostov. She is most talented, discreet, and deserves due patronage. S.'

"S" no doubt for Seldon. Lottie Chambers had come through, as promised. Now she had her entrée to Mrs Caille, one which might have her received rather than turned away. And perhaps Catherine would learn more of those who ruined the Weatherheads. She would be able to say to Levinia that she had pursued the thread, if nothing else.

She hauled out the finest of Madame Rostov's clothes, borrowed the rings again from Mrs B, and asked for advice.

"I know nothing of Muswell Hill," she said to her landlady.

"Write down address you must find." Mrs Bessovitch waited, then drew on her outdoors coat and was away. She returned an hour later having questioned, no doubt, Gersteins, Goldschmidts, Coopers and Cartwrights.

"Is easy, Katerina."

A parlour maid of a friend's neighbour had once worked… and so it went. Catherine received instruction to go by rail to Hornsey, and after that she had only to walk or take a hansom up Hornsey High Street, and keep going. Grove House, where Evelyn Caille lived in apparent exile, was halfway up Muswell Hill.

If she hesitated, she might keep that card of Lady Seldon's for days, or weeks. It ought to be done…

The Great Northern train was crowded, a situation exacerbated by a man trying to put two crates of chickens in one of the passenger carriages. People were feeling uncharitable, but eventually the guard's van was utilised, and the journey to Hornsey was simple enough. In character, she decided to take a hansom to Grove House, and sat back to enjoy the short journey from the small town centre and up the moderate incline into the wooded Muswell Hill.

Iron railings and horse chestnuts losing their last leaves; fields and men on bicycles. Recent, quite stylish houses had been raised amongst the trees, but Grove House was not one of them. Set alone down a lane to the north, it slumped between chestnuts, an amalgam of Georgian villa and later, awkward additions, as if the architect had forgotten what should be there, and had come back fifty years later to try and make rushed amends.

She paid the cab driver, and marched with false confidence to the lopsided porch which marked the main entrance. The bell-push made no sound that reached her, and so she knocked as well, for good measure. Eventually a man in a butler's uniform, but poorly shaven, answered.

"We do not wish visitors," he said.

Catherine had learned enough to know that this was an inappropriate welcome. "Mrs Caille is not at home..." might have been acceptable, but "We?" She tightened her lips and stared hard at the man.

"I come from Lady Seldon." Catherine held out the card she had been sent. "I am Madame Rostov."

He hesitated, but then took the card and read the back. "I don't..."

"It will be known," she said, "That Madame Rostov was refused at this house. Refused by you."

She spoke with her best mock-Russian edge, and it weakened him. He asked her, more politely, to wait a moment, "If she did not mind," and disappeared inside.

The grounds themselves were well-maintained, with even a spot of late colour in borders to either side. Scarlet dahlias and ivory-pale chrysanthemums still bloomed, all neatly staked and cleared of fallen leaves. It seemed an odd contrast to the apparent state of the building.

"Madame Rostov?"

Evelyn Caille stood in the doorway. Charlotte Chambers had described her. A nondescript dress, out of fashion; thin lips which reminded Catherine of Aunt Levinia. One hand played at tousled hair without colour—the other hung at her side, fingers tapping on her thigh.

"I am."

"Please, join me in the drawing room."

The house was clean enough, but its dark paint and heavy

furniture absorbed life, muted it. The butler stood by the drawing room door, watching. He had much the same effect.

"We shall not need you, Tanner."

Hesitation, and a slow withdrawal. Mrs Caille went to the door, and pressed it firmly shut.

"He listens," she said. "Let us sit by the French windows. He will hear less that way."

The woman moved like an actress, each gesture exaggerated. Even sitting, her fingers tapped against her left leg.

"He is my gaoler. I think you should not have come, though God knows, I have little enough company."

Catherine had not expected such directness. "Mrs Caille, I—"

"Evelyn. All I hear is 'Mrs Caille.'"

"Evelyn, then. Miss Charlotte Chambers was kind enough to arrange this introduction, and—"

"Let me spare us time, Madame Rostov. There is no force which could make Lucy Seldon disadvantage me, and therefore I can be sure that in some way, you are a friend. You do not need to present further credentials, or promise that you mean me no harm."

"Ah. I see." For once, Catherine wished that there had been a maid with afternoon tea, just to give her a cup or side-plate with which to toy.

"And if you have spoken to Lottie, then you must know that this is my exile. I have occasional visitors. I tend my garden. I see my son, Beresford, once a week, though Tanner watches us throughout. My husband permits this, subject to my complete compliance, and my pledge that I support whatever scheme in which he is involved. He intends this to continue, for as long as he pleases."

Evelyn laughed, a hollow sound so devoid of humour that those scripts, those planned enquiries and subtleties which Catherine had stored up over the days—they died. It almost seemed better to quit Grove House and forget that it existed, than hear this.

"I am allowed to attend very few functions. I must be bright and charming, or I will lose a week's privileges with my son—or more. Beresford is told, by a doctor in Frederick's pay, that his mother is not strong, not well."

"I…I understand."

"And do you understand that Tanner will report all he hears to my husband?"

Catherine shuddered. Frederick Caille's actions had caused the death of Charles Weatherhead and others, yes, and he had used all his power to crush the simplest wishes for remorse to be expressed, restitution to be offered. But those events were at a distance, and a year ago. Sat here, Catherine felt a new and direct horror of the man who had crushed Evelyn as well. His own wife.

Catherine was "Joshua's child." The daughter of a fragment of Frederick Caille. Control and subjugation. Veiled threats, and always something held just out of reach. A much loved son, or a chance for freedom. The same gleaming apple, never quite in reach. Do as I ask—am I not reasonable? It had produced her mother—produced her and reduced her.

It had created Evelyn Caille, as she now was.

"But come, you do not speak, Madame Rostov," said Evelyn. "Ignore my mood. I would welcome new conversation, on whatever subject you choose. I believe that Lottie mentioned you had a psychic gift, for example?"

The tapping fingers drummed out frustrated love, frustrated purpose.

"Yes, I—"

A creak at the drawing room door galvanised Catherine to act. She rose to her feet, and strode to the door, throwing it open. Tanner, the butler, started back, almost losing his balance.

"There is a darkness in this house," she said, looming over him. She thrust out her chin, and spread her fingers, like the conjuror she had seen at a show in Bradford once. "I, Madame Rostov, am here to bring release. How do I do this, when there are mice who chew the skirting boards? Do you have the gift, little mouse?"

"I am to—"

"You are to find your hole, and let me work. Do you understand?"

Tanner's face reddened, and he opened his mouth to speak again, but Catherine knew that impetus was everything. She had met his sly type before—they rarely had an appetite for direct confrontation. "Rarely," of course, was a hopeful word.

"Scurry, now. If I must speak of you to the Aether, to those who have gone before, what will they say?"

His cheek twitched, and he backed farther away. She did not yield, but watched until he left the hallway and disappeared into another room at the rear of the house.

In the drawing room, Evelyn Caille had her head in her hands, her shoulders quivering.

"I have gone too far," said Catherine. "I am so sorry to..."

The face which appeared from behind slender hands was that of a younger woman, one who had remembered, however briefly, how to smile.

"I may pay for that, Madame Rostov, but bless you, I have never managed to cow Tanner in such a way. I am in your debt."

Catherine sat down, and put her hand on Evelyn's knee. She herself was shaking slightly, not from laughter, but in realisation of what she had just done.

"You must call me Katerina," she said. "And when you are ready, we must talk more about your devil of a husband."

CHAPTER TEN

Clerkenwell, October 1886

In Clerkenwell the crows were fractious, black beaks stabbing even at each other as they vied for carrion and scraps. A dead cat provided them with amusement, as welcome as any forgotten crust of bread. Catherine wandered without purpose down Kings Cross Road and Farringdon, her mind too full to let her rest. Grove House clung to her, and all around were reminders—Clerkenwell was a land of dead prisons, from Coldbath Fields to the Middlesex House of Correction. All closed, their birds transferred to other roosts.

She knew, as she bought an orange from a barrow-boy, that she could not free Evelyn Caille. She could not harm Frederick Caille. She had heard enough to know that, truth or slander, there was nothing she could say that would affect the magnate. Evelyn told him of those who had tried. Ernest Glaive, a former partner and once well-respected, had ended up in Coldbath Fields. Court cases abandoned; reputations torn. Caille did not have all influence, nor did he always win, but he never quite lost.

The Liberals in Parliament, Evelyn had volunteered, would have had at him, but enough landed masters grew fat from Caille's purse. They said he would gain a title within the year. Many, such as Lord Seldon—Lucy's Harry—worked round the man and hoped for change.

"I might be Lady Caille, or bear some such fine monicker," Evelyn murmured, joyless at the prospect. "How grand I would be."

Catherine found a tea-room, and took strong coffee

for once. Evelyn had offered to find refreshments, but there had been so much to hear. To Madame Rostov, a vouchsafed stranger, the woman poured out a history of mistakes—an ailing father who had pressed Evelyn to accept Caille's offer of marriage; the subtle way in which her father's legacy had disappeared into her new husband's schemes and factories. He was seventeen years her senior.

"Strong and purposeful men attract—at first," said Evelyn. "A pretty wife—I was pretty once, Katerina—on his arm at the ball, and then a healthy heir…"

"What happened?" Catherine had asked, wondering at this woman's fall from grace.

"After Beresford proved bright and fit, my value fell. Frederick does not invest in shares whose promise is likely to diminish."

The afternoon had been painful. Catherine saw the shadow of her mother creep over the other woman at times. "Perhaps I should be grateful for…" and "There are worse lots for many, I know…" It was how she had watched her mother, Agatha, die inside, and how a precocious, rebellious girl had come to despise her own mother's weakness.

She shared none of this with Evelyn Caille. She said nothing of any Weatherhead, though she was so tempted to echo Aunt Levinia's views on Caille himself. She listened instead, and in listening, found hardly the barest hope that anything could be done, short of slitting Frederick Caille's throat…

A tea-room maid, tripping on an over-generous tablecloth, spilled tea on Catherine's green silk dress. The girl drew back, awaiting anger.

"It is not blood," said Madame Rostov. She stood up, taking the tea towel that was folded over the girl's arm, and blotted her dress. "It is not blood."

Confused, the maid fled back into the kitchens.

Catherine walked south once more—Clerkenwell Green, which had no trace of greenery upon it, and Farringdon Street

Station. The streets grew busier, men leaving their places of work to return to their homes or lodgings, or to gather in the chop houses, where women could not intrude. Top hats and tweed caps. Homburgs, the occasional wide-awake, and...the dark felt bowlers that now so bothered her. It was important not to look, not to peer and see if below them sat the face that haunted her. Haunted was now her word for it.

The streets became more familiar, and yet she did not remember coming this way before. The Blackfriars Bridge and her passage to Southwark across the river lay due south of her, a simple journey. A chestnut seller cried out nearby, startling her. She looked around, only to notice that beyond the hawker's barrow stood a man in a dark brown Derby and a neat, well-tailored suit.

And he saw her.

Pretending to fumble in her bag, she closed her eyes. When she opened them, the man was still there. Pale eyes blinked, and he moved away, down a narrow side-street. She knew this place. They were near to Smithfield, and the bloodied cobbles of her vision. Catherine pressed against the wall of a bank, drawing curious looks from other pedestrians.

He could not know her. Never, in dream or vision, had there been any sign that he was aware of her presence. She was an observer, a mind on the Aether, and no more.

"Are you well, madam?" A young clerk paused.

"I...yes, thank you."

She meant to find somewhere to sit and think, but instead she was drawn to the street into which she had seen him go. Madness, an inability to let this pass. She walked unsteadily across the road, earning a curse from a cab driver. Benjamin Street, cramped shops and rooms above; Albion Place the same. A woman clad in many layers of soiled flannel tried to sell her dried rose petals in penny bags, but she pressed past. He was at the corner, looking south. Two apprentices, hardly men, kicked a tin can along the road, and were admonished by an old man in mufflers.

She had no weapon, no guard set to watch her.

Constable Markham sees how deep the flesh has been cut, through artery, windpipe and gullet, down to bone...

As the snow-bound poles called to the compass needle, his presence called to her. She had to know, to learn something of the man behind her nightmares.

In clumsy imitation of stealth, she turned with him, still well back, into an even narrower street behind a Board school. A small boy stared at her, and spat. The bowler-hatted man was not there. Too many alleys surrounded her, squalid lodgings piled upon each other. She caught her breath, knew she should leave...

"You see me."

He stood in the shallowest of recesses, a bricked-in doorway. No taller than Catherine; tidy, polished, as he always appeared.

"Excuse me, sir. I mistook my way," she said, quick-breathed. "I have friends hereabouts, awaiting me urgently."

"Come, come. We know that you do not."

The weakest toss of a child's ball separated them. Two, three yards. Surely someone would come this way soon.

He took out his watch, consulted it. "A quarter after six."

"What do you want of me, sir?"

"Want? I am as the cat. Curious. I am a man who is rarely seen. And if seen, I am not noted. Why, then, do you act the Diana, hunting me down through these narrow ways?"

She edged back slowly, towards the busier streets. "I thought...I thought you one of the friends who expects me."

He nodded. "A quick thinker. I like that. Still, your words are sadly untrue. Let me see. You are from the North of England, by your voice—it is not hidden well enough—yet dress as a Jew, a Pole or perhaps a Russian. I am never followed, and yet you follow me. Mystery is not in my nature. Can you not satisfy my curiosity?"

Catherine swallowed. Her pursuit of him had been madness, and this conversation was a worse lunacy. He did not threaten or show displeasure—they were talking as if they had met on a busy street corner, and the weather had turned suddenly. He might have been asking her why the clouds had gathered so.

"Very well. I have…I have heard of you," she said, all trace of Madame Rostov gone. "And I was told you might be of service, but I realise that I am out of my depth. We should have no quarrel," she added more hastily.

"Go on." He brushed a hair from his shoulder, hardly looking at her.

She drew on the vision from before, when she had seen another make fatal errors in his dealings with Mr Dry.

"You are called the Tradesman."

His lip twitched.

"Ah. The tedium of men's minds. Bacon the Butcher; Spring-heeled Jack. They must have their names. I dislike such cheap names and epithets. I assume that a former client of mine has been discussing me?"

If he knew for a second that she had observed his deeds, that she had touched his mind, a knife would surely be her fate. But if he believed that she was a prospective client, she might live. At that moment she was willing to clutch at any assumption which favoured her.

She tried to keep the relief from her voice, her face. "Yes. Just so." She swallowed. "But they spoke most discreetly, a chance word only."

"And thus you have a commission for me?"

His pale gaze was assessing her, she knew. Client or victim, still in the balance.

"I thought…I am not sure now. I thought I did. But it is foolishness…" Levinia Weatherhead's pasteboard box. There was one name she could use, be rebuffed and perhaps win free. "I had a man in mind," she said. "But now I realise that he is beyond reach. I will leave, and say no more."

She prayed that it might be so.

He was quiet for a moment.

"I am intrigued." He looked around. "A constable turns that corner in seven minutes. He is slow and unreliable, but he will ask what we are doing. We are not 'in our place' down these alleys."

She edged back. "Please, do you not see? I was mistaken. I will not speak of this again, to anyone."

"No," he said. "The coin has almost left the purse, and having been Diana, you must now be Athena. You must let me hear your wisdom. To say that something cannot be done is to invite interest. Do you truly wish to leave this matter unfinished?" His lips smiled. "I have your scent now."

Six minutes only to the constable's heavy boots on damp cobbles. What did he mean by her scent? She wore no fragrance, no eau-de-toilette.

"What do you propose?"

"There is a quiet room in the Crown and Sceptre, a short walk from here. It is slightly—slightly—better in quality than the public bar. We should adjourn there, so that I may learn of the task that outmatches me."

A flash of spirit came to her on hearing the name of the tavern.

"And if you do not like what I say? Do I end in some alley hereabouts, a carcass to be found and hauled away that a harassed coroner may consign me to his notes?"

She thought she saw faint surprise, though his features gave so little away.

"A colourful image, but not an outcome I anticipate," he said.

⚰

The "quiet room," barely a cubbyhole with table and benches, brought her closer than she liked to Dry. He dusted his seat with a handkerchief, which he then carefully folded and replaced in his pocket.

"Brandy and one glass," he said to the boy who hovered nearby. The tavern was half-empty, their place concealed by thin partitions. When the drink came, he placed bottle and wine glass before her. "I observe that it stiffens resolve in some." He watched as she poured herself a half-glass, and took a hasty gulp.

Heat, and temporary courage. Catherine struggled to believe that she was here, that she had gone along with him.

"I consider your word unreliable," says Mr Dry.

More quickly than she should, she refilled the glass, and spoke of Fredrick Caille. She named his position, his power, his general malignancy, as heard from Lottie and Evelyn, added to from Levinia's clippings. When she began to explain the reasons why she might want Caille served due vengeance, Dry raised one hand.

"I have no interest in others' tawdry lives. Nor do I need the details of what set you on this path. You may spare me the rest."

Bold with spirits, she stared at him. Were his eyes almost black, or was it the way that they were set, peering from shadows?

"You see my mistake," she said. "God forgive us, there is no remedy against such as Caille."

"Is there not?" He sat back, motionless; she drank again.

Her head swam, fear and excitement trying to live within the same moment. She was ensconced with a killer, an assassin. Her visions had drawn her into ridiculous folly.

"I am sorry to have wasted your time," she said when he had neither spoken nor moved for some minutes. His eyes were open, but what they saw was beyond her.

He blinked. Once.

"I have come across the name. He is powerful, yes, but it can be done. You come to a craftsman, and ask for a work that transcends the usual, that presents true challenge, an opportunity to excel. What would I be if I turned you away, young lady?"

"Human," said the brandy within her, aloud.

"Possibly. But I will do what you ask, though you have not quite asked it."

"You…you will punish Caille?"

"I will remove him. It is what I do."

"How?" She craned forward, mistrusting what she had heard, and her empty belly griped, wrestling with the drink.

He sighed. "When you purchase bread, do you interrogate the farmer who sowed the corn? Such details are none of your concern."

Was it possible? That she had commissioned a murder almost by accident? She wondered, dazed, how such a situation could have arisen. But she was here, in this room, and Mr Edwin Dry was only feet away. Impassive, still watching.

"May I ask when, then?" Close to a croak, her throat tight. "When would this be done, if it can be?"

"Within the month. I have tools to prepare."

"And the price?"

"To be considered. Not great, I believe. What is in your purse?"

She rummaged and brought out a handful of shillings, a couple of half crowns. And then she found a sovereign, trapped in the lining. "Not nearly enough—but with time I might find more…"

He was paying no attention to her. He took up the sovereign, examining it.

"The monarch ages, but gold does not. We may call this a token, between us, of what is to come."

"My further payment, you mean?"

"The success of this commission," he corrected her. "An end to Mr Frederick Caille."

CHAPTER ELEVEN

Chelsea, October 1886

Safe ensconced in her Southwark room, Catherine could only turn the incident at Clerkenwell over and over in her head, without resolution. Mrs Bessovitch had a tendency to Russian stoicism, and to saying that things were "meant." Catherine was certain that the encounter with Edwin Dry would be described in such a way if she ever dared tell her landlady what had occurred.

Would Dry have killed her, if she had not come up with her preposterous suggestion, her commission? Had she escaped sudden death by the merest sliver?

If he knew that she had been "seeing" any fragment of what he did, that would surely have been the end of her. It was a realisation which sent her to the privy for some time.

Steadier, she ate toast and drank over-sweetened tea. There were surely only two outcomes. Dry would attempt the deed and fail, dying or be taken into custody in the process. Or he would succeed, and come after her for the rest of his fee. She had promised no specific sum, nor had he named one.

Would the Tradesman really work for the challenge itself?

In ignorance of what was to come, Madame Rostov had to work, and maintain a fragile position. This was Catherine's argument to herself, and how she tried to drive the matter of Frederick Caille from her mind. It was how she placed barriers around herself, thrusting Clerkenwell away, again and again. To Miss Bournelle's, and a quiet sitting in which many mysteries were explained, from the turbulent nature of the Aether to the reason why the dead may not wish to speak. All was concocted from Catherine's books and journals—or pure invention. Miss Bournelle, upright and stick-like, retained the discipline of a nanny, even if there was an affectionate nature somewhere beneath. Small errors and inconsistencies were questioned.

"Some who have the gift," said Madame Rostov, "wonder if there are influences on other Planes who may deliberately seek to confuse, to obfuscate."

As opposed to Catherine simply forgetting the name of Miss Bournelle's late friend in Holloway, and saying Janet instead of Judith. She was still prone to these mistakes. Fortunately the talk of "influences" served for the hostess and the two elderly couples who formed the rest of that night's circle.

"Will there be a manifestation, Madame?" asked a quite tiny, stooped gentleman.

"Madame Rostov is not a physical medium," said Miss Bournelle.

She was not. The complications of producing "psychic" matter from various orifices, or parading vague images of the dear departed, did not appeal to Catherine.

She survived the afternoon, and the dry, crumbling seed-cake which followed. The circle, all quite comfortable in retirement, pressed her to one pound and sixteen shillings, which she received with her usual show of reluctance. It would pay Catherine's rent, and a portion she would keep aside, in case she found Dry at her side one chill night.

The smallest part would appear at Levinia Weatherhead's bedside. The matriarch was no better, no worse. The doctor believed this the plateau before death, a time of quiet as the body gave up its last vestiges of resistance.

New clients were not that easy to find, arising in dribs and drabs and mostly by word of mouth. Coincidence and happenstance had taken her this far, but as she extended her knowledge, she learned more of the others who traded in glimpses Beyond the Veil. Showmen, who sat in vaudeville halls and had messages from "Someone whose name is J…J… might it be a Julia?" (there always was a Julia). Self-effacing women who protested they had no gift, and then filled a house with raps and strange creaking noises. Americans, quite the worse, with their colonial determination and panoply of trick devices—how the trumpets did dance and play themselves in darkened rooms! Her competitors seemed to have the knack of drawing audiences, one way or another.

Nothing had challenged the assumption which she formed in Keighley—that most spiritualist circles consisted of harmless folk, and that most mediums, psychics and their ilk were engaged in taking advantage of such people. Not all, though. Her own gift was genuine, when it arose, but her performances in general were not.

The dead did not speak to her—but those who brought death had certainly called, and left their cards. It was a thought that, as usual, she tried to purge from her consciousness.

Each visit to Stepney was an imposition she laid on herself. A duty.

No, not merely duty, she recognised. The fading end of her affection for Charles, the most decent of men, and a certain spite, a stab against her father, who had never lifted a finger to assist this side of the family. It was as if by clenching her teeth and doing what she could at Brantridge Street, she was challenging him. *I am better than you, Joshua Weatherhead,* her actions said.

She sat with the mostly insensate, wheezing shadow that was Aunt Levinia, whilst Clarissa patched and mended below. Jennie was usually absent. Catherine and her cousin shared few words, though she saw a little more of Charles and Clarissa's children.

Benjamin was a grave boy, isolated as the only male left in the family; Maisie, no beauty on the outside, had a generous manner and when not at school or collecting from the laundry, sat by her mother's knee and learned the ways of the seamstress. They seemed to view "Aunt Catherine," so much younger than Clarissa and Jennie, as a peculiar stranger who drifted in and out from the night, occasionally bearing gifts.

"You should not spoil them," said Clarissa.

"It was a florin. I suggested that they might have new socks for the winter, without bothering you."

"And when you are not around to attend to the state of their stockings?" Her cousin stabbed at a patch of thick hessian backing with a curved needle.

"Then they will still have warm socks for you to mend," snapped Catherine, returning to the cold, cramped room upstairs.

When she at last found an excuse to leave, and was in the act of pulling the front door shut behind here, she was surprised to find herself accosted by two women walking up the street.

"Oh, Catherine, good to see you," said the older one.

Catherine suddenly realised that the speaker was Jennie Weatherhead. She tried to gather her thoughts.

"Cousin, yes. Good to see you, also."

The other woman was more Catherine's age. Her locks dangled loosely, and one ankle was deliberately on show. A prostitute, by appearance.

"My friend, Ginger," said Jennie.

Catherine managed a polite smile. Friend, then, however that friendship had come about, but enquiry would have to wait. The last thing Catherine wanted at that moment was to be invited back into the tenement.

"I don't have time to linger at present, I fear. Perhaps soon."

And she sped on her way, eager to be free of Brantridge Street.

⚹

Her session that week at Lady Seldon's was awkward, with much unsaid at first. Amelia was oblivious to Madame Rostov's visit to Evelyn Caille; Lady Seldon and Lottie clearly meant matters to remain that way. Catherine guided them through automatic writing again, and there was consensus that Lottie had outlined not words, but the images of a giraffe and a lion. A visit to Africa in her future, they concluded.

She did not—dared not—attempt any genuine contact with the Aether. Because it was safer, and because she had few apart from Mrs Bessovitch with whom to talk, she showed them how one might tilt and rap at a table.

"You risk yourself, Madame Rostov, showing us these tricks," said Lady Seldon, as she knelt and watched Catherine use a wooden "clicker" on one knee to make the table speak. "Might we not wonder at the nature of your own talents?"

"Lucy!" Amelia looked amused and shocked. "Madame arms us against the frauds and mountebanks."

Lady Seldon shared a look with the smiling psychic. Yes, thought Catherine, there is a mind in that slim, privileged woman. And she wondered how many of Harry Seldon's votes and party stances were informed by his wife.

When Miss Baring-Smith apologised that she had an appointment to keep, and took her leave, the atmosphere changed. The maid who brought the sherry tray was dismissed, the doors to the drawing room closed.

"You saw Evelyn." Lottie perched on the edge of a divan, refusing a cigarette from Lady Seldon. Catherine had wanted to cultivate the habit of smoking pungent Russian cigarettes for her imposture, but her attempts so far had left her choking and slightly sick.

"Yes." Catherine stared into the swirl of her sherry glass. She had to remember that she was Madame Rostov. "It is true, she carries a great burden. Thank you, Lady Seldon, for your kind introduction."

She outlined a version of her visit to Grove House, giving them the colour of the situation, describing Evelyn's general health and demeanour as best she could, but omitting most of the conversation. She risked sharing the incident with the butler, Tanner.

"Do you think I did wrong?"

They thought on this.

"Tanner will report back to his master, or his master's closer aides," said Lady Seldon. "But no, they say that Evelyn rarely laughs these days. To be shown, even for a moment, that all is not under Caille's control will be good for her spirit. You did well, Madame." She lit another cigarette. "Amelia does not know of this, and I would be grateful if you did not enlighten her. The situation is...unstable."

"Of course." Catherine pushed away a tangle of hair from her face. "I am your servant, Lady Seldon."

Though quite what she represented in this company remained uncertain.

"I do still wish we could help poor Evelyn in some more substantial way," said Lottie. "If only we—"

"I will do what you ask, though you have not quite asked it."

"I'm sorry?" Lottie stared, and Catherine realised that her lips had spoken Edwin Dry's words out loud. Her glass fell to the floor, spreading a stain across the Persian rug. A brown stain like dried blood...

Madame Rostov struggled for words; Catherine Weatherhead fainted.

When she came to her senses, she was stretched out on the divan, and a mob-capped parlour maid was scrubbing at the Persian rug. She sought the mantle-clock, and saw that four, five minutes had passed.

"You had a turn, Madame. Lucy is arranging a carriage." Lottie sat on the arm of the divan, looking both concerned and excited. "Was that..." She leaned close enough for Catherine to smell the *oloroso* on her breath. "Was that a vision, a premonition? Did some spirit grasp and use you?"

"I...yes, yes." She sat up, smoothing down her dress. "It has passed, Miss Chambers, thank you for your kindness."

Lottie's voice was a whisper, her eyes on the vexed maid.

"Was it to do with Evelyn? That voice...it was not yours, Madame."

Catherine could not let her lives tangle like this. She could not. A practised medium would recover quickly, and would have experience enough to explain. She accepted a glass of water.

"This can happen." The water was cold, slightly metallic. It helped. "When the Aether is disturbed, when we allow ourselves to be open to difficult thoughts…all manner of influences, often the vaguest of things, may brush us. They mean nothing."

Lady Seldon returned, the butler Merrins at her heel.

"My carriage will take you where you will," she said. "Are you well enough to stand, Madame Rostov, or would you care to rest here a while longer? There is no haste, no haste at all."

"You are gracious, but I should search out my own couch, Lady Seldon." Catherine got to her feet. "Such moments pass quickly."

A chill October fog had clamped its hands around the world outside, each street light a distant star. Vague figures came and went along the street. By the two-horse carriage, its side emblazoned with the Seldon arms, Lady Seldon halted.

"I saw no giraffe, no lion. The girls are bored, and you bring stimulating new ideas to our little circle."

Catherine stood, one hand on the carriage. *But?* she thought. There was something else to come. Dismissal from her post as entertainer?

The other woman looked at her, grave-faced.

"I have sat and heard poor imitations of those who have passed, the garbled nonsense "brought" by spirit guides. There must be entire tribes of misunderstood Red Indians floating above our city, wondering at our denseness." She gave a sharp laugh. "Just now, though—you echoed a quite different sort of spirit."

"My lady?"

Lady Seldon stepped back, gesturing to the carriage driver.

"I believe that you have touched darkness, Madame Rostov, and seen into others' minds. There is no trick there, of that I am convinced. You may visit at your leisure, and be welcome here."

As Catherine took her seat, the carriage pulled away, and she pressed her mind to immediacies. Where to go? She could not be taken to Mrs Bessovitch's. None knew where Madame Rostov lived, and it had to remain that way. There was no doubt that a woman as sharp as Lucy Seldon would enquire of her coachman when he returned.

"De Keyser's, if you please," she said to the man at the reins.

De Keyser's Royal Hotel would do. There were many continentals there, and it was close to Blackfriars bridge. She could mingle unnoticed in the foyer, seem to recall something, and walk across the bridge to Southwark without notice. Or, given the weather, take a hansom from the hotel.

The Royal Hotel was a bulk of gleaming eyes, the lights from its windows struggling with fog that had grown denser, colder. When Lady Seldon's carriage had gone, she had the doorman find her transport, and was finally dropped at the end of the street by her lodgings.

She was calm, organised, and so when she gained the warm kitchen, to see Mrs B ensconced by the fire, toasting a muffin, she sat down and wept, uncontrollably.

Her hands would not hold the mug of milk and brandy she was offered; her mouth would not make words. Mrs Bessovitch went back to her muffin, turning it, and as she did so, she lent the room a lullaby, some Russian song in a low, slightly cracked voice.

At last Catherine lifted the mug, and drank deep.

"I may have done something terrible," she said. "And I have done it over a few cans of spoiled meat, and a woman I do not really know."

Her landlady gave her an enquiring look.

"It is the man, yes? The man who kills. I have seen that face of yours, when he has been in head."

"It is, in a sense. And it is about the one who killed my cousin Charles."

Catherine wiped her eyes, and a new flood commenced, not tears but words.

She spoke to Mrs Bessovitch of Harwich, *HMS Penelope*, and the fate of her cousin Charles. Some Mrs B knew, but not the whole. The tale had come up to Yorkshire, to be dismissed by her father as nothing to do with them, but Catherine remembered all, the details drummed into her by Levinia much later, or laid out inside the box upstairs.

On the sixth day of November, 1885, a blustery evening, the *Penelope* stood off the east coast on guard-duty, no more than ten miles from Harwich. Lieutenant Charles Weatherhead, accepting the hospitality of the midshipmen, sat down to a meal. With the last of the fresh beef used up by the officer's wardroom, and a supply-lighter not expected until the morning, they shared a meal of tinned meat, peas, and turnips from Harwich gardens. This was washed down with watered rum and a bottle of German wine, brought by the lieutenant as his offering.

By the end of the following week, he and three of those midshipmen were dead, the victims of food poisoning. Botulism, the Naval doctors said—a slow and painful death for those who succumbed. Several petty officers of the same vessel were hospitalised, but declared fit for duty within the fortnight.

Catherine asked for more brandy, less milk.

"Meat inspectors gathered at the Harwich Victualling Yard and opened over two hundred cans of meat destined for the Navy." She read out the facts from memory. "Not until they opened the twenty seventh can did they found one fit for human consumption. It was in the Illustrated News, all of it. They found ligaments, offal, tendons—some from what could only have been diseased animals, where the species of animal could even be identified. They found evidence that the cans had not been heated sufficiently, nor sealed with due attention."

"Tch." The landlady scowled. "To save pennies, they would risk lives."

"They took lives," said Catherine. "It was an embarrassment to the Admiralty, not one they wished to pursue in public. The relatives of Charles and the other sailors made enquiries— spoiled food was regularly supplied by the Harwich and

Deptford Victualling Yard. Regularly! The contract in question was held by Frederick Caille, a man with many such contracts, a man also involved in banking and industry at the heart of London. He denied any fault, so the families hired a lawyer to sue Caille and his company for reparation—and to expose his profiteering.

"There was no doubt. A hired investigator uncovered written evidence that Caille had a direct hand in the matter, instructing his workers to use sub-standard meat, and to process it cheaply. Temperatures were not met; the hygiene in the factories was appalling."

Mrs Bessovitch placed another muffin on the toasting fork. "So is proof for court, yes?"

Catherine was weary, but it was the first time she had told the entire story to anyone outside the family. She made herself continue.

"No. The investigator, a retired policeman, disappeared—the day after he wrote to the relatives' lawyer, to say that he had the proof. He was never seen again. No one ever discovered if he was bribed, or threatened. He might even have been beaten to ensure his silence. The result was the same—nothing tangible that could be used against Caille."

"What is happen to case, then?"

"Dismissed after four long months," said Catherine. "Two foremen were reprimanded, another dismissed. When the factories were inspected, they were clean, and all equipment new. Very new. Caille's contracts continued. He was begged for a gesture towards the bereaved; he laughed, and told them to seek such from the foremen involved—men he had instructed!"

"These men—"

"All three found work in South America within a week of the case being dismissed, and took ship accordingly. South America, where Caille has many business interests..."

"It is sad story. This is how your people, they are so poor?"

"The families were left penniless." She took the muffin from her landlady, and made to smear it with butter, but put it down. Here, in the warm, well-lit kitchen, it seemed possible to think, again. "My aunt—Levinia—even as she lies dying, wants vengeance on Caille. She wants him to suffer, to rot, for what he did to her son. For his arrogance, his utter lack of contrition."

"Is understandable."

"But is it understandable that she passes this burden to me?"

"Tch. What is little Katerina to do, with such a powerful man? And who is this woman, who you do not know?"

"Caille's wife." She gave her landlady a much abbreviated version of the situation.

The house creaked; the hearth spat. They sat quiet for a while on either side of the table.

"I met the bowler-hatted man who plagues my dreams. I did not mean to, nor do I know quite how it came about." Catherine pressed her knuckles together. "I met him. The one who kills without conscience."

Mrs Bessovitch nodded her head slowly.

"And you tell him, Frederick Caille is no good. You tell him he should kill this factory-man."

Catherine stiffened. "I…I was scared, confused. I did say it, though I'd had no such intention. It happened so quickly…" What else could she have done? Better an inept, foolish client than another victim.

"Is what I might do," said Mrs Bessovitch, surprisingly matter-of-fact.

"You might?" Catherine's eyes wide, she took in the plump, aproned figure before her, grey hair pinned back, a smear of butter on a rounded cheek. One or two crumbs of muffin clung to a chin that was beginning to whisker.

"Da. I tell you story now, very short. You hear me speak of my Aaron?"

"Your husband? Yes, you said he died, went overboard, at sea."

"Is so. It was mercy."

"He was not well, then—or troubled?"

"It was mercy for me, not poor Aaron." Mrs Bessovitch eased herself up, wiping her chin. She smiled, a fond expression on her face.

"Meant I did not have to use arsenic I buy."

CHAPTER TWELVE

Southwark, November 1886

Within the month, Dry had said. Catherine was left to wait and fret. She took small engagements, where she sensed that the clients were predisposed to be gulled or guided, wanting re-assurance rather than hardened fact. Was a mother safe in Heaven, would a child be granted God's grace? Yes, and yes, so many affirmations that she grew bored with her own tongue. The Aether did not tremble; the Veil did not part.

Each day she checked the newspapers—bought, borrowed, or glimpsed on an omnibus—waiting for news on the fortunes of Frederick Caille. And with each day her confidence took a blow.

At one lonely hour of the clock, after a particularly tiresome sitting, she conceived the idea that a police inspector might be the next to rap upon her door, accusing her of trying to assassinate an upstanding member of the business community. She constructed defences for anyone who might question her. She had been distraught, of course, at the condition of her cousins, and that had led her into folly.

Or, thinking on it, she could do better—all was but a phantasy to appease a dying widow, played to seem as if she had done the widow's bidding. She would laugh, and laughing, draw any officer of the law into the absurdity that Catherine Weatherhead could have anything to do with the lives of those who moved at the level of Mr Caille. Who was she but an insignificant young woman?

As proof of her erratic moods, she then became worried that Dry would come for her. An easier target than Caille, after all. He would remove her, now that she knew his face…

"I have your scent..."

When these anxieties tumbled out over the breakfast table, Mrs Bessovitch pointed out that she had given the bowler-hatted man no name, no address. They had not even met near where Catherine lived. How could he possibly find her, whether he did the deed or not?

Work lined her purse enough to meet the rent and spare a crown or two for her cousins. The atmosphere at Brantridge Street was cheerless. Levinia's sunken eyes asked questions which she could not answer—she had not mentioned (how could she?) the vaguest possibility that Mr Dry would complete his commission. Not mentioned that such a commission existed. The longer it went, the more deranged the idea, and the entire Clerkenwell episode, seemed.

There came a Saturday of especial tedium. Mrs Combes, a shrill woman whose husband had managed to escape her via the kindness of a rheumatic heart, was determined not to let the poor man have peace. It was Catherine's third sitting with her—between obituary notices and a few pence to Mrs Combes's truculent daily, Catherine had enough to keep up the charade.

She was also experimenting with the introduction of a Spirit Guide, a ludicrous notion sparked by Lady Seldon's comments. To stand out from her peers, Catherine's imaginary guide was a Mongolian. "Temur" was a shaman from a suitably vague period in Mongolian history, and was to assist her in locating poor Mr Combes, amongst others.

Much to Catherine's annoyance, Mrs Combes pressed for more detail than was to hand, and she had to bluff her way through parts of the sitting. She abandoned Temur, and concentrated on "seeing," hoping that her genuine gift might make itself known. Nothing but an intense headache resulted, and she had to end the session.

"There are other spirits, blocking me," she said as she left. "Darker ones, which do not wish us fortune today."

Mrs Combes's hand hovered at her throat. "I can't imagine why, Madame Rostov. I certainly have no stain to draw that sort of attention, and neither did poor George." She sniffed. "Unless you yourself have…"

Catherine was unwilling to follow that line of thought.

"Perhaps another day," she muttered, and quit the house without making the usual appointment for a further sitting. As she trudged homewards, she decided to let Mrs Combes find someone else to badger "poor George."

Light snow fell from a heavy sky, and her head…the non-existent Temur was beating his drum within. A pork chop did no good, and neither did brandy or one of Mrs B's powders. Catherine retired early, unable to undertake her usual research into potential clients. The room seemed smaller than before, more mean in aspect, and again she thought of the money which had gone to her cousins. The snow had stopped, and barely a breeze troubled the lodging house chimneys, letting the fire glow peaceably in the hearth. Those coals cost extra, and winter was coming.

Lying on her bed with her boots still on, she felt the blood pound through her temples, saw the veins stand out on her wrists, and knew that something dreadful was coming. This would be Islington and Clerkenwell again, in all their painful clarity, the opening of an inner eye beyond her control. She pressed her palms to her face, covering her eyes.

She could still see.

This was not the dusty room at Mrs Bessovitch's, but a vaster swathe of night, a London of sparse gas-lamps and yawning alleys. The Thames churned, sickened by its diet of sewerage and bloated bodies; the stars were hard, uncaring dots. She had no idea where she was, if she was anywhere.

Trembling on the bed, her mind embraced the night, the vision so clear that she might have been walking through a photograph, a photograph which lived. There were night-sounds around her, and she smelled the ordure of animals in great numbers, like the cattle farms of her native Yorkshire, yet she was deep in the city.

Her hands gripped the bed-frame, and she tried to guide herself, in vain. Her self, her focus, was drawn to a set of great gates, these closed but flanked by two gatehouses, crossed anchors carved upon them. Each gatehouse had its own lesser door, and the one on the left was open. Through this she swept, insensible of any contact with the ground, and there she watched the act unfold, that act she had set in motion without truly understanding…

Mr Edwin Dry walks calm and straight through the Deptford Victualling Yard, close by the Foreign Cattle Market. He pauses beneath the ornate bell-tower, and examines his half-hunter by moonlight. Sunday tomorrow, and hardly a light in the compound. Adams, the Superintendent, is home with his seven children, wondering if there is more he can trim from the budget to satisfy his masters; only one of the Assistant Victualling Store officers still holds late vigil, alone in an office by the high-beamed bulk of the cattle warehouse.

Dry has measures in place to engage and occupy any night rounders, to draw away constables who might wonder if they should check the Grove Street beat once more, rather than head for cocoa at the cab-men's shelter further down. And once such arrangements are agreed, he leaves them to others.

His focus is on the victualling offices—their precise configuration, those small variants on what can be gleaned from maps and descriptions. To the northwest, nearest the adjoining railway yards and stores, are the offices he seeks. Quiet places in brick buildings; good places for men to discuss matters of business which should not be widely known.

The Honourable Eric Seaton will not be attending tonight's meeting with Frederick Caille. Not long after dusk his youngest son, a babe of less than two, was taken from his nursery, the nurse chloroformed. The child will be found unharmed and none the worse for his experience in the morning, but Seaton does not know this, and in his panic, he has forgotten all other engagements.

Thus Caille and his bully boys sit in an Assistant Victualler's office and await Seaton in vain. Certain adulterants, meats of dubious provenance, will not enter the Deptford Yard later this month as a result. Mr Dry has already observed another man enter the Yard, but he knows this man and his purpose. Constable Retton from the local station, deep in debt to one of Caille's associates, a policeman bought and paid for should he be needed. If he runs, and runs fast enough, Mr Dry has no interest in him.

Pale eyes capture the scene and identify the side-entrance mentioned by his contacts. He moves through shadows—there is always the chance of a late cashier or drunken boatswain crossing the grounds—towards his goal. The lock surrenders with one twist of a wire. Inside, high-ceilinged corridors are pockmarked with office doors, all firm shut save one.

Mr Dry pauses. He brushes a trace of whitewash from the sleeve of his heavy outdoor coat, and places himself within himself, aware of each fold and pocket, each tool of his trade. He cannot be excited or fearful, for this is not his nature. He can, however, be appreciative that the endeavour is far more bold than his previous commissions. His client, the curious black-haired woman at the Crown and Sceptre, is of little interest to him. There are things which he will learn from this night, however the required outcome is achieved.

Which it will be.

The soles of his boots are coated in gutta-percha, and make no sound as he approaches the open doorway. There is conversation within; the bray of one who commands, and the whine of those who serve.

It is said that Frederick Caille's men are armed, for the magnate has a distaste of the lower classes which borders on fear, and a man of his stature has enemies. Two years ago an attempt was made on his life by an Italian who had fallen into disgrace—the result of financial dealings with Caille's bank. Mr Dry does not rely on firearms. They have an indiscriminate nature, and can fail or fire regardless of the owner's wishes. He is provided for tonight, though, with two small and well-sighted revolvers. Just in case.

He reaches into his overcoat, and takes out a curiosity, an American Civil War grenade which he acquired from a collector in Paddington. The heavy iron ovoid has no charge, but it looks the part. Leaning in, he tosses the grenade into the outer office, an action which brings forth cries of horror and surprise from within.

The bully boy nearest the door is transfixed, staring at the supposed deadly object; there have been bombings in London in recent years. The other shows more presence of mind and seeks to kick the grenade from the room. Mr Dry moves in, twisting to his left and away in a smooth turn which drives his slender blade into the stunned man's jugular and out again, avoiding the resultant red spray. His silent dance across the tiled floor brings him to the second man, who hesitates between this sudden assailant and the grenade. He is dying as he falls across the harmless device, and Mr Dry is already pressed hard against the wall by the inner door, waiting.

An angry query from within; an order. Police Constable Retton appears, slack-jawed at the sight before him.

"Run," says Mr Dry.

Retton's broken-veined face pales, but some fateful instinct, perhaps gained many years past when he was young and decent enough, makes him raise his official billy club and stand, blocking the inner doorway. He manages to deflect the first cut of the knife with his truncheon. A second thrust finds his belly, but heavy serge and brass buttons foil its intent; in return, the truncheon fails to connect with Dry's left shoulder.

Unfortunate seconds have passed. Mr Dry slashes across the tendons of Retton's stick hand, slides beneath a swing and drives the point under the constable's chin. The man's scream is choked by blood and steel, and the blade is free.

The first shot from the inner office comes close to taking Retton in the head, but the constable is done. He slumps to the floor, his arms outstretched and one leg gently kicking, a pithed frog on a finely tiled tray.

A second shot, wild.

"Who's out there? Show yourselves!"

An interesting situation. Caille was not reputed to carry a weapon himself, though Dry had prepared for the possibility. He reviews his knowledge of the offices. A grand window at the far side of the inner office gives access to the grounds. Caille can hide behind the desk and wait, or he can seek to speed his way from the room through that window. Dry crouches low by the doorway, listening to catch any sounds which might provide further information— the scrape of heels or furniture, the grate of...

A window catch.

Caille's two shots have relieved the need for quiet work. Dry darts forward, gripping the small revolver which was resting in its slide above his right wrist. He fires once at the figure halfway through the open window and rolls to the cover of the large oak desk. An oath tells him that the bullet has hit home, but the thud and faltering step on the gravel outside add the likelihood of a flesh wound only—or a slow, unreliable bleed.

Retton is not a large man. Mr Dry grips the corpse and drags it into the inner office. Sliding both arms around the constable's waist, he lifts it up to the window. This time the shot, which comes from a dark mass of shrubbery a few yards to the west, takes Retton in the chest, not that it matters to the constable any more. Dry is over the sill, outside and low to the ground even as the corpse falls back.

"Name your price, you bastard!" Caille yells from the bushes.

"It will be met by another." Mr Dry fires in the direction of the voice and the muzzle-flash from before.

"I can match and beat..." The words are interrupted by a wet cough, "...any amount of coin you've been offered. And the shots will have been heard."

Caille fires back, but Dry is no longer there. He moves with economic speed, sliding into the bushes to the right and behind them. The grey hunched shape of Caille is easily seen, and then Dry is behind the wounded man, sliding his revolver back into its mechanism as he moves. There are times when it suits him that a death should be a personal one.

A skilled journeyman must be close to his trade.

The garrotte wire is cold around Frederick Caille's neck before he can sense the presence at his back. Bleeding from a shoulder wound, the magnate lets his firearm drop to the wet grass.

"Why?" says Caille.

"Must there always be reasons?"

Mr Dry holds the garrotte tight with one hand, and wipes his glasses on Caille's jacket with the other, removing a spot of someone's blood. Either the man is too weak from pain and blood loss to struggle, or he is considering, at last, the possibility that all empires fall.

"Everything…" Caille manages, "Has purpose. What, damn it, is the source of your hate for me?"

"Hate?" Dry's pale eyes widen, and for a heartbeat a smile might have been about to form. "I am, sir, utterly indifferent to you."

The wire bites deep; the throat constricts. Two, three kicks; a low choking noise. Then Frederick Caille, a fine and mighty power in the great financial labyrinth of London, becomes no more than the sub-standard meat that he purveys.

A whistle in the distance, and the sounds of running men, but not too close as yet. The Deptford Victualling Yard is sizeable, and has many shadows. He blends, dances in darkness, noting small details as he leaves. On Windmill Lane he sights a female figure clutching her shawl as she hastens to be elsewhere. She would be the one assigned to distract the night rounders—the prostitute Mary Jane Kelly. The job was well enough done; she may be worth remembering, assuming the pox or the casual violence of the streets do not take her.

He does not hurry. He walks the tow-path of the Surrey Canal, and breathes in the night.

Twenty three days have passed since he met a woman in Clerkenwell.

CHAPTER THIRTEEN

Southwark, November 1886

She had not risen from her bed for two days, except to relieve herself. She did not wash; she hardly ate. The water carafe was always full, as if some house-sprite came when she slept, or when she lay in blind consciousness. Dried spittle marked her nightdress, and her dark mane of hair was unwashed, unbrushed.

"There are letters." Mrs Bessovitch, framed against the gaslight on the landing. "Again. I pick them up this afternoon for you."

Catherine did not speak.

She had killed a man—a vile man, true, and by another's hand, but the ease of it appalled her. You spoke into an ear, gave a name, and soon the one who bore that name was dead. It did not matter who. You could name a kindly matron, or a much-loved politician. You could take against a neighbour, or an interfering police inspector. She doubted that it made much difference.

The ease of it...if you knew a certain person.

The papers glared and sparked on the day after Deptford. Boys stalked the streets with extra copies, calling out the news with glee.

"Slaughter in the Yards!"

"Four dead by murderous hands!"

"Criminal gang leaves trail of blood!"

She smiled at that one—a mad smile, which she imagined could be found in many an asylum. Had there been a gang, had she by some means organised a crew of sticker-men and common bravoes, all ready to tumble with Frederick Caille and his guards…then she might have understood what she had done. But she had only said a name.

To Edwin Dry.

Mrs Bessovitch read to her at first. Each edition carried more, most newspapers convinced that a mob of incensed workers had entered Deptford Yard that night, surely a dozen men. The police and authorities responded, denying that it could be that number. "Impossible," said Scotland Yard. Despite regrettable delays, and disturbances elsewhere which had occupied some of the constabulary, no such mob could have been involved. Three or four skilled miscreants then, responded the papers the next morning. Editors and senior officers played numbers. As for who exactly would arrange such a thing…

Fenians. Jewish malcontents. French agitators and Balkan dissidents. A rival Anglo-Irish businessman, whose corned beef trade was under threat from Caille's industries. Catholics (though no sense was ever made of this one). A senior minister of Her Majesty's Government, deep in debt to Caille. Escaped lunatics, finding themselves discovered in the Victualling Yard and panicking.

They did not suggest a young woman from Southwark.

"It does not appear," said Mrs B carefully, on the third day, a Wednesday, "That this Caille will be much missed."

Editors and reporters then began to close sharp teeth on other matters related to the event. Scandals concerning Frederick Caille, certain cases of which few had dared speak until now. Reports that two of the dead men had extensive criminal records before their gainful employment as the magnate's guards. And with great reluctance, the Metropolitan Commissioner confirmed that Police Constable Alfred Retton did not have a spotless record. That he was under investigation for possible misconduct—which many took to be a way of explaining why he had been there, so far from his beat. There was no appetite for "avenging our own" in the constabulary, apparently. Not where Retton was concerned.

Certain politicians expressed sorrow and outrage—briefly,

and where it suited them; it was rumoured that others lifted brandy glasses in their clubs and cheered. Caille's business peers surveyed his empire, eager to partition that tempting sprawl between them.

Catherine lay helpless because she had been at Deptford, an unwilling observer, and had heard the final gasps of Frederick Caille.

Because she had heard that sound ten years before.

In Keighley.

It had issued from the mouth of a woman she admired, an unhappy woman in a bad marriage, who often read to a young girl, and taught her letters better than any school. Maggie Witten, the wife of Uncle Jack, her father's trusted friend.

Catherine had slept, had "seen" the trusted friend choke the breath out of his wife—and when she woke, much later, she ran downstairs still in her nightgown—shrieking the news that Uncle Jack had slain his wife with his own hands.

But no, that could not be, she was told. The Night Mare had crouched on the girl's chest, misleading her. Jack Witten had been with Joshua Weatherhead, drinking and playing cards in the back-parlour at the Weatherheads' house until ever so late. He had slept on an old settee in there—there was the rumpled blanket which had covered him. And here was Uncle Jack, returning from the privy…

Catherine would not be silenced, not even by blows from her father's hard hand. So they must go see. They found the body in Jack's plain, gloomy back room, Maggie Witten's face mottled and half-blue, the bruising clear on her neck. The cabinet and sideboard were in disarray, the drawers turned out. Fourteen years old, behind her mother's legs, Catherine saw all this as well.

"A thief, a burglar!"cried Joshua Weatherhead. "Surprised in the act."

"By God, it's true!" cried Jack, his strong, thick fingers over his mouth.

They bustled Catherine away, and made her close her

lips. The houses adjoined—a mild fever and strange sounds, perhaps raised voices, had fused into a dreadful dream. At first they were almost kind, but she was Mardy Cath, the "difficult" girl. The more she spoke, the less they heard. No one would hear that Jack had a hand—two hands—in the murder of his own wife.

Blood was not thicker than water, especially when the water was taken with whiskey and shared between two friends of long-standing. Jack and Joshua, drinking partners for many years. Inseparable. When there was a bottle around, at least.

Had Joshua Weatherhead known the truth? Or had he covered for his friend? It didn't matter. His daughter was instructed that she would not spread foul slander, nor speak of visions and visitations. She had no gift, nothing special—she was a trouble and a woe to her poor mother. Should she persist, there was always the cracked leather belt which hung behind Joshua's door…

After a suitable period of mourning, Jack Witten married a farmer's daughter, heavy-chested and without her letters. The murderous burglar was never found; Joshua and Jack were never quite as close.

"I cannot speak with the dead," Catherine moaned, alone in her Southwark room. The letters were on her night-stand; Mrs Bessovitch was gone from the doorway. "But I can watch them, hear them, being made…"

On the third day she awoke to the lullaby she had heard before, brought or borrowed from wherever Mrs Bessovitch grew up. Snatches of Russian, something else that sounded close to it, and the occasional word of English. The tune was soothing, if sad.

"Is enough, Katerina" said her landlady when Catherine opened her eyes. "Three days, is enough. Tch. How do you pay me if you do not work? How do you become famous lady this way? One man, four men, die. What is this, in such a world?"

Catherine lifted her hands from under the coverlet, looked at the pale blue veins.

"It is not Caille. Many would say that he deserved to meet his end that way. Many wished it, I think, if they could not see him jailed and ruined. It is…the sight, the knowledge that comes to me, with each death."

"Da. This I understand. But you are young woman, strong. What do you say to Mrs Gelderd, who loses seven children before any is one year old? To Pieter, who has stall by cathedral? Wife and children die from bad water, and in this fine country."

"But I…"

"You have worse than them? Because is in head, not in room where you can touch?"

Catherine searched for an answer to that, found none.

"See?" The other woman held out a clean dress. "You wear clothes, you come down for eggs. Tea. Toast. If you want be sad, go to cemetery. Tell Pieter's wife you are sad. See what she will say."

None of it was said in anger, or reproach, which might have driven her to pull the coverlet back around her. It was said because it was true, and she could not deny it.

"I will join you…shortly," said Catherine. "Truly, I will."

She took breakfast at two in the afternoon, awkward with the food at first and then ravenous.

"Enough," said Mrs B, when she asked for more toast. "Belly will burst, or get angry. Besides, where is money for this feast?" But that was said with a wink of the eye.

Fed, and then bathed, Catherine dressed herself and looked to the letters on the night-stand, not yet sure if she could face opening them. Seven were to Madame Rostov. Of these, one was the cream, quality envelope that usually marked a communication from Lady Seldon. The other six would likely be requests for her services—she thought that one of those was addressed in Mrs Combes's hand. A polite reply that she was engaged elsewhere for the foreseeable future would answer that one.

Two envelopes were addressed to Miss C Weatherhead. The uppermost was in Jennie's awkward writing, the other clearly from Clarissa. She opened the first one.

> *My dearest Catherine. Poor Mama asks for you again. I do not think she will be long with us, and I beg that you come to see her, though I know how hard this is. I reckon only too well how C can be Fractious and difficult. Apart from Mama, we are well, in our way, and B has been praised at Sunday School. I am engaged much away from Brantridge St, adding a little to the Coffers, but hope we will meet soon. Yr Affectionate cousin, Jennie.*

With less enthusiasm, she opened Clarissa's letter. It was somewhat blunter in its approach. Levinia Weatherhead would die soon, should Catherine have "time to spare" to see her before then.

She made herself read that morning's paper, with its continued speculations as to the "Deptford affair," though already this was relegated to the second page. Soon there would be other crimes, news from abroad, an announcement on butter prices, and so it went.

An omnibus; a brisk walk through November rain. The beggars and huddled figures around Stepney seemed set like statues in the downpour, with barely the vitality to call out their woes or needs. At Brantridge Street, Clarissa let her in immediately, taking her dripping coat and umbrella.

"Not long," she said. "I am…I am grateful that you came, cousin."

Catherine stood wary, but this was a genuine Clarissa, borne down by her situation and the shadow of Death in the room above. Her eyes spoke of sickness, exhaustion. Did her cousin not know that Frederick Caille was dead? Surely those would have been her first words, if she was aware of it?

"You should rest," said Catherine. "Find me some simple mending which will help, and I will sit with Aunt Levinia."

No argument, no caustic words. It was a year since Charles Weatherhead died—Charles who placed decent food upon the table, and tempered Clarissa's ways with his homely good nature. As she climbed the stairs, Catherine found herself missing him. And knowing that he would not have approved of what she had done...

Levinia's face was ready for the death-mask, the posed photograph. Her breath was hardly discernible—when it came, it was painful, laboured. Catherine sewed, addressing herself to simple tears in otherwise decent linen, and patches in inconspicuous places. Needlework would never be her strength.

The rain continued. She lit a candle rather than try to ignite the unreliable gas sconce on the wall. Her aunt turned slightly, and moaned. Catherine attended to her, and found part of the bed damp with urine. She slipped a torn tea-towel between Levinia and the linen, to take up some of the fluid. Should she lift her out of bed, try to change the bedclothes? She had no idea where fresh linen might be found in the house, and Clarissa slept in the other bedroom.

"Charles..." the old woman moaned.

"It is Catherine, Aunt Levinia. I am here."

"Catherine?" Eyes fluttered, opened a fraction. They were gummed, and Catherine wiped her aunt's face with a moistened cloth.

"Yes, I am here. Do you remember what you asked, what you demanded of me?"

Levinia looked confused for a moment. "What I...asked you?"

Sixty eight years stared at twenty four, the gap between so vast that it might have been oceans, or the sand-blasted wastes of foreign lands.

"It does not matter, aunt. You must lie easy."

The invalid's hand shot out, grasping her wrist. Catherine gasped at the unexpected touch—and the strength in that grip.

"I remember." Levinia's head turned to the window, the grey veil of rain. Some had entered through the cracked pane, droplets which caught the candlelight as they trickled down the glass. "I remember so much, Joshua's Child."

Catherine caught her aunt's wrist, returning the pressure. She felt the cold in her gut, and let it fill her eyes, her words. "I am *not* Joshua's Child. I am my own creation!"

Levinia coughed, shifting in the bed to look back at Catherine. An intelligence of old was awake in the old woman's face, a last flicker before eternal nightfall.

"Your own creation? What, then, have you wrought, girl?"

Catherine took a breath, a second breath, and tried to still her sudden anger. Her grip eased, though her aunt's had not.

"You burdened me, Aunt Levinia, with your pasteboard box and your hunger for vengeance. My father would have laughed, scorned such a burden and gone to his bottle or his account books, unconcerned."

"But you—"

"Frederick Caille is dead; the dogs fight over his empire. There. Are you content with what you have brought me to?"

"Caille is dead? This was by your hand?"

"By my instruction."

It was madness to say this aloud, and it would be madness if any believed it. A melodrama of ridiculous dimensions, too unfeasible to credit. The dying queen on her bed, and the faithful handmaiden who orchestrated her queen's revenge. Catherine wanted to laugh, to choke on bitter laughter.

Levinia stirred again, clutching the blankets with her free hand.

"Jennie says I will…be well, but I will not. Clarissa stitches a smile…on her face…and says all is in order, that we prosper. They are liars."

"I am also a liar," said Catherine. "All women must be. But in this, I swear I tell the truth, aunt. Caille was killed four days ago, and his men with him. My hands are bloody—though another served for the deed."

Wonder flickered across the old woman's face, and her eyes closed.

"Then I can rest," she said, more softly. "My Charles, my dearest Charles, someone has paid at last." Tears formed at the corner of one eye. "I have done a mother's duty."

Catherine felt her aunt's grip slide, and she too let go, stepping back from the bed.

She should have been relieved, her task completed. Instead she felt anger, that she had been pushed to this, had entangled herself until she could not escape. Despair, that she had crossed a street in Clerkenwell, when she could so easily have turned and spent her time on milliners' windows, wondering about a new hat for Madame Rostov—feathers, perhaps.

Frustration, that she was not now sat in a dimly-lit parlour, murmuring about the "dear departed" and earning her way through the credulous nature of Mankind.

There were no tragic queens, no handmaidens. An impoverished old woman lay on her death-bed in a damp Stepney garret, with lice in her hair. And a wilful girl from Keighley, who had read too many cheap and fanciful pamphlets, was swimming far out of her depth. Maybe she would drown because of it.

Levinia appeared to be asleep once more. Catherine blew out the candle, and took up the completed mending. No doubt Clarissa had a basket downstairs for work that was ready to go back out into the world…

"I never liked your father," said a weak voice from the bed. "Nor trusted him. Not in anything."

CHAPTER FOURTEEN

Stepney, December 1886

The newspapers have begun to speak of the Deptford Assassin. It is somewhat melodramatic for his taste, but it has a certain gravitas. He permits them to continue, though he would never describe himself in such terms.

For they have concluded that one man, of unnatural ability, slid in blood across the Deptford Victualling Yard. An Italian or Italian-American is their favourite suspect now, bred to the knife and the wire—a member of the "Red Circle" or some other such vicious and criminal organisation. Paid handsomely by persons unknown (rival bankers, perhaps) for his daring act of slaughter at the heart of Empire.

Giorgio Frazetti, a barber from Catford, is arrested, his razors examined and found to be entirely the wrong sort of instrument. Besides, Frazetti, it transpires, was thirty miles away that night, visiting on a sick cousin. The papers have not yet assigned the power of flight to the assassin.

The police do not comment, but it is said there have been telegrams to New York and Chicago. The Pinkerton Agency has been alerted.

Edwin Dry picks up the solitary gold sovereign that he gained by the venture. He is content, because he has satisfied himself, the only judge he recognises. It could be done, and it was.

Already he has catalogued small errors—the constable should have been removed immediately, for example. No warning. Those others who provided information and diversion had a certain value, but it might have been done without them. A journeyman must always learn.

He will keep the coin aside, to remind him. The black-haired

woman will have to be watched, of course.
He has her scent...

Josiah, son of Joshua, son of Joseph. A stooped young man in borrowed black mourning, the trousers slightly too long, the jacket too large, Josiah Weatherhead had the same untamed black hair as his older sister Catherine, his temporarily plastered down with hair oil and other preparations. His face, unlike hers, was weather-tanned. Anxiety swam beneath his dense eyebrows as he held his hat, dressed with black crepe, to his breast.

"I should not have come," he said as they walked, side by side.

Catherine wanted to snap at his meekness, but she restrained herself.

"It was a kind gesture, Josiah."

"Father said..."

She waited for the rest of the sentence, until she realised that there was no more, that it was there in her brother's face.

Father said.

This was Joshua's single token, then—despatching his son in pretence that they were all still family. There was no wreath, no letter of concern or condolence from the North. No offer of assistance. Just Josiah, thrust alone into the tangled skein of station, rail and junction, even though a pony cart from Keighley to an outlying village was usually the height of his adventures.

The mourners straggled from Bow Cemetery, with its great protective walls and its many—so many—mounds for the unmarked dead. Levinia Weatherhead lay in there now, silent in a public grave. A private plot was beyond the family's means, but the last of Catherine's money had insisted on an inscription grave. Levinia was buried with strangers, but her name was on the headstone with theirs. Better than the fate of most Stepney residents, heaped upon each other unmarked in a few feet of sour earth.

Jennie, supported on the arm of a hard-faced Clarissa, wept

throughout. Her brother was dead; and now her mother. It tore the heart to see her.

"The children, they look well," said Mrs Bessovitch as they quit the cemetery.

They did—Benjamin serious but with healthy red cheeks; Maisie unsure as to her role here, more interested in the finer monuments than the mean stone over her grandmother. Had others not been watching them, they would have been playing tag between the tombs.

Mrs B, named only as a "friend of the family" to anyone who asked, wore swathes of black muslin, her dress little different from her usual outdoor garb.

"You learn much of people at funeral, nyet? Today they wear special faces."

Her eyes was on the short procession of mourners behind them. Neighbours from Stepney attending out of curiosity, ready to criticise the arrangements, the clothes, the demeanour of family members. Tradesmen watching, wondering if this would leave their bills unpaid. And then there were the women who always followed funerals, slipping into the parade in their midnight crepe and worn silk. No one knew who they were, or cared.

Few present had any real concern for Levinia Weatherhead, the almost unknown woman from the sickroom at Brantridge Street.

Madame Rostov was not there, only Catherine. Madame Rostov brooded alone, for the time being. She had read the letter from Lady Seldon, though, the night before. Its core was direct.

I wonder at what vision or presentiment impelled
you to visit Mrs Caille, so close to her husband's
bloody, and well-deserved end—and what strange
currents flow beneath the surface of our lives.
Because you have expressed concern, and as we find
you an uncommon spirit, I am pleased to confide
that young Beresford Caille is to be reunited with

his mother, and Grove House is to be quit.

The letter ended simply.

In due time, we will expect the pleasure of your company in Chelsea. S.

A letter to neither a friend nor a servant. As there was surely nothing that Lady Seldon or the others could suspect, perhaps they took this as another indication that Madame Rostov's gift was genuine?

The gathering at Brantridge Street that afternoon was small, and awkward. Mrs Bessovitch, who had somehow found her way into the house without anyone asking or suggesting it, bustled about in the mean, ill-equipped kitchen, and lied fluently about knowing Mrs Merson, Catherine's imaginary employer. The children, stripped of their one set of decent clothes and back in outfits suitable for the Stepney slums, were sent out to play for an hour.

"I return...I mean, I must go back, to Keighley this evening." Josiah balanced a cup and saucer on his knee, the tea within untouched.

"To report to your father on our lowered circumstances." Clarissa's sharp voice cut across the room. "He will be content, I imagine, that he at least prospers."

Jennie's face crumpled into tears again; Josiah turned with dumb appeal to his sister.

"It is not Josiah's fault, Clarissa." Catherine tried to hold down her anger. "He lives under our father's roof, remember."

Where he did the books for the thriving ironmongery and coal trade that was Weatherhead & Son. Joshua Weatherhead the tradesman had long since become Joshua the prosperous West Yorkshire merchant. Gone were the farms of the Two Gentlemen, and with their sale, any ties to the land. Josiah was what Catherine might have become, a servant in their own home, had she learned from the belt and their mother's timidity. Had she stayed under their father's hand.

He lowered his eyes.

"To report on my sister. To satisfy Father that all is not too well with her, and that she will soon swallow her pride, return to Keighley."

"Oh." Clarissa's narrow cheeks reddened. "Cousin Josiah, I…it has been a trying day."

Mrs Bessovitch handed a linen square to Jennie for her tear-stained face, and a plate of tongue sandwiches to Clarissa, who took it, puzzled at its presence. There had been no tongue in the house, and little bread.

"To share blood is blessing and curse," said Catherine's landlady, and went to fill the kettle again.

Catherine shared a hansom with Josiah to King's Cross station. They sat side by side as siblings who had parted ways long ago. Uneven lanes and cobbled streets rattled at their teeth, the cabman too easy with the whip, the horse fractious.

"Is he hard on you?" asked Catherine as they turned from Whitechapel Road.

"No worse. He took the pledge, of course, and is a little the better for the lack of hard drink." Josiah fretted with his hat brim. He had no change of clothes, and she wondered if Joshua Weatherhead had given his son sufficient money to meet the cost of this hansom. "Better" would only be relative to how ill-tempered and controlling their father had always been.

"There are opportunities here for book-keepers—"

"Mother would not have it, not with you gone as well."

From another it would have been censure; a pointed remark on Catherine's abandonment of family. From her brother, it was no more than what it was.

Outside the railway station she hesitated, and put her arms around him. He smelled of hair preparation and defeat.

"I do mean it," she said, forceful. "I could find you a position, Josiah, I'm certain. It might take a few weeks, but…"

He slipped from her embrace, but took her hands in his for the briefest moment.

"Jack Witten remembers you," he said. She didn't understand why he had said this, until she saw the narrowing of her brother's eyes. "The drink will take him soon—rotten

124

inside, the doctors say. Rotten inside." This was added with a venom which was unexpected, completely uncharacteristic of the young man.

"I cannot—"

"I always believed you, Catherine," said Josiah. "About 'Uncle' Jack."

And he was gone for his train, and the long journey back to all she had fled.

Caille's death, Bow Cemetery, and the achingly cold start to December should have been an end to so much, but that hope was dashed within the week. She visited Stepney on a Thursday morning clear for once of rain, to find a constable at the door.

"Has something happened?" she asked.

The constable shrugged. "Don't know, miss. I was set to wait—the inspector is inside."

She pushed past him. Clarissa sat stiff and hostile in her sewing chair; a uniformed sergeant waited, apparently ill at ease, by the window. An older man in a long overcoat stood in the middle of the room. He looked to Catherine as she paused in the doorway.

"What brings ye here, miss?" He spoke with the directness of a born Scot. "We need neither pegs nor heather."

"My cousins live here. I am Catherine Weatherhead. Who are you?"

"Inspector Swanson, of the Metropolitan Police."

"Is there a crime?"

"Aye…or fair to say, there was. Ye ken the death of Frederick Caille."

"I read about it in the newspapers. The Deptford affair."

"Did ye? Bright lass. Then ye recognise the name well enough."

She might have sought the path of deference and a young woman's expected confusion, confronted by the bold and weighty officers of the law. She might have.

"Frederick Caille, the banker and industrialist who ruined this family? Why yes, Inspector, I 'ken' his life and his welcome death. My aunt Levinia, buried only a week past, would have had the man dragged through the courts in chains."

The sergeant, who seemed young for his rank, looked even more uncomfortable; the older man simply smiled.

"That sets us up well, then. I'm here to ask if any should have heard word, last month. Talk against the late Mr Caille, encouragement to ain gang or anither in these parts."

"The authorities still have no idea, then, who did this?" She was caustic, covering her alarm at this development.

"I wouldna ken, miss. I serve only, and have been called in to assist. My interest is ay the gangs of London Town—their feuds and the like. It was given to me to check any who had motive and interest. The Weatherheads of Brantridge Street, my colleagues say, have burned and boiled 'gainst Caille, wi' good reason."

"Why yes," said Clarissa, "We must be implicated. Because we are so powerful a family, with such influence." She gestured to the peeling wallpaper. "No doubt my late mother-in-law conceived the entire affair?"

"I did not say we thought ye were—"

Clarissa's temper was up.

"Yes, I sat and sewed my fingers down to blood and bone by day, whilst at night I ran a gang of bloody-handed villains!" She glowered at the inspector. "Or perhaps you think young Catherine here stalks the streets at night?"

The sergeant smiled, covering it with a broad hand; the inspector seemed unperturbed.

"Wheesht, now, Mrs Weatherhead. I came only to ask, to set my ear to the streets. No accusations, ye ken, none at all. In Catford and Southwark, in Spitalfields and Limehouse, my bonny boys are at it. Our duty."

"He deserved his death, and worse," Clarissa muttered. "If it had been my choice, I would have had him gaoled and rotting."

"Each must find their ain fate, madam, according to due process. There is sich a thing as the law."

Clarissa gave a derisive snort. "There was not when my husband was poisoned, nor when John Hollis and those others followed him into the grave."

Catherine swallowed, trying to remain steady.

"Inspector Swanson, you can see that there was no love for Caille here. Do you not think my cousins have been through enough?"

"Aye, maybe they have." He sniffed, and nodded to the sergeant. "We'll leave these guid folk to their thoughts, man. But…" He looked at Catherine. "If ever ye think of aught that might assist the Yard, I'm sure ye'll find me."

"I applaud your confidence, inspector."

When she arrived back at her lodgings, she was angry, worried, and most of all, tired. Her money was gone, and she must awaken Madame Rostov that same week. Mrs Bessovitch was generous, and patient, but not a charitable board given to handouts.

"There was other letter," said the landlady. "Came yesterday."

Catherine had forgotten that Mrs B was still picking up correspondence for both Catherine and Madame Rostov at the post office.

"Oh, thank you, Mrs B. I will get my affairs in order, never fear. I shall make a list, and see about more sittings."

"Da. I know you will."

Catherine took the letter and went to her room, easing off her boots. She turned the envelope, curious as to the precise, copperplate writing on the outside.

'Madame Rostov, Blackfriars Road Postal Office, Southwark.'

She tore back the flap, extracting a single sheet of paper. The writing inside was the same hand as on the envelope, but smaller and even more precise. It might have been set by a printer.

"It is done, and your coin will suffice. No further reckoning will be required.'

That was all. No signature. It did not need one.

Catherine tore the note in half, flinging the pieces away from her. She had told Dry neither the name she used, nor the means by which he could contact her. He had not asked.

She picked up the fragments and envelope with the fire-tongs, and gave them to the smouldering fire in the grate.

He knew how to find her.

CHAPTER FIFTEEN

Southwark, April 1887

Winter swept the streets of the city with snow and then dark, discoloured slush; ice and then great pools of water that rose to soak pedestrians with the passing of every wagon. Catherine took to using hansoms more often, despite the cost, and the habit persisted after the long thaw. She knew why. If she spent too much time walking the streets, she might see him.

Dry.

Every few weeks she wrestled with the idea of moving to other lodgings, but did nothing about it. She did not want to lose Mrs Bessovitch, or her comfortable room, and besides, what purpose would it serve?

He would come to her if he wished, wherever she was.

For all her initial concern, the months which followed Deptford brought no visions of bowler-hatted men, no sweat-filled nights of slaughter—and no unwelcome visitors. Her fears subsided as she reasoned there would never be any other business between her and the Deptford killer. Even the most lurid newspapers had abandoned any interest in the mysterious slaughter at the Victualling Yard. She was nothing to him, merely a passing client to be forgotten, and nothing so dreadful could happen that she might ever request his services a second time.

Madame Rostov remained a quiet figure throughout. She performed for the most ordinary of people a few times a week, earning enough to get by but not enough to prosper greatly. She attempted to touch the Aether as little as possible. Her sitters heard what they wanted to hear, spiced only when unavoidable by vague images that Catherine drew from…wherever. The vaguer the better, for she did not want to see murder again.

By Easter, she was almost recovered, but her inmost thoughts were often hard to focus. In her Southwark sanctuary she sat on her bed and darned a stocking. Her cousins, the whole Caille business of the previous year—that had surely been too much. And the Weatherheads were still a shadow over her, needs and obligations which were unlooked for and mostly unwelcome. If she abandoned them, though, she would be abandoning Charles…

She finished the darn and put her sewing materials in their box, packing away her concerns along with needles and thread.

Others would have to make their way as best they could, and she must concentrate on her own life. Brantridge Street might still be there, but it should not rule her.

The shadow of Edwin Dry should not rule her.

∼❦∼

Lottie Chambers adored, though did not always understand, poetry. Catherine understood much of it after a couple of readings, but gained little joy from doing so. Schemes of rhyme irritated her as being forced; the language used was maudlin, or excessively, ridiculously romantic. Often both.

Having grown bored of Robert Louis Stevenson, Lottie was currently enamoured of the blind poet Philip Bourke Marston, who she saw as a suitably tragic figure. His death in February had set his sad star in her heavens, and Lottie gave meandering recitations of Marston's work on a regular basis.

"You are *such* a Philistine, Katerina," she said, when Catherine asked that she be spared—at least until the following week.

For Madame Rostov was Katerina now in Lottie's company, almost a friend and certainly a mysterious figure to be trotted out when Lottie wished to make her mark.

They were usually two rather than four now. Lady Seldon was much involved in her husband's work, and in the Irish Question, she and his Lordship being in favour of Home Rule.

Amelia Baring-Smith announced her engagement to a Major in the Guards, not long after Christmas, and flitted back and forth between the capital and the country.

"I must go, Charlotte. Besides, your mother will return soon."

Mrs Chambers considered séances and spiritualism—any adventure of a supposedly psychic nature—to be too racy. Her own tastes lay in Sunday worship amongst good, stolid Anglicans.

"True. I shall read to Jemmy instead, this evening."

Feeling sympathy for Lottie's little sister, Catherine broke free of literature and stepped out, relieved, into a brisk April morning.

It was a difficult truth that her adoption by Miss Chambers, and by a few of Miss Chambers's friends, did not buy coal. Most assumed that she had some independent means, and that the spirits somehow paid her bills, much as parents or husbands paid theirs...

"Watch yerself, there!"

She felt the brush of air and horse-sweat as the brewer's dray clattered past, mere inches away, and realised that her eyes had been half-closed, her thoughts on other than the streets around her.

Money, once more.

The next day, a warm Sunday for April, she went to Brantridge Street with a handful of coins, suggesting they might be used to buy something for the children. The amount was less than usual, part of Catherine's new determination.

Clarissa took the offering with curt thanks, but no smile.

"And is Jennie well?" asked Catherine.

Clarissa shrugged. "We see little of her, excepting that she helps carry the mending back and forth to the laundries some days. These people for whom she cleans and skivvies seems to work her most nights."

It seemed an odd arrangement, but Catherine supposed the

family must take whatever work was on offer.

She thought little more of the matter until, after another brief visit a few days later, she spotted Jennie on a street corner by the Mile End Road once, laughing with a red-faced soldier. Her cousin wore a bright yellow bonnet with artificial flowers, one that Catherine did not recall seeing before. It was late afternoon, and people scurried down lanes and alleys, returning from one job or heading out for another. Children shrieked on doorsteps, and more than one drunk had already collapsed across the cobbles of the side streets, slurring imprecations to passersby.

She turned in Jennie's direction, intending to go over and ask after her cousin's health, but as she did so, she observed something in the man's stance, the shifting of hands and shoulders, which puzzled her. As she might read clients at a sitting, she saw not a courting couple but two people in the process of a transaction. She slowed, letting other pedestrians shield her as she went near.

The soldier was jangling coins in his hand, and leaning close, too close, into her cousin's face, an expression on his own face which seemed more like hunger than affection. An omnibus clattered by on the edge of the pavement, raising a string of curses from a flower-girl as its wheels spattered her with mud. The man glanced round at the noise, and saw Catherine looking at him.

He grinned.

"If a shillin' ain't enough for one dolly, maybe another'd be less fussy. What say you, eh?" He winked at Catherine. "Fancy a soldier-boy, stiffened with good mutton and the Queen's brandy?"

"Sheep carry disease, I hear," said Catherine, meeting his look with a cold stare.

Jennie paled at seeing her, and pushed the man away. "Later, Johnny—if at all."

His language was coarser than the flower-girl's, but he edged away from the two women, grumbling to himself. He was none too steady on his feet, and Catherine judged him to be no great threat. She took Jennie's arm.

"Come, cousin," she said, sharp and loud, "Let us walk awhile and catch up."

They left the soldier behind, Catherine marching Jennie down the road. She wasn't yet sure if she was angry or concerned at what she had witnessed.

Next to a saddlemaker's, an enterprising grocer had his awning up and was offering refreshments in a makeshift parlour open to the street. Catherine steered a silent Jennie to one of the three rickety tables, and ordered tea. A sign declared that samples of various blends were available "for the discerning customer."

"We have our own speciality, miss, blended here," said the grocer's assistant. "Or there are some pleasant Indian—"

"It's tea." Catherine passed the young man a handful of change. "Two cups."

She sighed, and took Jennie's hand.

"What were you doing, cousin?"

"You know what I was doing." Jennie's normally pleasant, easy face held a certain defiance. "I was earning."

"But—"

"I do not sew well, unlike Clarissa, and hereabouts are only the most menial, back-breaking jobs. I have used my imagination, Catherine, and done well enough."

Catherine's upbringing had hardly been sheltered. There were many prostitutes in Keighley, even on Fell Lane where they first lived, and there must be thousands more in London. They were part of the background on so many streets, especially in the East End. Nor was shame an issue that concerned Catherine. It was the risk—beatings and other ill-use; infection and impregnation...

Jennie must have seen some of this in her cousin's expression.

"Some of the men are nice enough, and most pay fair. I have had advice..."

"From whom?"

"I have a friend, Ginger—she was most kind when she saw I was set on this."

"She encouraged you?"

A blush of red high on Jennie's cheeks.

"She did not. She worried that I was too inexperienced and ill-prepared; she made known the pitfalls, and ways to tell a safe client from an unsafe one—all manner of issues a 'dolly-mop' must consider. The best protections to use, as well."

"Oh. Better that way, I suppose." Catherine knew she still sounded grudging, almost censorious. But who was she to dictate another's life?

"Exactly," said Jennie. "I bring money into the house, and am at no one's constant beck and call. And Ginger watches out for me."

The grocer's assistant, obviously unable to determine quite what class of customer he had—and whether his superior would want them or not—placed a tray of tea things on the table and backed away. Cheap china, but clean.

"So I have been careful—and cared for—as well as any could hope—"

"In the circumstances." Catherine felt weary. "Jennie, dear, if I could find a little more money—

"I would do as I do now." There was no doubting her cousin's resolve. "We must all make choices, not be constantly looking to others." Her expression softened. "Cathy, you have been more generous to our family than Clarissa wishes to acknowledge, I know that. And I know that you do it in remembrance of Charles. The children are the better for it. But we are not your burden." Jennie finished her cup, and rose. "Do look after yourself, Cathy dear."

Catherine watched a patched dress and a linen shawl slip down Mile End Road, only the bright bonnet standing out from those around her. The woman beneath the bonnet had surprised her and worried her. Was this another milestone on the Weatherhead road to a sad and worthless end?

We are not your burden.

Perhaps.

She spent the remainder of that day shopping. In an anonymous coat which had seen better times, she visited various modest milliners and haberdashers who had kept their shutters open in the hope of a few late sales. By evening she had everything she needed.

Mrs Bessovitch was in the parlour, ready to assist.

"You see," said Catherine, "The look is everything. I cannot wear the same outfit all the time, yet I cannot afford high London fashion, or whatever it is fine Russian ladies might wear at the moment…"

"I understand." Mrs Bessovitch held up some pale muslin. "A veil, yes?"

"I think so."

The two women pinned and stitched, exchanging only the occasional word. An old green jacket, slightly the worse for wear, received military frogging and braid; a broad-brimmed hat was steamed over the landlady's kettle and reshaped, acquiring a short grey veil and a rakish feather along the way.

"Madame Rostov will catch the eye," said Mrs Bessovitch.

"Just as Miss Weatherhead must not."

"I understand. Is clever, this you do."

Catherine refilled the kettle, this time for a cup of tea.

"These people don't want an ironmonger's daughter from Keighley pronouncing on the living and the dead. They want to sit with mystery."

"Sometimes is comfort only they want, nyet?"

"Yes, well, that too."

Her week held more bookings than usual, and she was nervous. Tuesday and Wednesday sessions, held in dull suburban drawing rooms, went smoothly, and a collection was held at the end of each, netting her almost three pounds in total.

To Catherine this seemed only modest recompense for long hours of reassuring words on the nature of mortality, and hints as to the fate of a missing cat, respectively. The furtive look on the husband's face, and the recent scratch marks half-hidden under his shirt-cuffs, made her sure that the truth would come out after she had left.

On the Thursday, she sat for a young woman whose baby had died of the croup, and her ability to perform deserted her. Her own youngest brother had died at much the same age.

"There is no spirit to mourn, or soul to wander," said Catherine, holding the client's hands. "Your child was taken back, innocent, untouched by the world."

This may or may not have been true, but it would have to suffice.

She took the half crown offered and left quickly, made uncomfortable by the mother's gratitude.

The crowning event of the week would be Saturday. A group of regular sitters from West Hampstead had asked if Madame Rostov would join them, though they did not ask for her to perform. She had considered the names cited—these were not the usual dowdy worriers or dilettantes looking for diversion. They were professional people, including a doctor, a town clerk, and the chairwoman of a number of charitable foundations.

Was she being assessed? She thought so. It was possible that at least one of the circle might be a journalist, or have connections to the Society for Psychical Research.

The first concerned her somewhat—most journalists preferred to uncover fraud, which made good copy. There would be no room for trickery—either she would be able to perform, or she must be honest and admit that her abilities were intermittent. Better to be written up as inconsistent than as a confidence trickster.

As for the second possibility, what little she read suggested that men and women joined the Society because they wanted the world of psychic phenomena to be real, not because they wanted to disprove it.

She could have pleaded other engagements, but it was the

second time they had invited her. She was not going to appear as if she had something to hide—that was how rumours started.

Mrs Bessovitch helped her assemble a muted outfit, and the cheaper rings went in a drawer. Catherine was to take the train to West Hampstead, where she would be met. The night was cold, and it spattered with rain, but the train was well-lit and comfortable. She made herself inconspicuous in a corner seat, her head cowled, and let the rattle of the journey soothe her. Late workers came and went at each stop, mostly clerks and office juniors by the cut of their clothes. One of them dropped his evening paper, and she caught sight of a headline.

Caille.

She swallowed, and read on. A banquet hosted by the Lord Mayor; a grand gathering of luminaries—by which they seemed to mean men of industry and money. The headline was less relevant than she had feared, the article itself only remarking on the fact that Frederick Caille, who had been a regular speaker, would be absent for the first time in ten years. True enough, unless they dug him up.

A man and a woman signalled her as she stood at the station in West Hampstead. They were middle-aged, quietly dressed.

"Madame Rostov? I am George Conners, and this is my friend, Mrs Bless."

"I am pleased to meet you." Catherine dipped her head to both. "Do we have far to go?"

"Only around the corner to Lowfield Road, a mere stroll."

She pulled her cowl tighter around her, and followed them to a recent terrace, a stretch of red and ochre brick frontages pierced with arched windows, lit against the night.

Conners ushered her into the front room of Number Eighteen. Introductions, and a cheaper sherry than that at Lady Seldon's, followed.

"Most mediums abstain," said Conners, as Catherine fortified herself.

"They do," she agreed. "I am not of their kind."

She could not interpret his slight smile.

"So good of you to come, Madame Rostov," said a thin, overdressed woman, Mrs Treach. She would be the woman of "good works," as someone had described her. Her husband, equally scrawny, nodded at her shoulder. He would be the town clerk. A Dr Mercier, a Mr Gayle and another man whose name she did not catch, completed the group. An unusual number of men for such sittings.

Conners seemed to be the master of ceremonies.

"Let us welcome Madame Rostov to our small circle of friends. Lady Seldon speaks highly of her abilities."

Which might be true, but did this come from general talk, or had they enquired directly? Did Lucy Seldon know these people?

"Am I to display my abilities for you tonight, ladies and gentlemen?" Catherine allowed a touch of practised Russian haughtiness to play around the words.

Conners coughed. "Only if the conditions are suitable for you, Madame. If you feel it would not be appropriate…"

"No doubt it will become apparent," she answered. She would have to tread carefully.

She was shown through into a large dining room, where a suitable table awaited them. They were observing her; she was observing the house. Despite the presence of appropriate furniture, of antimacassars on armchairs and fresh flowers in the hall, the place was too clean, unscuffed. The lack of certain little touches spoke to her…

"Is there a reason why this house is unoccupied, though it is made to seem otherwise?" She stared directly at Conners.

"Ha! Got you fair and square with that one, old man." The doctor laughed.

"Indeed," admitted Conners. "You are perceptive, Madame Rostov. We only use this place for sittings."

"And before each session, you check anew for wires and trickery, trumpets in cupboards and children hidden up chimneys."

Mrs Treach looked interested.

"Have you yourself been subject to investigation, Madame?"

"No. But I am used to doubt. Is that what the company brings to the table tonight?"

Conners stiffened. "Hope would be a more accurate word. We have come across what we would describe as the most striking psychical experiences, and yes, we have also been played. But our interest is genuine. It would be our pleasure to confirm Madame Rostov as a bona fide talent."

Catherine saw that she could melt and confess to her limited talent, or she could continue the front that Madame Rostov would normally present.

"Do I need such confirmation?" she said, chin raised. And she broke the moment with a broad smile.

"We are all friends here, I am sure."

She was sure that they were not. George Conners was, for some reason, observing her. As for the round-faced Mrs Bless, who had not yet spoken, there was something about her...a sketch Catherine had seen in the Illustrated News. The woman was a medium in her own right.

"You have the gift," said Catherine, one hand to her forehead, pretending that she had divined this fact from the Aether.

Mrs Bless smiled and templed her fingers before her.

"Shall we be seated?"

CHAPTER SIXTEEN

Hampstead, April 1887

The harmonium droned; six voices of varying ability raised an opening hymn, whilst Madame Rostov sat stiff-backed and silent.

"Behold a Stranger at the door!
"He gently knocks, has knocked before,
"Has waited long, is waiting still;
"You treat no other friend so ill.
"But will He prove a friend indeed?
"He will; the very Friend you need;
"The Friend of sinners—yes 'tis He,
"With garments dyed on Calvary."

Conners looked at her when they had finished and the harmonium was quiet.

"You do not approve of English hymns, Madame?"

"I have no voice for them."

"I find the vibrations most helpful in clearing the air for others to come through," said Mrs Bless. She had mousy hair, pinned tightly back, and a mole below her left nostril, the very vision of a strict but kindly aunt. "Such sounds alert them to congenial and receptive souls below."

"Perhaps Madame Rostov is receptive but not congenial?" That was the doctor, Charles Mercier, with a smile. His high forehead and neat beard gave him a studious appearance, as did the notebook in his hand, pencil ready.

"Are we a case study for your practice, doctor?" asked Mrs Treach. It was a cautious, prim enquiry.

"Mercier's an alienist," whispered the young man next to Catherine, the one called Gayle.

"I am a student here." Mercier put down his notebook. "Nothing more."

Conners lowered the gas, taking his place next to Mrs Bless. Faces and shoulders could be seen; most else was in deep shadow. The seven seated around the bare table were instructed to join hands, lightly, and Mrs Bless threw back her head.

"If there are strangers at the door, be welcome. We seek only enlightenment."

Conners raised both hands. "And if there are those who need guidance, who wish to move on, let them come."

Gayle, who seemed to have appointed himself Catherine's interpreter, leaned closer. "Sometimes there are troubled souls, stuck on this side of the Veil. Mrs Bless can assist them to be quit of earthly concerns."

Catherine's presentiments had been correct. These people were from the serious regiments of the spiritualist world, not the volunteers or yeomanry. She could expect any manner of attempts at physical manifestation, apportation or pronouncements from those higher Planes in which she barely believed. She doubted any of it would be genuine.

"For the benefit of the less experienced, Mrs Bless will now see if one of her guides will honour us," said Conners.

The traffic outside had stilled, the polite evening of the suburbs slipping into place. Maids might take an evening stroll, and men might straggle behind their dogs, but little else would be seen or heard. A sombre atmosphere filled the room. Mr Treach appeared to have a throat infection, and coughed occasionally, apologising each time. Gayle, to Catherine's left, smelled of alcohol and shaving lotion; the doctor to her right presented only a whiff of carbolic.

"There is a presence..." said Mrs Bless. "Lucy, is that you?"

A rap on the table then three more. Mrs Treach looked delighted.

"Sad Lucy is one of dear Mrs Bless's controls."

The guiding medium shuddered, smiled.

"Sad Lucy says that there are strangers here. One...one of them has a great gift..."

A few heads turned in the gloom to Catherine.

"They have seen sorrows, oh, such sorrows. We must pity them. What is that, Lucy?" Mrs Bless put her hand to her ear. "You see domes, and spires, all layered with snow, and narrow streets below—it is so cold…and the people, their tongue is strange."

"That would be Russia." Mr Gayle's comment was almost inaudible.

Catherine thought she should be helpful, until she understood what was happening.

"Moy staryy, staryy dom," she said, one of the phrases she had learned to parrot from her landlady. My old, old home. "Where I lived once."

The Treachers clapped. "How wonderful."

Had Mrs Bless been a horse, Catherine would have not have backed her on what she'd seen so far. The table trick she knew herself; and a pretended vision of a Russian city was safe ground when you had a Madame Rostov present.

More raps, imperative.

"Sad Lucy says that this night is one of importance." Mrs Bless put her hand to her ear again. "She senses…"

The act went on. Someone had suffered a loss in the family. Another was destined to find what they sought, and a third should no longer worry about his mother.

"Why is Lucy sad?" Mercier had his notebook and pencil under the table, barely visible even to Catherine.

"Because…" Mrs Bless hesitated. "Because there are so many whose spirits cannot escape this earth, this anchoring Plane. They burden themselves with their failures and misdeeds, not seeing that above them, all is Light."

"I see. Then all controlling spirits must be sad."

"In part." Mrs Bless did not sound entirely pleased. "But our friends above have joy, as well, for as they guide us, they see us shed our mortal concerns, and many do ascend. Especially those who understand." She placed quite a lot of emphasis on the last word.

In the hour and a half of her performance, Mrs Bless spoke for Sad Lucy, then another "friend" who was a long-dead American chief called Black Eagle, and finally a small girl whose spirit was somehow trapped. The small girl was guided into Sad Lucy's hands, and all was well. The table spoke from time to time, and the curtains rustled wildly at one point, though the windows were shut.

Catherine tried to gain the measure of those around her. The Treaches seemed complete believers, and so did the young man whose name she had missed. He was hardly more than a boy, but listened attentively to every word.

Conners she did not understand, because he seemed to accept even Mrs Bless's weakest moments as sound, yet his eye was on Madame Rostov at many points. The doctor was politely curious; Gayle was politely dubious.

The question was—did Mrs Bless have some psychic gift, augmented by trickery just as Catherine might do, or was she a complete fraud? There was no point in her trying to expose any fraud in public, as it might rebound on her. On the other hand, she hardly wished to be connected professionally with the Mrs Blesses of the city—she wanted only their clients.

It seemed that proceedings were coming to an end. Mrs Bless nodded to Conners, who opened his mouth to speak…

"There are hands at her throat!"

Heads turned to the young man next to Mrs Treach; Mrs Bless looked confused.

"What is that, Mr Hough?" Mrs Treach's eyes were wide.

"There…there are hands at her throat. Oh God—thick, brutal hands…"

The air thrummed, burned in Catherine's nostrils, and she gasped for breath.

Fever, the bare plaster of the attic.

She pushed away from the table. The young man called Hough was on his feet, dancing—no, he was jerking and turning, as if he could not control himself…

As if someone had him by the throat, lifting him up…

A fourteen year old girl cried out, using Catherine's lungs to vent her horror at what she saw.

"I believe he's having a fit," said Mercier, rising to take hold of Hough's arm. The young man sank to his knees, only spared the floor because the doctor had a grip on him, and a child-like voice sang out from lips flecked with spittle.

"No, Uncle Jack, no…"

One of the gas mantles flared and shattered, the bare flame casting a blue, flickering light across the company; Hough slumped and was silent, his chin on his chest.

The men carried him into the adjoining room and eased him onto a couch, one of them turning the lights up. Mercier took off his jacket, rolled up his sleeves and examined Hough for some minutes. Straightening up, he looked to where he had put his cufflinks.

"Chap's asleep. Perfectly normal sleep, as far as I can tell."

"An errant spirit," said Mrs Bless, clearly trying to control the situation. "Nothing to be alarmed about, friends."

"It alarmed me, I don't mind saying." Gayle had been examining the gas mantle, disintegrated in its holder. He stood in the doorway, white powder on his fingers. "Pretty old, that fitting. They get damned fragile after a while."

Conners had found another bottle of sherry from somewhere, and was pouring it into small glasses. Only the Treaches did not indulge this time.

"It can happen, when the conduits, the channels to other Planes are opened," he said. "We had not…Mrs Bless had not yet closed the session, or led us in our final hymn, you see. If there are troubled spirits who see the opening, well, there you go. It can happen," he repeated, unconvincingly. He looked pale.

Catherine stood back from the group, trying not to show how much she was trembling. Cold sweat ran beneath her undergarments. The boy had seen what she had seen, and it had taken hold of him. How was this possible? He could only have read it from her mind, surely? She wanted to run from Lowfield Road, to leave that very moment, but she knew that Madame Rostov would do no such thing.

"I say," said Mr Gayle. "Did I hear you call out, Madame?"

"I was…taken by surprise. Nothing more."

"Weren't we all? Damn queer business." He winked. "That wasn't part of the act, now, was it?"

Hough awoke moments later.

"Why am I in here?"

Mercier recounted what had happened; the young man shook his head, looking puzzled.

"Don't remember any of that, doctor. Not a jot of it."

"No history of epilepsy or fits?" asked Mercier.

"Certainly not. Nor in the family, neither."

Catherine stepped forward, her hands behind her back. She could feel her fingernails cutting into the palms. It was difficult to keep her voice steady, portraying herself as an interested observer and no more.

"You spoke...you mentioned a name." She made herself say it. "Uncle Jack. Does that name have some significance to you?"

"Can't say it does, Madame," he said, polite but awkward. "I mean, it's common enough, but I don't have an Uncle Jack— or even John, for that matter."

Against her better judgement, she joined Conners at the sideboard.

"This young man..."

"Reggie? Nephew of mine, always interested in spiritualism. Fancied a go, and I said he could attend tonight, if he kept his mouth closed and acted respectable. Never known him to have the gift, though. His mother will be furious with me."

Mercier strolled over.

"Quite a show, Conners."

"All genuine, all quite genuine."

Catherine glanced at the doctor. "You are not a believer, sir?"

He smiled. "If I did not believe, it would be most rude of me to say with Madame Rostov before me. A doctor, if he struggles hard enough, can be a gentlemen. I have, however, treated patients in a delusional state, caused by nervous exhaustion or neurological damage. The manifestations are much the same." He spoke in an amiable, everyday tone. "I practice at the Flower House private asylum, by the way, Madame. In Catford."

She would have said he was in his thirties, certainly under forty. Old enough to have some experience—possibly not old enough to become hidebound and inflexible. As Conners moved away, she thought of asking Mercier more, but Gayle, cheerful in his rounds between the others, paused by them. "Old Conners is Mrs Bless's commercial agent, you know? He wants to ascertain if you're a professional threat."

"And what did you come here to ascertain, Mr Gayle?"

"Oh, I'm a reporter. Didn't anyone say? Here to separate bombast and bluster from the real thing, don't you know? If there is a 'real thing'"

And he was off across the room, slipping into a conversation between Conners and the Treaches.

Catherine made her goodbyes, hardly noticed in the continuing chatter over the evening's events, and walked out onto Lowfield Road alone, despite the doctor's offer to see her to the station.

She did not trust herself to conversation, not yet.

～⊰✦⊱～

The weeks that followed were tainted by her experience at Lowfield Road. Madame Rostov continued her usual work, adding one or two "regulars" every so often. When at last she found the courage, Catherine enquired after the young man, Hough.

The Treaches informed her that he had quit such events. Apparently he had no recollection of what had happened that night, and showed no other signs of unusual behaviour or sensitivity. The letter from Mrs Treach suggested that the circle was rather disappointed with his departure. They made no mention of the episode having any connection to Madame Rostov.

Catherine had to assume that the boy was what she had been at his age—no more than an unwitting recipient of images from others, without rhyme or reason.

She hoped that it never happened to him again.

The matter of Uncle Jack and what he had done on Fell Lane was not quite finished, though. By chance or grand design, she received a letter from her brother Josiah in July, saying that Jack Witten was dead, of jaundice and a sudden apoplexy. His liver was found to be swollen and purulent; his heart laced with fat and disease. Their father had gone to the funeral, but it was poorly attended. Jack's second wife, Josiah wrote, had run away to the coast that spring, to set up home with a Flamborough fisherman. No one blamed the woman; some wondered she had waited so long.

Josiah's words conveyed no sorrow at the news.

～⊰✦⊱～

In September, she was asked to sit as medium for the same West Hampstead group. It was an invitation she accepted with great reluctance, and only after mention of "expenses" and an assurance that young Hough would not be present.

Neither Gayle nor Doctor Mercier were there either, their places occupied by two elderly sisters who had doubts about moving to Chelmsford and wanted to consult their late mother. Feeling rash, and aware of Mrs Bless watching her, Catherine indicated that their dear departed had passed too long ago, and was now far higher above than would allow for mundane communication. However, teasing out a little of the "dear Mamma's" nature as the evening progressed, she suggested that the move would be appropriate. It was obvious that they wanted to do it anyway, and this went down well.

"How marvellous you are, Madame," said one.

Mr Conners exchanged glances with Mrs Bless.

After the session he eased Catherine to one side.

"Madame Rostov—I wonder, would you consider joining in some modest explorations of the spiritual world before larger audiences. Mrs Bless has been asked to tour a number of Temperance Halls and spiritualist meeting places around our fair capital, and I confess that it will be much for her to endure alone."

"It is kind of you to ask," said Catherine. "But I am a quiet woman. I wish you much success, of course." She offered him a winning smile. "I doubt I shall aspire to such public affairs."

And that was what the other wished to hear. That Madame Rostov, if not to join his stable, was not competition for his existing protégée, Mrs Bless. Conners, underneath his professed beliefs, was obviously no more than a theatrical manager seeking to ride the spiritualist tide and line his pockets. Catherine imagined that he sought out rivals and possible accomplices— the Hampstead sittings were used to gather intelligence and occasionally for recruitment. Why not have journalists and sceptics present? They would help weed out the weak.

Catherine still had occasional ambitions, but not with Mr Conners.

That autumn the Illustrated News published a series of lengthy articles by Mr Philip Gayle, exposing some of the tricks of the "spirit trade." He questioned the bona fides of some mediums, and doubted many of the phenomena they produced, but he did not the attack the honest beliefs of most spiritualists themselves. His unfavourable references in one piece to a Mrs B were veiled enough that no one could be sure he meant Mrs Bless, though to Catherine it seemed obvious.

His final article came out at the start of November. Gayle had saved certain reflections for last.

'But there are some figures, such as Mme R—v and those like her in conduct, who should intrigue the genuine investigator. They stand apart in some way, with hints of true talent. They disdain the tilting table and floating face, the trumpet and the tambourine. As to whether they represent the future of spiritualism, few can say at this stage. We remain cautious but open...'

Catherine wanted to feel pleased at this assessment. She was at least surviving; Fredrick Caille and Jack Witten were dead, and she was largely free of her family. Yet she could not help but notice the date of the article's publication.

A year ago to the day, almost to the hour, she had sat down with a man called Edwin Dry and stared at the clean, neatly manicured hands of an assassin...

The Assassin's Coin
PART TWO

CHAPTER SEVENTEEN

Southwark, March 1888

He holds the blade, the exquisite blade. A perfect design, with razor edge and needle point, with subtle and balanced weight. It will kill, but it does not need to kill to be what it is, to be admired.

Alone in manufactured gloom, he places his jacket just so over the back of a chair, smoothing the lapels. His starched shirt collar is already on the chair seat, a white C against dark hessian.

He moves, his will extending from the pommel of the knife to its glinting tip. Here, and gone; there and up, to the side before his heart can take a second beat. The blade flies free of his hand and is regained, this time pointing down to pin, to trap...

And he is somewhere else, six paces further back, low and ready. There and not there. Flexing on the balls of his feet, angled like a Limehouse drunk but with complete control. The bullet that would have caught his shoulder is a wasted shot; the fist aimed for his head swings wild. The discipline of not being struck is as important as the one of striking true.

After an hour, a light sweat gathers in the small of his back, and the scent of it tells him that he has done enough for this night. Tomorrow he must attend to his wrists. They are the steely anchor chains for his hands, and must never be neglected.

He did not learn to move this way. It came with bone and sinew, muscle and ligament, a gift that only needed recognising, using to its full potential.

You take that which is given, and you hone it, like a blade.

You make it exquisite.

The arrival of spring, even a London spring, was welcome. The rain which fell on Southwark streets was warmer and less frequent, the air less fugged with hearth-smoke, though Catherine missed the broad, empty skies of her native Yorkshire.

Her client group had grown, but not as much as she had hoped—the occasional contact suggested by Lottie, but for the most part quiet people, solidly middle-class. Such folk donated towards her time in a manner commensurate with their lives— carefully and without excessive generosity—and had to be nurtured over months to be worthwhile. She heard of fortune tellers and minor psychics being taken under the Vagrancy Act, as a result of charging for their services, and was always careful to protest that no reward was required. Unfortunately, some took her at her word.

This would have to change. She needed to improve her game in some way. More than once she had seen a medium being ushered out of a house even as another was ushered in— there was competition in bringing "comfort" to the widespread congregation of believers.

Her visions of the bowler-hatted man, and the killings at the Victualling Yard, had dulled her spiritualist ambitions throughout the previous year, constrained her to the safest of practices. Much of her expected progress had failed to materialise, and she knew that it was her own fault. The plans she had made in her Keighley attic, the ideas which sprang from her early sittings in London—these must be re-examined in order to decide her future. Where she made ten shillings from a session the year before, she must make fifteen now; a two-guinea consultation must become a three-guinea one. Preferable four.

Attempting to become better informed, she enquired into telepathy, a term which was gaining ground over older concepts of "thought transference," and into apportation. She dismissed the latter, the movement of solid objects, as simple trickery, but she explored the other common practices of mediums with her more experienced sitters, never letting it be seen that she might know less than they did.

She came to no definite conclusion. She could not rely on

her gift, whatever it should be called, nor could she focus it, it appeared. It was in vogue to believe that some control or guiding spirit assisted the psychic. She had never sensed any such thing, and had good reason to believe that these controls were fabrications—or self-delusion.

She saw no conceivable reason why a "Mrs Peewit" or a "Running Bear" would hover over a medium, unreliably channelling fragments from another Plane. If these spirits had perfect knowledge, why share imperfect knowledge, imperfectly, to the earth-bound?

The wise Mongolian "Temur" was never summoned again as part of her performance.

She met Dr Mercier a second time at a séance, quite by accident. A group's regular medium had been taken ill (the rumour was drink), and Catherine accepted an invitation to take the man's place. Mercier remembered her, and was polite, almost gracious, in his silence for most of the sitting. A twitch of his eyebrows here and there marked his doubts, and she took the unusual route of talking to him afterwards. She had a feeling that Mercier was one to be headed off before he dreamed of deeper enquiry.

"You did not challenge my comment on Miss Wright's sister," she said.

They stood on the pavement outside the terraced house where the session had been held, nodding as the other sitters passed them, dispersing into the cool evening.

"It was a reasonable assumption, Madame."

"Or word from the Aether, channelled through my admittedly limited abilities."

"That too is conceivable." His expression amiable as ever.

"But less likely, in an alienist's view." Catherine laughed, pulling her fur collar closer.

Mercier pulled out his half-hunter. "Unfortunate that I have a patient in an hour's time. I would have enjoyed discussing these matters with you, Madame."

"And exposing my little tricks?"

"I dislike false logic, poorly tested theories, and errant fraud. I have no firm opinion on Madame Rostov. I might almost say that she promises less than most of her kind, and delivers more."

He bowed, and hailed a passing hansom, which clattered to a halt by them.

"You have a means of conveyance?" he enquired, one foot on the running board.

"I shall be borne aloft by the spirits, doctor."

Or, thought Catherine as she watched the cab pull away, she would save a few pence and walk home…

Mrs Bessovitch asked why Katerina did not have a young man. Was she, as the landlady put with her usual turn of phrase, "more happy with the other ladies?" In truth, Catherine had avoided the issue most of her life. She had to go back to her grandparents, the Two Gentlemen, to find anything of promise within her own family, any example of genuine love and affection.

A kiss on the cheek from Lottie Chambers was more appealing than the looks of most men she met. They so often seemed that they might wish to acquire her, like a fine and unusual piece of furniture. Or a sculpture, which if they polished it enough would be suitable to show to their acquaintances.

The fad for spiritualist enquiry had largely passed from Charlotte Chambers's circles. This was to be expected, but by some strange quirk, she and Lottie still saw each other. Catherine remained Katerina Rostov, the interesting "older" woman, and they continued to read to each other three or four times each month, with the occasional afternoon entertaining Lottie's younger sister, Jemmy. The planchette and board came out for idle moments; nothing of consequence was revealed.

"I had word from Evelyn Caille," said Lottie one dull afternoon at Cheyne Gardens. "She is to take Beresford abroad for a few months, after so many months of trying to sort through Caille's business affairs." She scowled. "He left such questionable dealings behind as may yet raise more court cases."

"Is she well, in herself?"

"Better than I have seen her for years." Lottie plucked at her hair. "She asks to be remembered to you."

Evelyn Caille's remembrance came in the form of a small velvet-covered box, which contained an assortment of rings, some of which appeared quite valuable.

"She admired your old-fashioned rings, apparently. In clearing out Grove House, she found these, and begs that you should take them as a small token."

"You think I should?"

"Katerina, she would be offended if she heard that you refused them."

Catherine sighed. Taking out the smallest, a simple gold band, she placed it by Lottie's side.

"Give this to Jemmy when you see fit. Then this underserved profit is not mine alone."

"If you insist. Evelyn also asks that you forgive her for not contacting you this last year. She could not think of the words to say."

"Why would that concern her?"

Her friend's smile was hesitant.

"Did you not know? She believes that Madame Rostov was her salvation. It was following your visit that she began to gather her own courage—and then, so soon after, there was the affair at Deptford. It was as if you were a...what is the word, a harbinger of her freedom."

Catherine made sure to look at her book, at the wainscoting, anything but Lottie's face.

"I did nothing," she said, almost a whisper.

I killed four men.

It was after this meeting that she began to receive regular images of Edwin Dry once more. Having hoped that the bloody events in the Victualling Yard had been the climax of her visions, it was a bitter blow. The episodes came when she was deeply tired, or trying to sleep but failing; only rarely did they occur during séances, and by now she had learned to suffer this, to complete the sitting without panic.

Her only comfort was that much of the intensity had gone. She saw neither murder nor blood, but brief flashes—fireflies in the night, brightening and dimming, sometimes not even truly remembered when she woke. A snow-specked street with empty windows; his progress across the river on a waterman's launch; the looming chimney of an anonymous factory. Once she saw him moving through great crowds, untouched and unnoticed, as if he were an inexorable force as yet undocumented by this scientific age. He was out there, though his activities no longer seemed to have relevance to her, for which she was grateful.

Yet she read the papers each day, and shivered if she saw any report of a suspicious death…

More promising change arrived by accident, the result of a call to visit a young woman in Vauxhall, Mrs Ameley, the widow of a borough finance officer. She was some vague relation to Miss Bournelle's neighbour, and was distraught—her husband had committed suicide.

They sat across from each other in Mrs Amely's large parlour, tea-cups perched on their knees. The house was well-appointed but appeared in disorder, and there was no sign of a maid. Mrs Ameley had draped black crepe on every conceivable object, from the mirrors to the plaster figurines crowded on the mantelpiece; black window blinds were pulled almost down, shutting out the world.

"He could not bear his thoughts, Madame Rostov."

"Thoughts?"

"It was the same with his father. Deep moments of undeserved gloom, without rational source. I found him…" Mrs Ameley stirred her tea, adding a third spoonful of sugar. "I found him weeping one night, and all he could say was that the sky pressed upon him; the earth awaited him. He was not a lunatic." Said with sudden force. "Melancholy gripped him from youth."

"You cared for each other?" Catherine had known a woman in Keighley who had been that way. Close to vagrant, without relatives, she was committed to a public asylum and never seen again.

"We did. He worked hard at his job, and I hoped…I hoped that it would pass, with time. But this last winter brought him low, and whilst on borough business in Folkestone, he…he threw himself from the nearby cliffs. That was three days ago."

"I am so sorry."

Mrs Ameley's hazel eyes were filmed with tears. "Is he at peace, Madame Rostov? Has his torment passed? I feel I must know…"

Had this recommendation not come through the reliable Miss Bournelle, Catherine would have left, pleading that "the spirits will not settle today." What real comfort could she bring with genuine sorrow abroad in the house? A departed uncle, or an annoying mother—she could weave words around them easily enough. She could tell people that their faithful greyhound was at rest, or that their cousins felt no pain. A twopenny priest could have done the same. Mrs Ameley's grief was raw and recent, quite specific.

"I will seek," she said. "But I may not find. There is no map for the Aether, and I use no contrivances.

Mrs Ameley put a fourth sugar in her tea, sipped it and grimaced, pushing the cup aside. "I have a table ready in the dining room, which is suitably dark and quiet. There should be a hymn as well, should there not, or music? I have read—"

"I am Madame Rostov." Catherine raised a hand heavy with rings from Mrs Bessovitch and Evelyn Caille, stemming the flow. "The visions will come, or they will not. Clear your mind, and think of your husband. Tell me of him."

Haltingly at first, but gaining confidence, the young woman spoke of Edward Ameley. Catherine listened, opening her mind, searching for those rare impressions which could come to her during such sessions. Mrs Ameley's voice became a litany, a life recited from a distance, as Catherine sought to find the essence of what the dead man had been.

Other minds, she was convinced, roamed the Aether—perhaps all were living, and there were no lingering dead, no disincarnate souls…

She gripped the arms of the chair, caught suddenly by other eyes…

The line is too heavy. The feathered hooks are fat with mackerel, but it is still too heavy. He hauls on the winch and wonders. Once they took a shark, a rasp-skinned streak of grey which had drowned on the tackle. Drowned, aye, that a fish could do so—suffocate was the word, said old Doctor Johns, who often saw the small boats in…

There is no shark with a pallid, lifeless hand, nor one which wears torn cloth above the wrist.

"We have a man!" he cries to his brother at the tiller. "We have a man!"

The body comes slowly, and though it has been roughly served by the sea, the face is unmarked—a short moustache above full lips, leached of colour, and large grey eyes, never to close. The expression is of pale serenity…

Catherine choked, imagined saltwater in her lungs, and was back in Vauxhall. A parlour, a fallen cup, a broken saucer. The woman across from her looked shocked.

"Madame Rostov, are you well?"

"They did not find your husband's body."

"No, the police suggested it…it may return with the tides."

For a moment she matched what the young woman had said about her husband—his appearance, his bearing. This was not coincidence.

"He has been found. The fishermen will bring him in."

"Oh dear God!" Mrs Ameley pressed her hands to her mouth, took them away, placed them there again. She seemed as if she did not trust herself to speak.

"His pain has fled," said Madame Rostov. "His pain has fled, and now he sleeps. Grieve no more for him."

What else could be said?

The kitchen at the lodgings smelled of fresh bread and caraway seed; coffee and something else which lingered. Fish, of the oily variety. She hoped that it wasn't mackerel. Mrs Bessovitch laboured and cursed in the small back garden, calling down divine punishment on the cats which scratched up her herbs.

Catherine had found—in a manner of speaking—a missing man. It had not been intentional, but it sparked a thought. She had read a headline in Mrs B's paper a few weeks ago— "Medium assists police in baffling case." She had dismissed the article beneath—her view was that most results were either predictable or meaningless. When predictable, the self-proclaimed psychic had put snippets of fact together, as she might "read" a client, and come to a logical conclusion a half day before the police would have done so themselves. When meaningless, they had supplied such nonsense as could apply to a hundred cases, and thus lost little face in the process.

Her Vauxhall experience was different. There was nothing vague about what she had seen. A new possibility for a headline appealed to her as she buttered a piece of warm, crusty rye-bread.

'Madame Rostov solves Southwark Mystery; Police Commissioner expresses gratitude.'

Perhaps this was one route by which her name might spread, and by which fatter purses might join her client group?

CHAPTER EIGHTEEN

Southwark, April 1888

Superintendent Denis Neylan of M Division believed in the Living God, the Rule of Law, and that he and his men were serving both when they walked the streets of Southwark. He made this plain to Catherine at their first meeting.

"If you..." He pointed a stubby finger at Madame Rostov. "If you, Madame, are privy to the Voices of those who cannot find their way to the Lord, then you are Blessed. There may be purpose for you, even here in the Bastion of His Justice."

Neylan spoke with the use of many obvious Capital Letters. He would be a lay preacher, she imagined, a tee-totaller, making love (she wondered if he called it copulation?) to his wife at exactly half past nine every Monday evening. Probably after a prayer. Madame Rostov's approach would have to be adapted.

"I am a fallible instrument, Superintendent." This brought an approving nod, one which also betrayed the fact that the portly officer wore a hair-piece. All is vanity, Saith the Preacher. "Sometimes I can uncover truths and bring comfort, sometimes not. I do not dissemble when there is nothing I can do."

"Good. Ability must always listen to Humility." He paced in front of his office window, one eye on the street. "I dismissed a fortune-teller who came to me last year. I believed that by coming to me, he sought to place himself at the hem of Justice, and thus evade it. I had him followed, and not long after, I gave him a month for Vagrancy. He gulled coin from decent folk, claiming that he could predict the years ahead."

"The Future is closed to mortals," said Catherine, her own language becoming more portentous to match Neylan's.

"It is. The Past and Present are our rightful domains, as He grants. I shall consider your offer of assistance to the Southwark Constabulary, Madame. Should a suitable case arise, you will be notified. Leave your details with Inspector Mallick."

Anonymous again on the busy Borough High Street, Catherine tried to weigh what she was undertaking. She knew from the newspapers that members of the public swamped the police when wicked deeds were done. Some claimed to be witnesses, hoping for reward, and were not averse to naming their neighbours out of spite. Others might be better served by Dr Mercier and his fellow alienists, confessing to crimes they had not committed. A few were "morally outraged," a phrase which amused her.

And then there were the spiritualists, offering assistance…

If she could be considered first, be the woman who the police came to, rather than leaving her to join the throng at the police station desk, she would have the advantage. It was hard to tell if the forthright character of Superintendent Neylan would be help or hindrance.

She walked south, diverting through an empty alley in order to come out at the other end as Catherine Weatherhead. With hair tied down, rings gone, and wearing a dowdy hat and plain coat, there was no hint of the Russian psychic apart from the same cracked leather bag, which she draped with a woollen shawl to make it less obvious. She was an actress now, and the two parts she played must never be apprehended by the same audience.

Madame Rostov was the star. Every time Catherine loosed her hair and put on the many rings, she was reminded that no one in London cared a fig about the ironmonger's daughter, or about Mardy Cath, the "odd" girl once of Fell Lane, Keighley. Excepting Mrs Bessovitch, of course.

Madame Rostov was also an intimate performance, one maintained best in private parlours. Catherine had lost confidence that she could put on the shows of which she had dreamed in her Fell Lane attic. The more she heard of Mrs Bless and her adherents, the less she wanted to be known as part of such a movement. Bluff and obfuscation she could contemplate, if not overdone, but the grand show was too much.

Perhaps another, slightly less astute Lady Seldon would come along, and be her patron? For whilst Lady Seldon believed Madame Rostov had a gift, she was immune to showmanship and quite able to spot outright fraud.

In the meantime, she would hold her modest séances, and try routes such as the police, possibly even the newspapers. Tomorrow she would adjust arrangements so that communications for Madame Rostov went to a post office elsewhere, in order to muddy the trail. Holborn might suit—a relatively easy walk, and an easier cab ride, from Blackfriars Bridge. An agent would have made more sense, but agents, she understood, took a percentage.

Remembering that there was occasionally correspondence for Miss Weatherhead, rather than Mme Rostov, Catherine enquired at the usual Southwark post office, and found there was a letter dated the twenty fifth of March, from Clarissa. It thanked her for "going out of her way and being so generous" when marking Maisie's eleventh birthday. It was polite, but managed to be snide and begrudging at the same time—appropriate, perhaps, for Catherine had come close to resenting the postal order she had sent.

Clarissa wrote that George Street would never be to their taste, but that they were making do. According to the letter, Jennie was still engaged as a part-time maid for a Jewish family outside the area; they saw less of her, but the extra income helped.

So the pretence was still intact. Clarissa knew nothing of her sister-in-law's true activities. Catherine did not visit her cousins any more—had not been to George Street, wherever that was. Somewhere in Spitalfields, apparently, which did not add to its attractions. Levinia's death had almost severed the ties between them. Under other circumstance she might have spent a little time with Jennie, but even she was at least fifteen years Catherine's senior. What they might have shared was difficult to see. Stories of Charles, and the Weatherheads at Harwich, of times lost.

Lost was lost.

The concept of becoming a respected consulting psychic had more and more appeal.

A fortnight after her visit to the police station, Madame Rostov returned to Borough High Street to enquire if anything had been done about a recent case of a factory foreman who had failed to come home after work. With his wife and colleagues being mystified at his disappearance, it seemed a good opportunity to test herself. When she explained her situation and the possible use of her talents, an ageing sergeant politely told her the matter was in hand, and they needed no "public hinterference."

The foreman's body was eventually found on the mudflats of the south bank, with a fatal fracture of the skull, probably caused by falling against a bollard by the river path. She attended the inquest, which recorded the incident as "misadventure." No one seemed very bothered, not even the wife.

Feeling discouraged, Catherine undertook a series of small sittings. A few shillings from one session; a guinea from another. She had cab fees to bear, to appear respectable, and still she needed new boots. London was hard on the feet. She frequented certain tea-rooms, where the "Russian medium" began to be recognised, and that was more expense. Madame Rostov could not ask if there were any stale buns left over from the previous day.

Her dreams were absent, or dark.

He understands the dead.

He is a student of what makes them so.

The subtle difference between the tainted froth of poison on the lips, and the slack saliva which comes from a natural fit or illness, for example. Not that venoms and toxins are fit tools for a journeyman, except under duress. They are the recourse of serpents, of thwarted and disappointed lovers.

The proper angle of a thrusting blow to heart or kidney, and the quarter inch, often less, which would give an opponent long enough to make a last blow in return.

The foolishness of assumptions, of believing that a single shot is enough.

The drum of a choking man's heels on polished floors.

The slow pressure of a pillow across the face.

The smell of disease.

As a carpenter knows timber, so Edwin Dry knows flesh.

At the end of April, Catherine received a note from Inspector Eden Mallick, of M Division. She was requested to call on him, should she be free to do so, the following day. With nervous fingers, she penned a brief reply that she would be there at ten in the morning.

Mallick was a tall, lugubrious man whose right eyelid had a disconcerting twitch. He showed her through to a cramped office.

"I am not Mr Neylan," he said, with gloom. "Matters of spirit and soul, would that I had time for them. Days plodding the Southwark streets, followed by a dried-up steak and kidney pie…"

"You do not hold with mediums, or with séances, inspector?"

"Don't hold with them? Know nothing of them, Madame. And care less, but the Superintendent will have his foibles. A case vexes him, and he says we shall explore all routes—'The Lord will shine His Light on the correct one.'" This in a passable imitation of Neylan's voice.

Catherine smiled.

"The Superintendent believes I may be of use?"

"He's a rare bird. Anything that sounds right and Christian goes in his armoury." The eyelid twitched and shook. "You must have had the proper cant when you met with him."

"I am no fraud, inspector," Madame Rostov was sliding

into her own. "The gift comes; the gift goes. At least I will not deceive you."

"So you say, so you do say." Twitch. "Well, Madame, we have a gang of lads—the Compass Rose Bravos, they call themselves—who parade around South Street and the Compass Rose public house. Mostly machine and factory boys. They drink overmuch, and offend the Superintendent with that and their language."

"Not a fertile ground for spiritualism."

The corners of Mallick's mouth turned further down.

"There was a shooting, two days past. A girl from the Union Boys, a rival gang, was wounded in the leg, and a Union fellow lost the sight in one eye. All were at fault, I expect. The gun has been found, you see, but we have no proof of who fired it. Neither side will speak; Mr Neylan will have one or more of them go down, as an example." The inspector gave her a sideways glance. "Mrs Neylan, a most righteous woman," He extended the "righteous" to stretch across the table between them, "Is on the Holy Trinity Ladies' Virtue Committee. She will be pressing him..."

Catherine's thoughts flickered, as unpredictable as the inspector's eyelid.

"If no one is killed, or wishes to speak to their late mother... ah. Perhaps I have it. Mr Neylan wishes me to guide him to the one who used the gun?"

"Aye."

She could express her regrets, say this was not her line of work. But they had come to her...

"An unusual request. Let me meet with such suspects as you have, Inspector Mallick. And if there is nothing, I will tell you so, plain."

"We have them remanded for disorder, in the cells. They will get a fine only, if that, unless we have better proof."

He led her to the cells below, where carbolic and stale alcohol vied with each other in the narrow corridors; one small cell contained only a pool of bloody sick.

"Not a place for a lady," said Mallick, noticing the vomit. "Maybe I should have them brought up to the interview room."

"It is no matter."

"Aye, well. Here are the likely boys from the Compass Rose Bravos. Not so bravo now."

The end cell held five youngsters of sixteen or seventeen years, clothed in cheap suits and sullen looks. They were the spit of boys who had plagued her around the backs of the factories at home—the half-poor, which meant they wanted more but could not quite grasp it. They had wages, but not good ones. Decent enough boots waited too long for new soles; collars had to be turned again and again. Boredom was washed down with drink, and tempers to follow.

The taunting gangs, following her through the muddy streets; Ellie, who had rickets at twelve and yet threw handfuls of dirt at Mardy Cath. The men who swore and urinated—and looked at her as they did so—at the back of the Cavendish Hotel. Slow Charlie, wondering why she would never touch him "down there" again…

There was always a weak one. He would be her way in. These boys were certainly not ready for the bone-china cups, almond biscuits and harmonium of a séance.

"Inspector, I will require a separate room, the weapon that was used, and…that boy on the left." The one who would not meet her eye, whose back was turned slightly from his comrades.

She stepped closer to the cell bars.

"I am Madame Rostov. Mr Neylan, the Superintendent of this place, would know which one of you fired on other children." She used the last word with scorn. "His men have better things to do than slap your faces, and so he calls on my gift."

"What gift's that, then, lady?" a sly-faced lad called out. "Summink under yer skirts?"

Someone snickered and she swivelled on one heel, surprising them with a cold stare.

"I am a psychic of some ability. I have dealt with death before, and worse miscreants than you. Do not toy with me."

Uncertain, they went quiet.

The available interview room was small and airless. The constable who had charge of the boy, whose name was apparently Ally Parfit, pushed him down onto a creaking chair and took up position behind it.

"It is Alastair?" She took her own place at the table, where lay the unloaded revolver. It was mud-spattered, and looked in poor repair, but the inspector assured her it had managed to fire twice.

The boy said nothing, and the constable cuffed him across the back of the head.

"Yes, miss," muttered the suspect.

"Madame. Madame Rostov." She took up the gun and stroked it, making a show of running her fingertips over its length. "Ah yes, this weapon has killed," she said, as if to herself.

"We didn't kill no one."

Cuff. "When you're spoken to, lad."

It was hard to tell if the constable was zealous, brutal, or both.

She asked for Mallick to be brought in, and achieved a reluctant agreement from him that she could sit alone with the boy.

She had one chance to impress.

When the policemen had gone, she lowered her head, and placed both hands on the revolver. For a long moment she was still, and then she gave a theatrical shudder. Watching Mrs Bless's performances had been good for that, at least.

"I turns me 'ead," she said, aping the talk she heard on Southwark streets. "I turns me 'ead, and I sees 'im; 'e has that barker up, pointed at me cannister. 'Fire,' says Parfit. Fire and—'"

"Raggy said that!" The boy protested, slapping the palms of his hands against the table. "It were 'im as found the barker, an' gave it to Ned—I never seen it 'til then."

"Easy to lie when one boy has an eye missing and a girl may not walk properly again."

"I'm not lyin'—you're lyin.' That 'Says Parfit' game, you made that up. You're some Ikey's wife they paid to nark on me…"

He subsided, confused and close to tears. Catherine put the revolver down.

"Violence confuses the Aether, makes many voices speak across each other. Is it so, then, that a boy called Ned had the barker—the gun—and he took the shots?"

He was quick to grab the lifeline. "He did, yes. I done nothing."

"Nothing?"

"Didn't 'ave no barker, never," he said more carefully, avoiding the question of any other role he might have played in the Compass Rose Bravos.

"Wait here."

She went outside and found Mallick trying to light his pipe in the corridor.

"Is one of boys you hold called Ned?"

"Ned Ginny, a butcher's apprentice, though not a good one. He's the big red-head in the cells. Why?"

"He fired the shots. The revolver came from a boy called Raggy. I don't know if Parfit will speak openly against them, but I assume you can work with the information?"

Mallick gave up on his pipe.

"The spirits told you all that, did they, Madame Rostov?" Twitch. Twitch.

"You do not believe, inspector, and so my explanation would mean nothing to you." She said it with a smile. There was no need to antagonise him, not if further work might come her way. "After all, if you get Ned Ginny to talk, you will have pleased your Superintendent—and Mrs Neylan as well."

He squinted at her, stilling his twitch for a moment.

"Aye, there's that. And Raggy? Hmm. That's probably the

printer's boy. We let him alone, but I know where to find him. I'll not say I catch your game, Madame Rostov, but still…I'm obliged to you."

"Pleased to assist the constabulary, inspector."

He showed her back to the front desk, where a short-dark-haired man was screeching at a sergeant about missing spoons.

"She's gorn and taken them all, the bitch!" he yelled, until the sergeant gestured a constable over, and the man quieted.

"Eden Mallick—any news, laddie?" Someone called from across the busy room, and Catherine halted. She knew that voice. It was the policeman who had come to Brantridge Street, asking about Caille's murder.

"Aye," said Mallick, loud enough to carry. "We'll have the right lad lagged and in prison linen soon enough, Donald. But I fear there's nothing more to it. A petty enough falling out, no great game underway."

"Pity, pity." Donald Swanson pushed through a group of quarrelling women. "And this lady, did they trouble her too?" He looked at Catherine, a look which turned quizzical. "Ha' we met afore, lass? I thought for a minute I kenned yuir face."

A long time had passed since their meeting in the damp, cluttered front room in Stepney, and under such different circumstances. He would not, could not, recognise Catherine Weatherhead.

"We have not, inspector."

"Chief Inspector," said Mallick. "Chief Inspector Swanson here is with the Criminal Investigation Department. He has an interest in the gangs of our fine city, and wished to know if the Compass Rose Bravos might become a problem worth his notice. Donald, this is Madame Rostov. She is…" He faltered.

"A psychic, Chief Inspector. A medium, of a sort. Mr Mallick is shy of the word, and shy of the path I tread."

"Ha. Eden Mallick tapping on tables, there's a wee change. That'll be old Neylan's doing, I'll guess."

The inspector's usual mournful look returned.

"He tasks us sorely, right enough." Which was not said so

loud that any of the other officers round the front desk could hear. "But better we fear God than dance a Highland tune."

She could see that the two men, much of an age, were well known to each other.

"Madame Rostov, eh." Swanson tipped his head to her. "Be welcome, Madame. The Force needs all it can muster some days."

"You approve of my profession, Chief Inspector?"

"Not greatly, Madame. Shysters and charades, for the most part, begging yuir pardon. But if Mallick here has found ye of value, then we must ay learn new tricks, ye ken."

"We are in agreement on that, sir."

And she made her exit. What Donald Swanson might learn if he gazed upon her face for too long was not to her liking.

CHAPTER NINETEEN

Southwark, July 1888

Three welcome gratuities from the Southwark police in less than three months. With the fees passed to her through Inspector Mallick, and the donations from her sittings, she met the arrears on her bed and board, though Mrs Bessovitch always waved the matter aside as not pressing. The extra money would also help with the hansom cabs needed to maintain Madame Rostov's reputation and distance. A medium who turned up late, limping in worn boots and soaked with rain did not command respect.

From what fund the police paid her, she did not know. Monies set aside for informants? Unclaimed rewards? True to the law, she never claimed openly to any at the station that she could succeed. She never asked for recompense. That was the necessary game.

The money had no taint when she spent it at the milliners, purchasing Madame Rostov a sombre, wide-brimmed hat, or when she settled her own account with the butcher—she could not expect Mrs B to buy every mutton cutlet that was cooked for her lodger.

In mid-July she was called back to Borough High Street for a minor "case" that she suspected had more to do with Mrs Neylan, the police superintendent's wife, than any wished to say. That woman's occasional appearances at the station were viewed with dismay, involving as they did more perfectly straight collars and brightly polished boots than even her husband demanded.

"Boadicea would have surrendered to that 'un," the desk sergeant confided to Catherine the week before.

She sat alone in the same small room where she had questioned Ally Parfit, a missing persons report in her one hand, and a distinctive child's hair bow in another. According to Mallick, the police had no suspicion of foul play, only that the child, Ellie Smith, was an active and generally disobedient eleven year old of good family. She had wandered off the previous evening, in a huff over a meal, and might be at large anywhere in the borough. Nothing had come back from officers on the beat, or from the general public. The father had offered a reward.

The report described her as well-dressed in a new cotton smock, long of limb, and with short curly brown hair. The red velvet bow, far larger than was considered stylish, was included with the file as being identical to the one the girl was wearing when she disappeared, and had been shown to each constable as he went out on his rounds.

This time the images came easily, free of violent taint or the horror that had once attended many of her visions. A lonely place seen through blurry eyes, but a skyline which Catherine knew, not far from the Walworth Road coal depot. It could not be mistaken, for the factory chimney there was in perilous condition and had a number of bricks missing near the top.

They found Ellie Smith exactly where Madame Rostov said, not abducted but a victim only of venturing into unsafe territories. Even now the authorities were preparing to harry the owners of the old factory, demanding that they seal the premises against further accidental intrusions. A fractured arm for Ellie, after her fall, and tears of relief for her parents.

The matter was concluded smoothly the same day. Granted, her involvement would not reach the newspapers—Superintendent Neylan would have none of that—but she held Inspector Mallicks's most recent speech close to her breast. "A tidy enough job," he'd said with a double twitch of the eyelid. "We'll no doubt see you again." None of the usual scepticism.

Eden Mallick was not an imaginative man, which made her success all the more satisfying. He was methodical, and she could work with that, as long as she only went along with him when she was sure she had a genuine insight. There was no point in treating him as she did her usual clients, playing on their need or their gullibility.

There was, though, a slightly unpleasant taste to the incident when she thought it over. The Smiths, respectable and vocal, were such that the police bothered mightily with their concerns when their daughter went missing. Catherine had no doubt that other children met death by accident every week, sought by few and mourned by even fewer. Were Benjamin or Maisie to wander off, she doubted the police would even note it, unless there was a general outcry from Spitalfields.

But this success was currency of another sort for her, to be used in her sittings. Hints as to her status.

"I do, occasionally, assist the constabulary," she would say, and make it sound as if she did so at her own discretion, not only when she managed to get the police to take her seriously.

～⚓～

All in all, she should have been elated, but what was it that still held her in its grip, this cloud of doubt? She never made any declaration that the Future was open to her, not even at her most extravagant sessions. Madame Rostov was no Nostradamus, to be able to predict such things; she had no more known what was coming for her than she knew the results of next week's races. That last would have been a welcome gift.

Late in the month she undertook a lengthy morning sitting in Bermondsey, which went adequately, but provided only seventeen shillings. More disturbing, the hansom took her there by Blue Anchor Lane, where a canning factory sat in gloom. Not so far from here to Deptford, the face of the factory said to her. Not so far to the world of the late, unlamented Frederick Caille.

Business concluded, she saw no sign of a cabman, and thought she might go to the Old Kent Road, where there would be hansoms in number. Her early life around Fell Lane and the poorer parts of Keighley had left her with little fear of walking alone—she knew how to run, how to kick, and how to place a boot between a man's legs, where his pride was easily bruised.

The streets were crowded, and tiresome. Bermondsey was not an area she knew well; better to be back in Southwark proper and on territory she understood, for all its failings.

"My apologies," she said absently as she bumped into a woman on the pavement in front of her. The woman turned, and Catherine recoiled. That face…

"Do you support us, ma'am?"

The words were slurred, issuing from lips dragged to one side by a swollen lower jaw, the tissue grey and unhealthy.

"What?"

"The strike, ma'am."

Catherine steadied herself, seeing that the stranger was a girl, really, no more than sixteen or seventeen. Above the disfigurement, the eyes were brown and gentle.

"Lil has phossy-jaw," said another, older woman in a heavy shawl, coming up at her side. "On account of what they do make us work with."

"Phossy-jaw?" Catherine tried to look at the girl, Lil, without showing her feelings. There had been something… "Oh, phosphorus."

"That's right."

She had seen the news. The match-girls' strike.

"This is what it does, the damned stuff," said the older woman.

"I'm so sorry." Catherine reached for her purse, but the woman stayed her arm.

"It ain't brass we ask for, but that you do talk of us, and tell others. We only ask fair pay and fair conditions. Bryant and May, they do profit as we suffer."

Catherine took a smudged leaflet from the younger one, stammering agreement that she would indeed spread the word. The girl's face disturbed her more than she expected, and she found herself rushing away without decorum, possessed by guilt and horror in equal measure.

Her second sitting of the day, near Blackfriars, went badly, perhaps as a result of her disturbed mood. Whatever talent or gift she possessed was elusive, silent. Mrs Ledworth was a demanding client, who would only sit between four and five pm, would not suffer others to be present, and cavilled at minor discrepancies. Catherine had paid the woman's daily to pass on snippets of information, but the daily was often drunk by the time she disclosed anything, and was unreliable.

Worse, Catherine kept imagining Mrs Ledworth, who was pale and patrician, with the sort of terrible affliction that affected the match-girl, Lil. In the gloom of the Ledworth's parlour, her mind took a grip on that cold, flawless face and distorted it, causing the lower jaw to crumble and bulge, the lips to part with discoloured spittle…

"Madame Rostov? I think I pay handsomely for your attention, do I not?"

Catherine blinked. The woman was fool enough to talk of pay, as if Madame Rostov were a tradeswoman, to be bought. That was how the fraudulent were taken, charging for nonsense.

"It is a troubled time, Mrs Ledworth," she said. "The Aether swirls, shifts. Do you think we can order such things?"

Her client was clearly dissatisfied, fussing at the lace around her shoulders.

"There are others mediums who might be more suited to my needs, of course—"

"There are." Catherine straightened in her chair, let her wild black hair frame a direct stare at the other woman. She knew it could be effective. "But they are not Rostov."

Mrs Ledworth hesitated.

"If—"

"I have recently been with the police, a matter of a doomed girl, foully treated, whose soul was almost lost…"

Catherine extemporised a tale of tragedy, of black deeds, embellishing Ellie's Smith's accident in the disused factory into a story of such villainy that Mrs Ledworth was captivated. Hints were given that the matter would not be widely reported because of the girl's connections. Ellie's parents were transformed from prosperous drapers to some echelon of high society, and the play was complete.

Mrs Ledworth was duly impressed, and insisted on providing a donation for the session after all. Catherine had no doubt that a further distortion of what she had said would soon be winging its way around the Ledworth's social circle. She left with relief, and this time she did take a cab, all the way back to Mrs Bessovitch's.

Her landlady was solicitous, seeing the weariness in Catherine's eyes.

"Come, I bring steak and dumplings, is good for young woman," she said, ushering her into the kitchen. "You sit."

"I ought to rest—"

"Rest after," said Mrs Bessovitch. "You are big girl, you need feeding."

Catherine smiled. Her landlady was a little shorter than her and twice the weight. It was said she once laid out a truculent boarder with one blow of her fist.

They ate together, and talked of their day. Only to Mrs Bessovitch did Catherine tell the truth of her activities, or admit how mercurial was her link to the psychic world, augmented of necessity by a keen eye and a lot of gossip.

"This is why you do not sit for me." The old woman smiled. "There is no gossip of Gilda Bessovitch—no one would dare."

"Very true." The steak was tender, a cheap cut but simmered for hours, with great floury dumplings, heavily-peppered, floating in the broth. She cleaned her bowl.

"I will sleep, for a while, I think."

"No crazy widows tonight, heh?"

Catherine gave her a look of reproof. "Or grieving parents, distraught sisters."

"I know, I know. Some of them is sad, true. Go rest."

The bed had been made, the room tidied. Mrs Bessovitch, whilst the best of landladies, had an inquiring mind, and Catherine was careful to keep any private papers well out of sight.

She unlaced her boots and lay on the bed, wanting only a dreamless rest. Instead, there came what might have been more use at the Ledworth's—a murmuration of voices, the disorganised fringe of other places. Tired and vulnerable, she pushed away the whispering, but found that the face of the young match-girl haunted her still.

Catherine jerked in half-sleep. There had been a smell, too, on the girl's breath—disease, the rotting of the flesh…

He raises his head, draws in the air, and knows his surroundings. A flash-house on the corner, ripe with drunks and counterfeiters; an abattoir close by, dogs fighting in the gutter over discarded innards. There is a pig-yard a quarter mile beyond, where beasts are brought for a final week of fattening; his fine nose is not needed to detect that. He stands on the edge of Bermondsey, and a walk which will consume half of the evening. Mr Dry does not take undue exertions, but his is a demanding trade. The walk will stretch sinews and strengthen muscles, prepare him for a commission later in the week.

He is, in general, satisfied. Many things are known to him, from many sources, and like the modest clerk which he appears to be, he files each fact according to its value. The Member of Parliament for a certain borough has a mistress, and his visits to her leave him open, away from his friends and servants. The director of Kimmet's Light Engineering is beholden to a money-lender who grows ever more demanding, and there may be work to be done.…

And on the streets, ah, it's there the plague is spread, through the veins and arteries of the city, carried by judies and dippers, fine dandies and stiff-collared baronets. Distrust, greed, and betrayal. All are carriers, and all may have need of him.

If they can meet his price.

By the abattoir, one dog triumphs, dragging ruined meat into the shadows; the other, thwarted, sniffs and scuffles at a gate in the alley.

At leisure, and not immune to curiosity, Dry goes over. The value of knowledge, in even the smallest things, should not be discounted. He may need to pass this way again, one day.

He leans down and touches the hound's back, gently. It looks to him, whines, and slinks away. If he had a morsel on him, he would be generous. The dog, as a species, is not given to such vice as humans hoard.

The gate is fixed by a latch which yields easily. There is a whiff of putrefaction in the alley, not strong but enough for hounds and Mr Dry.

The yard beyond, no more than four strides across, contains stacks of staved-in barrels. They once held vinegar, he suspects, but have been abandoned for years. They are not the source of what he can smell. He slips between the barrels, towards the rough brickwork of the far wall.

The body is that of a pig, one of moderate size. A sow. It lies with its back against the wall, not quite prone. There is no blood. The throat has been slashed, the result of several assaults with a long blade, with only one cut deep enough to reach the vertebrae.

Dry examines these, reconstructing each blow. From the left and from the right. Violent, but inefficient. One accurate cut would have sufficed. No experienced slaughterman would waste his energy so.

Lower down the pig's body, there are mutilations. The abdomen has been opened, and some of the internal organs are visible.

He stands in thought for a moment, and then leaves, securing the gate again.

Someone has been playing. But to what ultimate purpose?

CHAPTER TWENTY

Southwark, August 1888

So Dry had truly returned.

Not in passing images, which she could for the most part dismiss, but with the same stark immediacy as at Deptford, and there was a clarity to the experience which once again was close to pain. Catherine could almost smell what he smelled, feel the movement of each individual finger. His thoughts were ice, even though she barely skimmed them. Not evil, as she understood it, but ice—cold and crystalline in their reflection of the world around him.

The image of the mutilated pig haunted her.

Edwin Dry haunted her.

She cried off the few bookings she had arranged for early August, staying close to her lodgings. Somehow it was no surprise when on the eighth of the month, she read of a brutal slaying across the river.

The late editions of the newspapers dwelled on Martha Tabram's position as a prostitute and a drinker; they dwelled on the terrible nature of her injuries. The woman had been discovered at five in the morning on the stairs of a tenement building in Spitalfields. Numerous stab wounds had brought her life to an end at the age of forty. Surely not his work? Catherine could not believe that Dry would have used such violent excess—unless…

She put down the paper, and held firm to the kitchen table, steadying herself.

Robert Louis Stevenson. The first novel Charlotte Chambers had persuaded her to read, so long ago. Was it possible for the bowler-hatted man to be two killers in one—the careful, precise assassin, and the maniac, letting loose his frustrations? A dark Jekyll; an even darker Hyde, emerging when the ice cracked.

No, it was too much to entertain. For all that Catherine knew, Tabram was the victim of in-fighting between prostitutes, a chance robbery which ended in violence, anything. A meeting with a client gone wrong—common enough from what she read. The squalor of the streets and those who must live on them. Doctor Mercier had said after one séance that there were many in his asylum he thought safer company than those who roamed free. She would say a prayer for Jennie that night.

Mrs Bessovitch bustled into the kitchen, headed for the kettle. She noticed the paper.

"Everyone talks. Was Southwark girl, her."

"Martha Tabram?"

"Da. She drink much, move to Whitechapel. Commercial Road, last I hear."

Catherine took the tea things from the shelves behind her, cradling Mrs B's old gilt-painted teapot in her hands.

"A dreadful end."

"Is over. That is what 'end' means. She will have peace."

A spoonful each and one for the pot. Decent tea, not dust and shavings. The Southwark police had paid for it, which gave it extra savour.

"Was your land in north so different?" Mrs Bessovtich sniffed the milk.

"Less people, less murder. Otherwise, I suppose not. Keighley has its slums and degradation—in part of Leeds and Bradford, only the doughtiest constable walks his beat alone."

"I was in Kiev once."

Catherine wasn't sure where Kiev was. Part of the Russian Empire, certainly.

"And conditions were bad there?"

"Maybe. But I was young girl. We go to grand affair— many rich merchants, fine house with many rooms. Do you know what happen?"

"No. I hardly could."

"True. Well, we have good time, enjoy ourselves. Then we go back to small hotel. Next day, is news. Fine house was too near new railway cutting. Rain, heavy rain, in night, and back of house slide into big hole. Many rich merchants now dead in ruin."

She squeezed half a lemon into her lodger's cup.

It was, once more, one of Mrs B's strange parables.

"I suppose you mean to say that no matter how lucky you may seem, how rich you are, the end can come without warning? We are all mortal."

The landlady raised her eyebrows. "Nyet. I say, do not go to Kiev. They are not good builders."

That evening Catherine retired early, ostensibly to read something that Lottie had lent her. It appeared to be a book of children's stories by a man called Wilde, former editor of *The Woman's World* magazine. As the titles included happy princes and nightingales, she put it to one side. There were no princes, happy or otherwise, in the Spitalfields tenements where Martha Tabram was found. She closed her eyes, breathing in the musty but not unpleasant scent of the bedding and the old clothes in the wardrobe, listening to the late omnibuses passing outside...

As she drifted, Dry touched her mind—the brush of a crow's wing and the first snow, then the uncomfortable opening of a vista, something scratching at her nerves. He did not know of their connection, she was sure of that by now.

So where was he?

Chimney stacks and roof-peaks; high attics and a cross upon one peak. He knows the building, though he doubts the value of purpose. That rich and poor might live in Christian harmony— which is to say, that the rich tolerate the poor and the poor do not rise up. He rarely entertains politics—it is not his trade.

Commercial Street and George Yard. That is where she was taken, in George Yard Buildings. He has the pocketbook of a sergeant who attended, and the whispers of journalists from all around. He has word from the street.

This is the first.

Or the second practice run, if that is a more appropriate term. Too many blows, too little sense or purpose. That may be refined, as the killer progresses on his path.

Dry cannot name him, describe him, or predict exactly what will happen as a result of this deed. But there will be others. It has started with a sow and then a street woman, a prostitute. The sex of the victim is important. The next one taken will also be a woman, and the work done will be animalistic, brutal.

Unnecessary.

The journeyman is economical in his work, at one with his tools, and respectful of his materials. The unnecessary should never occur.

More, Dry senses that there is emotion at play. Lust or anger, much the same. This man is gratified not by the precision of ending a life for a genuine purpose, but by the protracted act, the involvement. He kills like the sullen, angry boy, who kicks a dead beast long after life has gone.

It is distasteful.

Those who take pleasure in such things—they are not journeymen. They are amateurs and lunatics. They besmirch his careful trade.

And this is only the first.

He will need more information, if he is to understand what is to come.

Catherine gasped, knocked over the water carafe with a flailing arm. Half-conscious, she became tangled in the linen and she panicked, forgetting where she lay. She was unable to escape a tiny attic, unable to unsee dear Uncle Jack, alcoholic malice on his red face as he strangled his wife…

No, she was in Southwark, not in Keighley. She lay there for a moment, her heart pounding.

The double image had given her a glimmer of understanding.

That had been the moment, had it not?

She took a half bottle of brandy from the back of the wardrobe and sat on the bed, letting a hot mouthful burn her throat.

What she had seen, what she had sensed that night in Fell Lane when she was fourteen—brutal murder, only yards away from where she slept—had been the start. The first real wound in a young girl's mind. Otherwise she might have gone through life receiving flashes of nonsense and dismissing them.

Perhaps it would have healed and been forgotten, but the repetition of circumstances at the Islington séance had stripped her of the possibility. It had allowed a quite different killer into her head, one who unlike Jack Witten had murder as his trade.

She was a psychic, yes, but one who knew nothing of departed souls or ethereal spirits. The dead were gone, as far as she could tell, leaving a maelstrom of impressions in other people's minds. She knew Miss Bournelle's late aunt because she could sense—on occasion—what Miss Bournelle and others had retained, the memories and impressions.

That talent, however unusual, might have served and caused little distress, but it was not alone inside her.

Her real knowledge was not of the dead, but of that which made them so.

The violence of the living.

She had a weakness, a wound inside her. If at times she could twist her abilities enough to be of use, such as with Mrs Ameley's drowned husband, or the missing child, it was a matter of luck and circumstance. A small consolation for the greater burden.

Catherine Weatherhead was damaged.

~~⚕~~

She plucked up the courage to write to Charles Mercier. She had questions of a spiritual and possibly medical nature, she wrote, and she hoped he would oblige.

Dr Mercier replied to her letter immediately, saying that he would be most pleased to meet with Madame Rostov. Not far from Flower House private asylum were tea-rooms which he described as "popular with the quality"—she was welcome to join him there an hour after noon on the seventeenth.

There was no direct train, but by changing twice, she made Catford well in time, and found the Prince Albert Tea-rooms, which occupied the ground-floor of a Gothic building which must once have been a school or workhouse.

A tall, prim-looking woman intercepted her in the doorway, and asked what "Madame's preference might be." Unwelcoming eyes had noted Catherine's worn furs and dress.

"I am at this establishment," said Catherine, with a more extravagant touch of the mock-Russian than usual, "To meet with my colleague, Doctor Charles Mercier."

The prim woman had lost the high ground, even more so when Mercier himself rose two tables away and tipped his head to her.

"Madame Rostov! How charming that you could attend."

This display brought two maids at once to take their order.

"The manageress is a talented snob," murmured the doctor. "Remain in 'court' fashion, and you'll have her begging you to patronise the Prince Albert again."

Initial conversation was easy. They talked of Mrs Bless's touring performances, and shared their mutual doubts about the woman. Mercier was tolerant and good-humoured as ever. He brushed his fair hair back with his hand on a regular basis, trying to tame it, and kept one eye on the other customers.

"I have a curiosity about people," he admitted when she pointed this out. "You still have my full attention, Madame."

"The cake here is over-iced, and over-sweet."

"It is."

They both laughed.

"You had matters you wished to discuss, though. I do not believe they involved patisserie."

He rested his bearded chin on his hands, the picture of an attentive doctor.

She spoke of a client she had encountered, and the client's concerns. Of visions which this invented figure had. The woman, said Catherine, was distraught, unsure as to her next steps.

Mercier listened, nodded, listened again.

"Are we talking of the 'departed,' intruding upon her thoughts? Of the souls of the dead?" he interrupted at one point.

"No." Catherine.

"Good, good."

What did he, as a psychologist, an alienist, think of someone who had visions which appeared to show actual events, violent ones—not predictions, but genuine occurrences, as they happened or perhaps a short time later? Yet the individual was not there, could not know of these matters. Was this a mental disorder she was describing?

"Not necessarily." He looked more serious. "I understand—I believe I understand—your predicament. You say that you yourself do not belief this lady to be partaking of matters 'beyond the Veil?'"

"Dr Mercier, I will try to be honest, and say that which I would not say at a sitting. Nor must it leave these rooms, I beg you. You see, I have no great conviction that there is life, conscious existence, after death."

"Aha!" he clapped his hands together, drawing looks from others in the tea-rooms. "I knew that you were cut from different cloth, Madame Rostov. No tambourines, rickety tables or halting 'spirit guides' who cannot finish sentences. You are, then, a follower of thought transference, or as some now prefer, telepathy."

"If I am a follower of anything," she said, cautious. "I have read a little on the theme."

"At least it is a potential discipline, not a re-enactment of witchcraft and such mummery under a different name. It may be nonsense, of course, but no black cats or monkey skulls are required."

Catherine paused, working out how to take his comment. He seemed to mean no offence by it.

"We may differ on some points, doctor. But I have never had a cat."

"So, you wonder if your client is either a telepathist, or mentally unstable and confused. Such things can be explored through experimentation, but most experiments connected to so-called psychic phenomena are, well, phenomenally flawed." His smile faded. "I cannot, naturally, say much more without your client becoming mine. Barring misfortune, I suspect that will not happen.

"Let me propose that if it is not the transference of thought, then it pertains to my own studies of the interactions between mentality and physicality, between the mind and the mechanisms by which we feed it information."

She pushed her cup to one side, then back, trying to grasp what he said. She had read so much that at times it confused her. Bluff had grown far more informed over nearly two years, but she was unschooled in the formal talk of medical men.

"More simply?"

"Your client is receiving quite normal stimuli, but is not processing them well. Permit me a demonstration, Madame. Put your hand forward, on the table."

She did so. Mercier unclasped his tie-pin, and without great force, pressed the point of the pin into the back of her hand, enough to cause mild hurt. She felt pleased that she did not flinch.

"Where is the pain?" he asked.

"In my hand."

"No. Your hand does not understand pain, not a bit. The pain is in your mind, your brain. Your hand recognised intrusion and disruption of the dermal layer. It was telling you that you have been breached, and should be aware. Your mind, however, translated this and called it pain."

"Yes…I think I comprehend."

"I expected that you would, from what I know of you. And so, this client has encountered stimuli, akin to my pin. These stimuli may be a melange of visual and auditory ones, olfactory and tactile. She may not have noticed them consciously— take, for example, a murmur of words overheard on a train or glimpsed in another's newspaper for only a split-second. When they reach her brain, it does not know what to do with them. With the added confusion of memory, it seeks to form a narrative, much as a dream constructed of random images might appear coherent at the time."

She watched the ebb and flow of customers in the tea-rooms, the thousand interactions of each minute.

"You are suggesting that such visions are the mind's attempts to make sense of...to organise these things? Things we are learning without realising?"

"You should have been a student of psychology, madame. I would say Bravo, but I would not want to appear condescending."

"A medium must be a student of psychology, doctor."

"As must every salesman of snake oil." He smiled with genuine amusement, and she smiled back.

"I'm sure that is true."

They took more cake, and had the pot freshened.

"But I may not have helped, Madame Rostov. Our beliefs intersect, possibly, at points, but do not meet. Still, it has been fascinating to have an open debate for once. Alienists and neurologists can be as inflexible as spiritualists."

"You have given me much to ponder, doctor, for which I thank you."

Their meeting ended with lighter conversation and few comments on his work, after which he rose, and they shook hands.

"Flower House demands me."

"And I have clients of my own for which I must prepare—though I shall say nothing of stimuli or physicalities. Good day, doctor."

Catherine did not know what she thought on the journey back from Catford, and by the time she reached her lodgings, she was too tired to sort out the tangle of her mind.

She slept free of visions or nightmares for once, and was thankful.

CHAPTER TWENTY ONE

Southwark, August 1888

Mercier must have known, Catherine was sure, that she was speaking of herself in the tea-rooms, speaking of Madame Rostov. And he had tried to assist her, to present an alienist's, or a neurologist's, explanation, one which would not alarm her.

That he was wholly wrong on certain key points brought clarity to her own thoughts. Not with Maggie Witten, nor with Philip Tether, the man outside the Crown and Sceptre, the priest...not with any of these could she possibly have gained the detail of information that had been in her visions. She had no disorder, no confusion of the senses or the way in which her brain organised the stimuli it received; she knew that she was not mad—she and Mrs Bessovitch had seen the newspaper columns which matched her visions so precisely. Her gift or affliction was real, and her mind was doing its best with what came to it.

Which was all she could ask. Damaged but sane.

Strangely cheered, she replaced a button on one of her boots. She bought blue paint, refreshing her night-stand with it, and read a fatuous adventure story borrowed from Lottie Chambers. As the month simmered around her, she went to the local park and listened to the brass bands. She even smiled at a strolling singer—a pretty lass with a freckled, up-tilted nose—who expressed her admiration of Catherine's raven hair.

She tried to be a young woman.

As a young woman with rent to pay, food to buy and undergarments which needed replacing, she returned to the dim parlours and expectant tables of the medium's world. A friend of Lottie's engaged her for an after-dinner entertainment, which netted her more than ten guineas. The guests were somewhat pompous and irritating, but the coin was true.

Police work raised its head occasionally. She failed to find an absconded and violent debtor for Eden Mallick, but did discover, through an accidental blur in the mind of a boot-black, the whereabouts of a hammer which had been used to club down a local tobacconist.

And in unguarded moments, she saw the Deptford Assassin as he prowled…

In Spitalfields there are few places, so very few places, where eyes do not look and ears do not listen. Even in abandoned courtyards and alleys which go nowhere, a window is open above, or a beggar lurks close by. He sifts fact from malice; truth from wishful thinking.

The woman before him—Mary Jane Kelly—picks at her lace sleeves and tries not to meet his gaze. She has already been more useful than most, and he remembers her from Deptford, though she never saw him that night. She knows what he did there, and what he is capable of. She has many encumbrances—fears, small enemies and desperation—but is bright enough. Prostitutes can be excellent listeners.

He takes the folded sheets of paper from her.

"On Friday, again, as usual?" she asks. She wants the money, but there is more than that. Dry wonders when she will speak of it openly—the matter is clear enough to him. She wants him to kill a rival of hers, a woman called Gorse, but she cannot yet bring herself to say it. He can wait.

Gorse, who also knows the streets, might have suited him, but he has observed her. She is duplicitous, and beholden to the worst of the local gangs. He has no doubt that she would try to play him. She would fail, of course, but he is not inclined to waste the time.

Mary Jane Kelly will do. That she fears his abilities and yet wants to employ them puts her firmly in his grasp.

His stock of information grows, and serves many purposes. Not all is accurate; not all is precise. Those who gather it do not know what it is he seeks—which is as it should be. As he has put word out among certain prostitutes and alley girls, so does he make quiet enquiry concerning the rough hands from Smithfield and the slaughterhouses.

He makes progress.

Catherine received not only fragments of Dry's search, but also other intrusions which confirmed the Deptford Assassin was still about his usual work. In mid-month she contracted an infection of the throat, which laid her up for a couple of days and carried with it a slight fever. Her room was thick with the smell of endless hearty soups brought up by Mrs Bessovitch, and the sharpness of the chamberpot. At the height of her croaking discomfort, she dreamed without sleep...

The history of Father Emmanuel Groves, and his "tendencies" is long and sordid. Mr Dry finds himself irritated by the protestations and weak rationalisations which the man makes as he realises his likely fate. On his knees, the priest has sudden remorse for dreadful acts. That such acts have been committed upon children does not help his case with Edwin Dry.

"I do not believe in the confessional," says Dry. "Neither does the mother of young John Berrowes. And so I have her coin in my pocket."

The priest dies quickly, the wire sufficient, and the commission is complete. He cleans the garrotte on a discarded surplice from the vestry, and wonders as he does so at the dirt around the groove it has left in the man's thick neck—do priests not wash?

He has time yet before dawn, time to spend in those narrow places which snake out from around the church—the alleys, lanes and cul-de-sacs littered with hopeless lives. He will walk a while. London, his city, is of a considerable size, and even he cannot be everywhere, but he needs the feel, the smell of the streets.

There will be another death soon.
Not by his hands, but by the one who still practices.

Following her recovery a day or so later, she searched through the newspapers, and found grim confirmation of what she had seen. A Fr Emmanuel Groves, of St Luke's Presbytery, Hoxton, had been discovered murdered in the vestry of his church, on the evening of 27th August—a garrotte had been applied until death occurred. The Hoxton Courier of the following morning had much more on the subject.

'On apprehension of Mr Geo Clegg, the husband of the Presbytery cook, the constables in question were subject to a litany of astonishing accusations against the deceased, including certain appetites of the flesh which plagued the priest. Inspector Taylor, presiding over the investigation, informed us that he could not provide more detail, nor would we wish to print it, lest we overwhelm our readers' sensibilities. Clegg is not considered a suspect, and we learn that he and his wife have been offered alternative positions by the Church authorities, who would also not comment to this journal.

'One Mrs Grace Berrowes, a widow and seamstress resident in the parish, remarked to our reporter that God did indeed understand justice, but she would not elaborate. Readers may remember that the body of Mrs Berrowes's youngest son, was sadly found last year in the Regent's Canal.'

Catherine had seen and heard enough in her visions from Dry to understand the nature of the late priest's deeds, and his way with the children who were supposed to trust his position. She would not weep for Father Groves.

Yet she thought back to the solicitor Philip Tether, who had not seemed to be involved in anything of great mischief. The bowler-hatted man took the guilty and the innocent. For every Frederick Caille or Father Groves, was there also a victim merely of someone else's ill will—deaths commissioned out of jealousy and spite? Rivals in love or business; inconvenient relatives and inconstant friends. She thought this likely.

Edwin Dry was not justice, even if he sometimes served it. He simply killed people.

⚔

The erratic nature of her abilities still vexed her. She could not "read" the thoughts of others as a discipline. She could not shut Dry out, or filter what came to her. Her learned talent to interpret the expressions and general demeanour of clients was more reliable. Could she learn control over what she possessed?

She took many of Mercier's comments seriously, reading up on the subject of telepathy once more and even recruiting her landlady to help. Late one night they sat in the front room and experimented. Mrs Bessovitch drew a number of figures or words on pieces of stiff paper cut into squares, and the two women sat apart, facing each other.

"What is on card?" Mrs B asked, making sure that she was not near the front room mirror. The landlady could see what was on the card; the side held up to Catherine was blank. As was her mind. After two or three minutes, she shook her head.

"A fish…a sea creature?"

"Tch." The landlady turned the card around, to show a crude drawing of a dog.

"It is an animal," Catherine said, knowing how feeble she sounded.

The next card was the word "Kettle," to which Catherine had suggested she saw the image of a horse. And so it went for another dozen cards.

The landlady laughed.

"Katerina, is all trick. In theatre, there is other man who can see card, makes signal with fingers. This is not you."

"Perhaps I wish it was."

Alone in her room, and smarting from her failure with the cards, her mind swirled with doubts about everything, from lemon tea to the suicide of Mrs Ameley's husband.

She had one certainty, which stayed with her throughout days of seeking to earn her living, with her on omnibuses and in hansoms, whether she stood on spit-covered cobbles or the plush carpets of a respectable household.

The Deptford Assassin was moving, probing.

A woman was slaughtered on the thirty-first of the month. Another prostitute, as the newspapers were quick to add. Mary Ann Nichols—a cut throat and several savage wounds to the abdomen. Her body was found slumped by a wall on Buck's Row. Not far from the London Hospital, which had sent a doctor to Levinia Weatherhead and pronounced that there was no hope.

Some papers mentioned the earlier death of Martha Tabram; some did not. One even raised the case of a murder from the preceding April, a death of which Catherine had not heard—an Emma Smith, killed in Spitalfields. She should probably look that up at some point—Mallick would know of it.

Catherine was taken by the shakes for a moment, and had to push the paper away.

Edwin Dry had expected this death.

Was there something she could have done? She had no idea who was doing the killings, where they would happen or when. No details at all. The thought of going to Superintendent Neylan and predicting that there would be violent death in London, and amongst the Whitechapel slums of all places... it was ludicrous.

Despite her visions, she had nothing of substance to share.

Closer.

Many possibilities have been explored, discounted, but London is a swamp of lustful, intemperate men from every station of life. Not that he considers the female of the species immune to such things.

A mile from Brick Lane he finds a man crouched over the body of a woman, a few yards from the noisome sprawl of a brewery. The man's hands are thrust up under the woman's ragged skirts, and he looks up as he realises that they are not alone.

"The kind of cove who likes to watch, eh?" The man laughs. "They don't charge when they're this drunk."

Dry moves closer, sees the steady rise and fall of the woman's chest.

There is no sign of either knife or any intent beyond base passions, and he leaves them to sink deeper into their own vices.

Such vices are not his business, this or any night.

CHAPTER TWENTY TWO

Southwark, September 1888

Only a week of September had passed when Catherine encountered two pieces of news which troubled her, for very different reasons.

The first was the murder of Annie Chapman. Mutilated, and in Whitechapel, on the eighth day of September. It seemed impossible that it had happened again, so soon after the killing of Mary Ann Nichols. The streets were now ablaze with talk of the deaths in Whitechapel. Rich men walked the streets at night, some said, seeking out fallen woman to carve; others talked of Jews, taking out their twisted frustrations on gentile women—or even workers seeking to raise sentiments against the Jews. There was a single madman; there was a gang. A doctor had gone insane; a slaughterhouse man had been cheated and now took his revenge.

Southwark may have been south of the river, but it was still not so very far from Whitechapel and Spitalfields. The dolly-mops and professional prostitutes began to walk in pairs, or find meagre wages from other activities for a while. Superintendent Neylan commented that "offences of the flesh" were down, and Inspector Mallick, tasteless as he could often be, opined quietly that Mr Neylan would make a good suspect—righteous in his condemnation of the prostitute's trade, and in thrall to an overbearing woman.

"I'm sure I did not say that, Madame," he added. His eyelid flickered with unaccustomed vigour, and he grinned.

They stood by a cab-man's shelter, cradling mugs of tea in

their hands. It was a convenient way of avoiding the bustle of the police station. She had met the inspector as a courtesy, concerning a woman the Superintendent wished to charge with duplicity. The woman had asked a half-sovereign a time to tell the future, working from a basement near the Compass Rose, and a disappointed customer had reported her. Mallick wanted to know if Catherine had anything to add, or knew anything of the woman. She did not.

Their business concluded, talk of the murders had been inevitable.

"Scotland Yard seems to have no ideas, if the press are to be believed," she said. "But they must surely be gathering intelligence on such a horror?"

"Aye, Donald's awash with reports from every eager watchman, constable, and sergeant from Cripplegate to Limehouse—and numerous letters from the public. Names are made or lost on cases like these."

"Donald? Do you refer to your Chief Inspector Swanson?"

"They gave him oversight last week—he must sift the lot, and find a diamond in ten thousand pebbles. Poor fellow, I don't envy him."

"A thankless task, I imagine."

What might Madame Rostov report to Swanson? That she knew a second killer strode through Whitechapel, sniffing after the first and watching?

She would be ejected from his office within the minute.

Her second piece of news, received later that same day, cut deeper for being so personal. It was a letter from her younger brother Josiah, and came to the lodging house, which puzzled her until she remembered that she had sent Clarissa her true address weeks ago. So few wished to contact Catherine Weatherhead that it had seemed pointless to keep up the rigmarole of going to the post office if her cousins needed her. Josiah must have had it from them, meaning no harm.

The letter was short.

*Dearest Cath. Father has read of the dire murders
which afflict the capital. Be warned, he comes for
you, and will have you back in Keighley. In haste,
Yr Josiah.*

She had made one simple mistake. She had assumed—absently, foolishly—that Clarissa and Jennie would keep Mrs Bessovitch's address to themselves.

And they had failed her.

Cloud came with Joshua Weatherhead; cloud and a mean rain which dampened but did not wash the city. The sky matched the ache at Catherine's temples, the same sensation that she had when the barometer swung wild. Pressure within; pressure without.

He arrived before ten in the morning, a single rap on the front door of the small Southwark Terrace. Isaac Green, a snot-ridden seven year old, had been paid to watch for a large stranger heading in the direction of the lodgings, and had been given a description. The child did his duty, and they were forewarned.

"You still have choice," said Mrs Bessovitch. "You keep out of way—I say I do not know where you are gone. Or…I do not let him in. Is my house."

"I will face him." Catherine tugged savagely at her hair, bound it back with an elasticated band. "It would have happened—this year, another. Let it be done, and done with."

"You really do not know why he comes?"

"Josiah said that my father wants me back up north, but not the true reason. I doubt that it is to do with my own welfare. That Josiah should even warn me is a surprise. My brother is not…brave."

Mrs Bessovitch spat a boiled sweet out into her palm, stared at it and then put it back in her mouth.

"Katerina is brave."

"No, I'm not. I ran before. I will not run today."

The landlady shrugged, and trudged down the hall to let the man in. Catherine heard short words between them, and then he was there in the kitchen doorway.

"I am in parlour, Katerina," said Mrs B. "I wait, if you need."

There was more grey than she remembered in his long black hair, and in the meagre beard which clung to a chin grown corpulent in its own right. His waistcoat bulged, pulling on the buttons of mother-of-pearl, and his trousers were of fine material but an inch too short. He was only half of his father, sharing the late Joseph Weatherhead's large frame but not the old man's angular lines and strength of feature, which had gone to Catherine.

"Meet all your guests here, do you?" said Joshua, glancing around the cluttered kitchen without enthusiasm.

Catherine, standing by the small range, wished that she had one of the fire irons to hand.

"You're not a guest, Father. You brought yourself—I did not ask for you."

"True. But now I'm here. You look different, lass."

Joshua's smile owed nothing to that of his father or his daughter. It was pinned to thin lips, a merchant's smile without meaning. Buy from me. Nothing had changed in almost three years.

"I'm fed well, cared for." Catherine pointed to a chair at the table. "Best tell me what you want, now you're here."

They sat opposite each other, chess-players without a board. He would have his pieces to hand, no doubt.

She made herself look at his face. His eyes, a muddy grey and crouched beneath heavy eyebrows, were raised to hers.

"Your mother's not well," he said. "She could do with you near, Catherine."

"You travelled more than two hundred miles to tell me that? You could have written."

He flexed his fingers, placed his hands on his knees. "Mebbe I came to make it clear. You never listened to owt unless it were said twice, and then more."

"She has Josiah."

"The good he is. Counting doesn't make caring. She's your mother too."

"And your wife."

The pressure around her forehead was getting worse. She stood up and fetched Mrs B's brandy, two glasses. She needed drink to prop her up against his presence, even at this hour of the day and in her own home.

"Tea's more than enough for a man," he said.

"Tea, then." She glared, poured herself a glass of spirits, and set the kettle on the hob. Sitting down again, she took a mouthful of brandy because he would not, because he did not want her to.

Joshua's expression shifted, much as when a customer moved from one rack of goods to another, undecided.

"I can read, you know, lass. The stories we're seeing from London—such bloody murders. God must weep at these women being cut down. Another only a few days ago, they say."

"God should do something about it, then."

"You'll not use His name like that!" He reddened. "It's man's evil as walks the streets here. Even if they were…women of a certain nature, they might have been saved for His mercy."

"You have money, Father. You should endow a mission."

"I do enough at home. Temperance and prayer, there's many look to me in Keighley."

She eyed the brandy, managed not to refill her glass.

"What do you want of me? Just have it out."

"I told you, your mother needs you."

"Get her help—another maid, a nurse."

"She needs a dutiful daughter." He turned away from her hard look. "Besides, lass—what's happening down here, wouldn't you be safer back home? With your family. We worry about you."

There was an undercurrent—what had Josiah said of her

circumstances?

"You think I'm a prostitute, perhaps? Risking myself for a few shillings down the back alleys, like these other women?"

"I had a letter from Clarissa, saying you came and went with shillings—not that she's seen you for months. You've no civil tongue, and could never mend nor sew proper. You're no companion."

"And so you think I let men up my skirts?"

He looked awkward for once, perhaps sensing he'd been wrong on this estimate, if nothing else.

"Mebbe I worried, like a father does. A girl in this place, this Godless den of thieves…"

Back to the almost reasonable appeal, which he did so well when he had a mind to. She filled the teapot, and pushed it towards him across the table. A cup and saucer from the dresser; milk from the shelf above the sink. Teaspoon and strainer clattered on to the polished wooden surface, and she frowned, thinking over his earlier words.

"And why did cousin Clarissa write to you at all?"

"Money. They only write, any of them, for money. Said I owed Levinia, that I'd wrung the best from both sides of the family." His eyes narrowed. "I worked. I worked, and made what we have. Thomas, he had no need to go south, marry Levinia. He could have had a share in the business."

Tom Weatherhead had died before she was born. A respectable travelling man, father of Charles and Jennie, dead with his heart at an early age. Levinia had ruled since then, until her end.

"You could spare it. You could make them a gift, for the sake of family. I have done my part, despite you."

"And what would I leave you and Josiah? The Lord does not reward the profligate, but the frugal and careful."

She could see his blunt thoughts. He would arrive in London, the dutiful and caring father, and sweep her up, put her back in her place by the hearth and the range—until he could trade her in marriage and add to his empire. There would be some merchant somewhere in West Yorkshire with useful assets and a dolt of a son. He was only here because he had a scheme laid out—or because his own wife was becoming more of a burden than an asset. He had never had time for the weak and the sickly.

"How many shops now?" she asked, sudden and direct.

"Five, and one more in Leeds to come." He looked pleased at her question. "Wholesale as well. And the coal trade brings in a fair rate."

"Then go back and look after them. Leave me be, Father. I'll not return."

"You will." His broad, fleshy face was dark again. "I came this far, and you'll do your duty. You're an unnatural child, Catherine Weatherhead, to leave your mother without a daughter's love, to abandon good family for…for this!" He waved a contemptuous hand at the room in which they sat. "Never a thought for what is proper, for the needs of others. For—"

"What do you know of anything but your own greed and comfort?" She swept her arm across the table, dashing the tea things to the floor. "Oh, you sanctimonious bastard! If I could—"

Pain. The ache which had been clinging to her temples, gathering behind her eyes, released itself in one needle of memory, one vision…

She saw him.

Joshua Weatherhead, more than ten years younger, and the houses on Fell Lane, from the Union Infirmary to the terraces, neat enough. The Weatherheads, and next door, the Wittens. Joshua and Jack, always close and often in drink together, before Joshua took the pledge.

She saw her father.

He belches, rises from his bed, restless. Damn, he's left his watch in the back room, where Jack is sleeping off the drink. He stumbles down in stockinged feet.

Jack isn't there. The back door is open. Joshua rubs at his eyes and looks out onto the small yards, left and right. The door to the Witten's is open as well.

He should go back to bed, but he wonders. Padding from his yard to the next, he looks into the house next door, the moon holding up a lantern for him.

The act is almost done, the woman sinking to the floor, lifeless. Joshua gasps, and Jack looks round. No surprise, no penitence.

"I did for her, Josh. No bairn from her in ten years, and only harping about the drink, the cards, the rent—never a rest for a man."

"You'll hang."

Jack smiles, steps over the body and comes closer, almost outside.

"Will I? For a thief what came in the night, while yet I slept at my old mate's house. A thief what was taking his due, and being surprised in the act, rode the life out of the one who saw him. Would you give me to the law, Josh, or help me?"

Broken sleep, a belly of dark ale, and a man Joshua had known all his life. Laughing Jack—Uncle Jack to his own children. And Maggie Witten, she'd not been so bad, but she was gone now. A lumpen shape on the carpet before them. Nothing he could do about that.

They pull out the cupboard drawers, and scatter spoons, letters, fragments of lies across the floor. Joshua picks two decrepit silver candlesticks.

"He'd not leave these. There's good metal to them."

"Hide 'em, then. They'll go to Bradford when all's quiet, fetch a crate or two and still change for us."

Uncle Jack takes a screwdriver, quiet, to the back door latch, scratching all around.

"That's how he came on her," he says.

Joshua hesitates. He hears a plan in his friend's voice, one which surely did not spring newborn from this ugly night…

Maggie Witten never liked Joshua anyway.

He turns over a chair, tucks the candlesticks under his arm.

"We slept through it," he says. "They'll find her soon enough in

the morning, and wake us."

"Oh, to lose my poor dear darling wife so," says Jack Witten, and the moon sees a narrow smile on the man's face…

Catherine managed to stand. She managed to stand because she had Madame Rostov, who knew how to be in control, to be imperious. To walk the Aether, and bear the sight of murder.

"What is it, lass?" Her father looked puzzled.

Had this been in her these many years? Buried thoughts, the other half of young Cath's vision. A knowledge of her own father's complicity, of his lies, that she had pushed aside in desperation. Or had she read it from him here and now, in a moment of anger across a kitchen table?

She had known. It had coloured her life in Yorkshire, and played its part in driving her to London.

"Did it trouble you?" she asked.

She held on to performance, to Madame Rostov with eyes of grey ice and wild, unmanaged black hair, the heavy rings glinting on her fingers. She imagined the rings, even though they lay boxed upstairs in her room.

"What are you talking about?"

"Did it trouble you, seeing Aunt Maggie lying there, stripped of breath, of life? Did you wonder, as you ransacked a cupboard and grabbed at the candlesticks, if you should have checked? Or perhaps you had light enough to see her mottled face and know that she was gone. Did you?"

Her belly was hard, her blood rushing to strengthen her. Her father's hands were veined claws, gripping his thighs as if he could not release them; his face was soured milk, pale and poisoned by her words.

And the words would not stop.

"You took the belt to me for lies and slander, for having thoughts which came from the Devil and his sendings. You marked me, and you let others mark me. 'Touched,' they said, and you let them say it. Chapel every Sunday, where Cath sat slumped and sullen, whilst her father, the industrious Joshua

Weatherhead, sang out—upright, decent.

"Here I am, father. The 'unnatural child' you helped make. Is this what you want back at your hearth, to order and to use? To break, like you did my mother?"

"You can't speak to me like this, you—"

"Can't speak to you? Oh, I can, and more." She advanced on him, laid her shadow over him. "Maybe there are other secrets? Shall I look deeper, and lay out your finest moments for you?"

This lifted him from his seat, a hand raised as if he might strike out at her.

"I'm your father, you ungrateful whore! You'll show respect—"

"I could have you killed." Said soft, but clear.

"What?" He halted.

Philip Tether, the man of bluster at Clerkenwell, the priest at St Luke's—she had seen them slaughtered. She was tainted, and knew the trade of death. And always Frederick Caille. A man of business, proud of his status. Like her father.

"This isn't Fell Lane; not your coal-yard or your little empire. This is London. You came for someone who no longer exists. Here, I could have you killed, and they would never find you. Not like Aunt Maggie—you remember? You would be ended and unmourned."

"You're insane. I should—"

"Leave my house," said Mrs Bessovitch from the doorway. "You upset my Katerina."

He looked from one woman to the other.

"Two candlesticks," said Catherine. "Two battered silver candlesticks. Did they ever go to Bradford, to the pawn shops, or a publican who asked no questions? You and 'Uncle' Jack must have drunk deep when they were safe away."

"I...you don't..." Unmanned, uncomprehending—or beginning to comprehend something with which he could not cope. He edged towards the doorway, and Mrs Bessovitch stepped aside.

"You will not come here, to my house," she said. "You understand this?"

He was gone, the front door creaking behind him, the thin rain at his back.

The landlady set the brandy glasses upright, tutted at the broken cup on the floor.

"You are not good for my crockery, Katerina. Maybe I add this to your rent."

She poured out spirits for both of them. Catherine could not speak. She took her glass and drained it.

The clouds grew thicker, and darkened the street outside.

⁂

That night she talked of her mother, and Mrs Bessovitch listened. She talked of a poor marriage, founded on the money which her mother brought with her, and the slow loss of will. Of a weak woman, easily swayed and ordered, who had clung to her two surviving children as if they were little dolls with which to toy—until they grew too old for the game.

"Did you not love her?"

"Love did not live with us." Catherine and her landlady were close to drunk, down to gin from around the corner. Catherine hated the taste of gin. "Josiah played longer than I, knew how to say the right words to keep in favour. And he dwells under it still, caught between pathetic need and harsh command. Poor Josiah. I should have loved her, yes, like any proper daughter. I am unnatural."

"Is true," said Mrs B, and they laughed until the gin ran from Catherine's nose.

Later, she was very sick.

CHAPTER TWENTY THREE

Spitalfields, September 1888

Three have now fallen to the unknown knife.
Tabram. Nicholls. Chapman.
The authorities prevaricate and bicker. They debate who was cut down by whom, how many murderers there are. A gang of low-lives, working in concerted effort? A single madman loose upon the streets, or a conspiracy?
Their debates are pointless. The three deaths have the same sense, the same feel—this is the professional assessment of the journeyman, deep in his craft.
And he is able to make another assessment.
He himself can take life in a hundred different ways. He can deem a commission to be of no value one week, interesting the next. He can wait for a month, or for a year, before he acts. He can improvise. A door creaks and a child's hoop lies across the cobbles in Clerkenwell; as a result, a man who has walked the same way home for ten years decides to go another way and take the omnibus...
Each plan is the right one until it is not.
He understands change. It is the essence of his world. The ability to consider, and to change. Without this, he could not do what he does.
The newcomer is likely to be deficient in this field. Dry sees stubborn pattern, not flexibility. Emotion, not intellect. The bloody acts may develop in intensity and focus, but they are steeped in specific needs, wreathed in warped and personal judgement.
There will be a story, of course, behind the one they call the Whitechapel Murderer. It will be a maudlin, confused one. The same story is available in every public house, heard from drunken Lascar seamen and penniless students; bitter apprentices and

thwarted accounts clerks. Each tale is some terrible indictment of humanity. Jealousy, betrayal, brutality.

And each is, in the end, quite dull.

Ten thirty-seven in the evening, and Whitechapel is ripe with life, despite the killings. The prostitutes cling closer to the street-lights and the tavern doors, but trade must continue. Bellies are still empty—throats rasp for ale and spirits. One mouthful of a man's spend, spat out when he's away down the street, and then a welcome gargle of gin.

Dry slips from one dank alley to another, noting crumbling bricks which would offer a toehold, a broken window where the frame could be cracked without undue noise. These observations are stored away. As ever, he times the constables as he goes. Colchester Street to the Jews' Cemetery. East and south, quartering Stepney without haste. Each nest of streets has a smell, a prevalent wind of poverty or ambition.

The night is a circle, carrying him back to the pale, dawn-touched bulk of Christ Church in Spitalfields. He admires architecture which is of use. What use this is, he does not know—he has no interest in religion or spirituality.

A ragged shawl and missing teeth reach out to him on Dorset Street. When the owner of shawl and teeth sees his eyes, she huddles back into shadow.

Mary Jane Kelly lives close by. His gatherer of intelligence on the comings and goings of men who cannot restrain their manhoods. Are some of their clients more violent, more frantic or sly than most? Do any have a penchant for the knife, even in play? Something will betray the newcomer.

To be alone and pure in his craft, to work without the need for others—that would please him. There may come a day. For the moment, for such a sprawl of streets, he makes reluctant use of those he must.

The police double their patrols and scatter inspectors, down to the dullest placeholders from idle stations, across the breadth of the East End. Scotland Yard is unhappily alert. Reporters and vigilantes creep through the streets, followed close by the mission *faithful, seeing this as chance to hoard souls. All in all, too many eyes are open for his liking.*

But the sun lifts behind Christ Church, a coral tint to the chimney smoke, a soft glow which will be beaten away within the hour.

Even Dry must sleep.

A day with a blinding headache, after a night where the Deptford Assassin flickered in and out of her dreams, showing her places she had never been, would never go. Catherine took salts and a tonic, made one trip only, to buy chocolates and violet water for Mrs B. These she presented, her head still throbbing.

"I am sorry to bring this to your door," said Catherine. "Yesterday, I mean."

"Tch. I have seen worse than your father. Go bathe, Katerina. Sleep some more. And do not disturb me. I have much chocolates to eat."

The newcomer has no clear scent. A minor problem, for which adjustments must be made. That is to say, he is so close to the streets and the filth that there is nothing which marks him in a crowd. If he is a man of note, he has walked among the beasts for many nights; if a beast, he is as yet indistinguishable.

Method and persistence. It may not be the third, or even the thirtieth. There are many men in London.

On a sultry Stepney night, a thick-shouldered seaman looms over a woman, pressing her against the Board School wall. Metal glints, but the blade which clatters to the ground is a pen-knife, the tip broken away. The woman who is being serviced has a shallow cut to her cheek, the mark of a drunken bully.

Dry moves on.

Off Anthony Street he watches a thin girl being beaten by a Greek or Levantine; a half mile east he sees two men puking into the gutters whilst a third watches. He waits, but when they have done emptying their guts, they join their companion and kiss.

Nothing of importance.
As he pads away, Dry holds a question tight to himself,
unanswered. It is a question he does not like. There is no commission
in play here.
When he identifies the Whitechapel Murderer, when he truly
knows the man and his nature, has assessed the potential there and
has the measure of how far the killer might go…what next?

Catherine woke cleaner and clear-headed. There was
something she needed to do. An afternoon session with the
miserable, priggish Mrs Ledworth, which would net her ten
shillings if she was lucky, and then a private matter.

At four in the afternoon she took an omnibus, all trace of
Madame Rostov abandoned, and made her way to Spitalfields.
She would have words with her cousins, for giving her address
to the family in Yorkshire. And there would be, should be, the
inevitable coins to be left, a token for Benjamin and Maisie,
despite her irritation with Clarissa. She hadn't seen any of them
since they left Brantridge Street.

Quite where the George Street lodgings were, she was
unsure, but there were maps in her mind, shadowy ones that
had not come from her own experience. The bowler-hatted
man had passed down these streets, many times, and recently.

There was Christ Church, as clear as she had seen it in her
visions. Box-like, surmounted by the tall Gothic steeple—and
all around it the alleys and lanes which Edwin Dry walked.
This seemed no better place than Brantridge Street, and she
wondered how low Clarissa and her family had fallen.

Martha Tabram. Catherine shuddered. She had paused by
the Christ Church graveyard, now more a public green, and
the thought had come—the connection she had never made.
Tabram had been found in George Yard Buildings. Her cousins
must live close by the site of that brutal murder, yet it was never
mentioned in Clarissa's infrequent letters. To avoid her pity at
their circumstances? She thought of Jennie—how safe was her
cousin in such surroundings?

"Miss Weatherhead? Miss Catherine Weatherhead?"

Catherine looked around. By the churchyard wall, an old woman in shawl and clogs was beckoning to her. A scrawled placard, which Catherine could not read, was propped against the stone wall.

She went over. The woman seemed familiar from somewhere. A jaundiced, toothless face, the hair grey and straggling.

"I am Catherine Weatherhead, yes."

"Mrs Hollis. I was at poor Levinia's funeral."

"Oh. I…I hope you are keeping well." It seemed doubtful, looking at her. Memory ground slow like a mill-wheel, and she tried to smile. "Yes, Mrs Hollis. I apologise—I did not recognise you for a moment. Your son—John?—was on the *Penelope*, with my cousin Charles."

"Served with that good man; died with him," said the old woman. Spittle gathered at the corner of her mouth. "But my dear, I was so sorry about poor Jennie."

"Jennie? Is she ill? I heard nothing from Clarissa."

Mrs Hollis's eyes widened, faded colours against the yellow-grey that tinged her cheeks.

"I only meant…it's no matter."

"Something has happened." Catherine focused her attention on the bent woman. There was terrible news underneath the torn lace shawl.

"It's not my place—"

"Tell me, please."

Mrs Hollis glanced around, a rabbit pinned in lantern light. "I could so do with a wet, my dear. Anything…"

The King George public house was shabby and mostly occupied by working men, taking an early dinner from the bottle. Their dull eyes marked Catherine as she pushed past them, but there were alcoves at the far end where a few women sat. Some were entertaining, clutched by costermongers and barrow-boys; others hunched over half-empty glasses, showing no interest in anyone.

The barman provided two glasses of pale ale, eyeing

Catherine as he did so. She was not in the mood.

"Is there aught you want to say?" she snapped. He scowled, and turned to another customer.

Pressed into a corner, with the smell of Mrs Hollis thick in her nostrils, Catherine sipped the weak, sour ale.

"What has happened to Jennie?"

The old woman tried to drink, some of the ale spilling from the corner of her mouth.

"We spared Clarissa," she said, a plea for understanding. "We all did spare her, for the loss she'd taken."

It was a bleak tale that unfolded. Mrs Hollis knew that Jennie Weatherhead had never served as a maid—that it was entirely a fiction for Clarissa and the children—and that life on the streets had been hard.

"She admitted it to me last year," said Catherine, remembering her fears at that time about the path on which her cousin had stepped.

"It were Jennie's choice, dear," said Mrs Hollis. "Girls around here, they do make best."

The woman continued in a rambling tale of rivalry, the gangs who drew tithe from the street women—and the violence of the men they served. A toothless saga which took Catherine into places she wished not to visit. She did not want to see her gentle cousin in that story, but choice was denied her. The old woman's words had only truth in them, however mixed and mumbled.

"Emma Smith," said Mrs Hollis. "The name she took, see. But she were not made for that trade, poor soul. And in the end they had her, fist and stick. Oh blessed Lord, they had her, and put an end to her."

Catherine knew the name. Emma Smith. She remembered the comment by Eden Mallick. She had heard of her own cousin's death, and put it to one side, ignorant, considering it the sad fate of a stranger.

"Then Jennie is dead," said Catherine. Flat, drained of feeling.

Mrs Hollis wept. Catherine could not. At last the old woman looked up.

"We kept it from the family, like I says. And Easter hardly passed. With poor Charles and my Johnnie gone, then Levinia—what could we say? Better to say that Jennie had left, maybe found something better, than to talk of such a day. I laid a few flowers, such as I could get."

Mrs Hollis stared into her empty glass.

"White roses, mostly. They weren't the best…"

"Are…are Clarissa and the children well?" It was all she could think to ask.

"As they can be. The air is not good on George Street, but they have a roof, and Clarissa has her mending."

She could not see them. She could not go there and lie, now she knew of Jennie's fate. She found a half crown from her purse, laid it on the table.

"For your troubles."

"I would have done it anyway." A flash of dignity from the old woman.

"Take it. Have another beer in Jennie's memory."

The half crown slipped under the shawl.

"I think I were supposed to ask you something." Mrs Hollis frowned. "About what happened a while back…"

"Write to me." Catherine wanted to hear no more. "The world has my address these days."

It was unbearable.

She rose and tried to push her way to the tavern door.

"You looks worth a shillin' or two, girl," slurred a corpulent man with tattoos down his forearms, blocking her way. He grabbed at her shoulder, his dirty fingers digging into her flesh. "I knows a room nearby…"

To have faced her father down and buried a murder from long ago, only to find another death had come close to her.

The instincts of Keighley alleys, and the certainty of Edwin Dry, wrapped her fingers around the neck of a beer bottle on the nearby table. She swung, shattering the bottle across the man's skull and sending him reeling back, blood in his hair. A few men growled, but most laughed. They did not stop her leaving.

Her hair wild, her thoughts as dark and unmanaged, she fled for Southwark.

He has no sentimentality as to the slaughter of women— parson's wives or prostitutes. They are human beings, and can sin, can cheat and lie. And they can achieve through those approaches, or through virtue and bold works, if they choose. They are no different from men. He sees no reason why they should not vote and hold high office, be mistresses of banks and great industries.

That the stranger has chosen women—and street women—as his victims is merely a mark of the man's own weaknesses. Another sign of sullen, twisted prejudice.

Edwin Dry does not entertain prejudice in his work. Deptford came from a woman; not a month after, he took ten pounds from the towering black first mate of the merchantman Bewcastle, a man whose captain had swindled him of his due. The captain's permanent retirement came quickly.

All are equal when there is a commission.

All are equal before the blade.

CHAPTER TWENTY FOUR

Southwark, September 1888

She asked.

Catherine sat at the Borough High Street police station, and she asked Mallick what he knew. Was the death of Emma Elizabeth Smith, on the night of the fourth of April 1888, considered to be the work of the madman now loose in Whitechapel?

Not knowing why she asked, he reeled off the broad case—as he had it—without concern. Where Emma Smith had been attacked, and how she died two days later in the infirmary. It was painful to hear, but she tried to show no great emotion.

"Unlucky, that's all," he said. "Maybe she crossed one of the gangs. They take a cut, see, and if you're late in paying... well, they get rough. If you look like you're going to stand up to them, they get rougher. Set an example, like."

It was not Jennie's world. She would have been ill-equipped for such men, however much—as Mrs Hollis said—other women had tried to help her.

"Unlucky." Catherine thought of how much could be said with such a short word. "And so many like her."

The inspector shrugged. "There are men who'll pay, always men who'll pay." His eyelid twitched more rapidly, a distracting sight. "It's not as if I like it, Madame. I've a daughter, going on twelve years old. Not as if I like it, and not as if there's much we can do."

"You're married?"

She had never thought to find out anything of Eden Mallick's circumstances. He was somewhat shabby, as a rule, with a creased collar and a waistcoat button missing at that very moment, the sort of things he hid from Mr Neylan when he could.

"Fifteen years, and contented enough."

There was little else to say about Emma Smith, who had once been Jennie Weatherhead. No point in telling Mallick the dead woman's true identity or circumstances.

Oh Jennie, to end up so! Catherine was angry, and...she was trying to avoid what else she knew she felt.

Guilt.

Would a few extra shillings have turned Jennie in another direction, and kept her off the streets? Joshua Weatherhead could have paid his dues to family, and acted on those Christian virtues which moved his lips but not his wallet. Or Catherine might have managed to help more, with care—even if she had to force the money on them. Extra sittings in the early days, a chance that she could bluff her way through to more substantial donations. For that matter, she might have found a way to beg Lady Seldon and the others for a small remuneration.

Though Jennie was gone, Clarissa and the children had to survive. Perhaps there was a favour of a different kind she could beg, a last gesture in the memory of Charles Weatherhead, and poor Jennie.

Family.

⁓❦⁓

Madame Rostov presented her card in Chelsea, and was welcomed in. Charlotte and "Katerina" kissed, followed by the ordering of cakes and tea with lemon. Lottie had become enamoured of the drink since she had seen Madame Rostov liked it so—Catherine still did not—and now it was always tea with lemon.

"I did not entirely understand Mr Rider Haggard's piece," said Catherine, passing the book back to her friend. "This Ayesha ruling over her black subjects—an odd choice. Is it meant to be clever, a satire on the Queen?"

Lottie giggled. "Is it? Goodness, I must read it again. I never thought of that. Anyway, your timing is excellent. Lucy is coming in half an hour."

A cat yowled in the hall, and Jemmy ran in, breathless.

"Tiddy doesn't like the new game," she said, and mocked a curtsey. "Good day, Madame. Do psychic ladies have cats to attend them?"

"They may," said Catherine. "But it is not required."

The girl grabbed a piece of iced sponge from the cake stand and ran off again.

If Lady Seldon was soon to be there, then Catherine's request—her purpose in coming—should wait until then. She talked hats and books with Lottie, and made light fiction of a recent sitting, where the old man who was hosting almost passed away in the middle of it.

"A heart tremor—nothing serious in the end, said the doctor. Such was the man's panic that he near died of fear."

Lottie wondered aloud that if the man had died in mid-session, his spirit might have spoken there and then through Madame Rostov. They debated the technical issues as if it were a game.

"Speaking of the psychic world, dear Katerina, I met a fascinating young man on the Embankment, a Mr Thomas Carnacki. He has recently taken a place on Cheyne Walk, and would you believe—he is a student of what he calls 'astarral vibrations,' which apparently—"

At the moment Lady Seldon was announced, whereupon a maid brought extra tea things, and fresh scones.

Other lives.

Two weeks ago Catherine Weatherhead stood below Christchurch, to be accosted by a ragged old woman, and to break a beer bottle over a man's head. Two weeks ago she heard of her cousin Jennie's brutal wounding and subsequent death. And here she sat in comfort, attended by servants, nodding her head in greeting to the slim, capable Lady Seldon—whose cream silk dress and lace trimmings would probably have paid a year's rent for some.

"You do not care for the style, Madame Rostov?" The other

woman noticed Catherine's gaze.

"The dress is most pleasant, Lady Seldon. You will have to forgive me—I recently undertook a small task which has given me thought. I am distracted."

"Do tell. I have little enough distraction from committees and Harry's work. This escape to Lottie's is one of the few I will have this week."

Lady Seldon could not be played, not easily. Catherine would serve up fragments of the truth, well-larded for present company, and see what might come of it.

"I had cause to visit Spitalfields," she said. "You know that I occasionally assist the police, when there is reason to think that the Aether holds answers that the streets do not."

"With some success," said Lottie, smiling.

"It is unpredictable, I fear. Still, I had to sit with some there, poor souls. And I came across a well-spoken woman who was so down on her fortunes that I wonder she can manage another winter. The widow of a naval officer, left with two children and only a half pension, if that arrives at all."

"She should apply to the nearest Mission, or the Widowed Women's Charitable Board, perhaps?" Lottie looked to Lady Seldon, who waited on Catherine.

"Her husband has gone, and she clings to pride. She was a seamstress once, and takes in mending. But imagine, from her own little house to a hovel in three years, and in Whitechapel, with murder all around at this very moment…"

The older woman put her plate down, her scone half-finished.

"I doubt you tell us this for instruction, Madame. A seamstress? Was the woman—is the woman—skilled with needle and thread, with materials?"

"Undoubtedly. I have seen her work."

"Would you vouch for her character?"

Catherine thought of Clarissa, and all that she knew of her cousin.

"Yes. Hard working, and steadfastly honest. She would

rather her fingers bled than that she took charity. Even though she has suffered from childhood with her breathing, as well."

Lady Seldon nodded.

"We have never acknowledged," she said slowly, "The considerable amount of time that Madame Rostov has spent, indulging our curiosity concerning the spirit world. Or the inconvenience this must sometimes have caused. You might say that we are in your debt, Madame."

You might well say that, thought Catherine. But then again, this elevated circle had also offered social advantages to Madame Rostov, and to Catherine. She should not complain.

"There is no debt." She met Lady Seldon's eyes. "I do not ask for favour. I mention, only, a matter which has bothered me."

Lottie touched Lady Seldon's arm. "Lucy, you might—"

"I might. And I imagine that Madame Rostov thinks I might, as well. She is no fool." She smiled at both of them. "We are all politicians. I shall enquire, and write to you. There may be a place for a hard working seamstress in such straits—possibly somewhere that might be more conducive to the raising of children than the stews of Whitechapel. Is that satisfactory?"

"It would be a mercy for those concerned."

"Good. Your penance for raising a serious matter, Madame, will be to hear of Harry's latest row with Salisbury, and the uproar at Horse Guards. It will be instructive for you both— and it will allow me to say what I really feel, instead of nodding politely at every Godforsaken dinner table in London…"

The field narrows yet again.
There is initial promise in a medical man, who flits between a fine town-house off Finsbury Square and the byways of Spitalfields, bag in hand. Dry watches the comings and goings of women who visit a ground-floor room behind the Brick Lane brewery. The reasons for the man's furtive passage become obvious. The doctor

removes the threat of new, unwanted life from women's bellies—for a price, no doubt. Nothing suggests that he conducts more extreme surgery in the Whitechapel alleys.

A lanky, square-jawed Jew prowls late past Christ Church, but only to meet a woman—married, Dry suspects—of his own religion beneath leafless trees. A student from Lincoln Inn stares at women as he skulks his way past—Dry follows him as well, but it seems that he is here in the East End to see his family, perhaps preferring that his classmates know nothing of his origins.

He pays little interest to public rumour. Jews, Poles, and Germans; actors, surgeons, and occultists. Any or none of these groups and individuals could display the behaviour he seeks. Edwin Dry is an educated man. A poor Jew in the East End is more likely to be knifed than to wield the blade.

For some, this work would be tedious; for him, these nights provide information which may be of use at some other time. He knows his city all the more because of them.

His routine shifts as he sees fit. Human behaviour interests him.

As long as they do not insist on talking.

She knew what the Deptford Assassin was doing. Whether her mind drifted on an omnibus, or she woke from night-sweats, it was the same. The bowler-hatted man was quartering the East End, observing, and his observations haunted her. She took strong drink late at night; it did not help. She immersed herself in sessions for the middle-classes, but even then she was not free.

In Vauxhall she was supposed to speak of a brother lost in war, and instead received images of huddled men, drinking in a Spitalfields tavern. She quit that sitting, with apologies, saying that malevolent spirits were on the Aether. Which they were.

One desperate evening she asked Mrs Bessovitch to stay with her in the parlour a while.

"I want to see if there is another mind there to be touched," she said. "The Whitechapel Murderer."

"Is big thing to do. And I am not psychic woman. What use am I?"

"To watch over me."

"Da. That I do, willingly. You want trumpet, maybe? Fancy board with letters?"

Catherine struggled to smile. She squeezed Mrs B's hand.

"Your company will be enough. I plan no tricks."

They sat with the gas-lights turned low, comfortable in loose clothing and the two over-stuffed parlour chairs. Mrs Bessovitch's knitting needles clicked and clacked, a reassuring rhythm.

Catherine sat back and closed her eyes. She had no set ritual, but sometimes there was a way to empty her own mind, to leave space for whatever might come.

At first she drifted through idle thoughts, from sad memories of Jennie to wondering if she had left a missing earring under her correspondence. Should she buy lamb cutlets again; had Josiah suffered for writing to her...

Gradually she pushed these aside, trying to look into those wicked London nights where a killer roamed.

She is fear and the weight of the ceiling and the hand raised the heavy hand which has a stick but it does not this night and no there are tears and she has tried and this is his doing that she thought was his wish but it does not work it does not work she is lies and she is fear...

Catherine gasped, shifted, but dared not open her eyes. What was the grey face above, the red snarl filled with white teeth? Conners. Mr Conners from Hampstead, his wrath engaged with Mrs Bless...

She is lies and she told him so but she did not know she could not know and the soldier the soldier who cried out who shouted and the audience which hissed and booed and she had done had done her best oh so very much to please...

She tore away from images she did not want to see, and from the idea that Mrs Bless might deserve sympathy. Why those images had come she had no idea. What Conners did, what Bless pretended—these were not her concerns. Only...in the process, she felt pity, because she could sense that Mrs Bless might have a genuine gift, a slight one, and had squandered it, seduced by Conners's grand schemes and tours.

Her search. That was what mattered.

There were minds and a maelstrom of thoughts out there... Fruitless.

It was half-expected. She had not sensed Jennie's death, after all, nor Martha Tabram's, nor those murders which followed after. She received only vague flashes of other lives, insights she could not use, and a muddle of unconnected images.

"I cannot sense him," she admitted at last. "It is as if he does not exist."

"Yet you see this other man." The needles clacked, and paused. "The man who wears the hat, who kills so neat."

"Edwin Dry, yes." She opened her eyes, breathed in the calm and quiet parlour. "Perhaps...is it possible that I cannot see both? That the presence of one masks the other?"

"Or is your own daemon, this Dry," said Mrs B. "So is not room for second daemon."

"I suppose that is possible." She felt dejected. "And there must be accidents, without any purpose. Minds meet and blur upon the Aether, and once in a hundred thousand times, they stay, bound and burdened. Unlooked for. My burden appears to be Mr Dry."

"Is Sud'ba, they say in St Petersburg. Fate."

"Are you really Russian, Mrs B?"

"Russian, Pole, Czech. I am many things." The landlady smiled. "I am Jew, most holy Orthodox, and so on. Even good Catholic once. I have travelled. It is best —on surface—to be whatever is useful, whatever does not bring more problem. Is why I understand there is Miss Weatherhead and Madame Rostov. Useful."

"Is why we are such friends," said Catherine, mimicking her landlady's accent.

But her brief humour soured in the depth of night. At this moment, to be rid of Dry and to "see" the Whitechapel Murderer would have brought her some satisfaction, however savage his deeds. Then she might have been of use.

⁓⁘⁓

A letter from Doctor Mercier, arriving unexpected, included a pamphlet on the work of Washington Bishop, an American mentalist.

> *Though I place no great faith in so-called psychic disciplines, you may find this of interest, considering our occasional discussions on the matter. Mr Bishop states that his performances are based not on spiritual insights, but on close reading of the psychology and physiology of his subjects.*

A touch of the truth, thought Catherine. After so long a period of observation, she was closer to being able to place her fellow "psychics" in firm categories, fit for cardboard folders in any records office.

There were the open, sometimes even brash, mentalists, who claimed no powers beyond concentration and practice in legerdemain—they mystified and entertained by trickery, but did not mislead. She had nothing against them.

Then came the frauds, who flew the false flags of spiritual learning and ab-natural insight to cover their mentalist tricks. Their nonsense was drawn from the betrayals of the sitters' words and faces, common sense and such other information as could be easily gathered beforehand. Their sin, if that was the term, was that they did not admit it.

Next, if there were to be a stated hierarchy, came the Rostovs of the world, where inexplicable gifts came and went, requiring either periods of admitted failure or the employment of techniques used by the fraudulent. She believed that there were others of her kind, walking that thin line.

And above them…the truly sensitive, perhaps. Those whose talents had no explanation, who might well be able to seek out and converse with spirits, even the disincarnate souls of the dead. She had heard gossip of, but never met, one of this tier. She imagined that at the very least, they might have what she possessed, but be able to tune and turn the gift at will.

It struck her that there must be others who had attempted to do what she had, to sense this new killer. Curious, she brought out a selection of the various spiritualist magazines she received, all of which lay under her bed, by the chamber pot. She had not read any of them for weeks.

It did not take long to identify the prevailing wind. Spiritualists were imploring the authorities to listen to their disparate and often contradictory voices. They clamoured at police stations, and wrote to the newspapers, and yet nothing they provided appeared to be of any use.

The *Medium and Daybreak* journal carried a typical report, from a séance held in early September at a house on Kentish Town Road.

> The medium, Mrs C. Spring, was controlled, and appeared in great pain all over her body, as if suffering from severe wounds in the body; also went through the action as if cutting her throat. One of the sitters (being impressed) asked the control if it was the spirit of Mrs Nicholls, the woman who had been murdered at Whitechapel a short time ago, and the spirit answered: "Yes."
>
> It seemed that Mrs Spring, genuine or not, had stayed on safe ground, as the medium continued, "The fiend! The fiend! I am not the only victim; there will be others yet. More, more, before long, and of a more brutal kind.

The police are asleep; in fact, it requires soldiers to keep watch. There is a gang of them. 'Tis a secret society.

The further Catherine read, the less faith she had in her profession.

By Upper Swandam Lane he kills a man, a Chinese standing watch by the Wheel of Fate, one of the opium dens near the wharves. Kelly's reports noted a client prone to lashing out, who rarely managed to perform. He was described as middle-class—a clerk or overseer in a cutlery firm—fair-haired, with a light beard and a temper, often to be seen in both Whitechapel and Limehouse.

The den's sentinel against police raids does not want to let Mr Dry into the Wheel of Fate, and presses the issue with a long, curved Eastern knife.

"You do not come to smoke," says the man. "I see your eyes."

Mr Dry is not a soldier or street brawler. Fighting is not his profession, and he avoids casual violence, but the Chinese man is insistent.

When it is over, Dry steps across the body and down crumbling steps which lead to an unmarked side-door.

The sentinel has died for nothing. It takes mere minutes to discover that the cutler's poor sexual performance is due to his persistent ingestion of opium, and that the man lacks the strength or co-ordination to be the Whitechapel Murderer.

Another name has gone from the list.

The last day of September 1888 was a Sunday. A few minutes after eleven in the morning, Mrs Bessovitch returned to the house with a newspaper. She placed the paper on the kitchen table next to Catherine's plate of toast, without comment. The headline said what was necessary.

Two more women had been murdered in Whitechapel.

CHAPTER TWENTY FIVE

Southwark, October 1888

They speak of "Jack the Ripper." There is a letter from the killer, signed thus but with no certain provenance. A ludicrous title, which may even be the creation of a minor journalist, eager to progress in his trade. Dry sighs and tuts. There is a stranger, a murderer in Whitechapel, yes, but such vainglorious names are for the credulous. A cheap affect, to give prominence to those who are commonplace. Any cat's meat man with a grudge could have done what has been done thus far.

More Jews are assaulted. They might as well mob Limehouse and find a random Chinaman or Lascar to adorn a lamp-post.

Dry pads the daytime streets, listening, sniffing the air. He is close to knowing this slaughterman who stirs the police, the newspapers and the mob so. As he surmised, there will be nothing about the killer that matters, excepting that he does what other weak men have only entertained in their cups. There will be deep-seated hatred for a mother, a wife, a girl who slighted him—and inadequacy.

This will not be a creature of his kind.

The authorities make no progress. Is Edwin Dry alone in understanding what might need to be done?

At times he wonders if he himself is the first journeyman or the last.

Catherine was allowed one shred of good news to set against her concerns. A letter came to say that Lady Seldon had spoken to a friend of her uncle, the friend being a Royal Navy captain who had retired due to injury. Unhappy that a fellow naval officer's family should be brought so low, he had an offer.

The old lodge house by his house in Kent was empty—tiny and in poor repair, admittedly, but serviceable.

Subject to his housekeeper meeting Clarissa and approving, he would be willing to relocate Clarissa and the children there. Duties would include linen repairs, mending of the servants' clothes and such similar, minor tasks as were needed.

Catherine went to see her cousin, knowing that this could not be done through a note. The meeting was not easy. The family's place on George Street was a slum, if a clean one. It was worse than Brantridge Street, and even though Catherine knew that larger families lived in worse conditions, it was hard to bear. She showed Clarissa the offer from Captain Meredith.

"You have done this?" asked Clarissa.

Catherine steadied herself for the lecture on charity and interference. It did not come. Her cousin sat down by her mending, and twisted her hands together.

"I have hated you, Catherine—for your father's wealth; for your youth, and for your kindnesses. With Jennie gone, no doubt to tread her own path, away from my complaints, the children's needs and this dire place..."

Catherine could neither bear to speak the truth concerning Jennie, nor conceive of any coherent lie.

"No doubt Jennie...had her reasons. Or a sudden opportunity, we might hope."

"No doubt. I do not blame her."

It seemed awkward and unnatural, but Catherine knelt at her cousin's side.

"See, Clarissa, take this opportunity—for Benjamin and Maisie, at least. Be free of this place, and let them breathe the Kent air, not the London smog. Charles would have wanted it."

A remark which would have brought bitter words once, but Clarissa nodded.

"You are right." She eyed Catherine with sudden worry. "This is... genuine, to be trusted?"

"It is. The woman who arranged it is a chance acquaintance,

above our station, much vexed by social conditions. She would not toy with me, I assure you."

She took an envelope out of her bag.

"Five pound notes are in there, Clarissa. If you will not take them, I shall find Benjamin and give them to him. Or if I must, to Maisie. Dates have been offered, and the money will see you to Captain Meredith's residence in good order."

"The housekeeper will not want me, sour and wheezing as I am."

Catherine stood up.

"Buy linctus, and sew a fixed smile to your lips."

Clarissa's cheeks were flushed. "I do not know what I should say to you—"

"Say nothing. Do what is needed." Catherine picked up her bag, pausing at the door. "I shall write to you, cousin—in Kent."

"And I shall reply," said Clarissa, seeming close to tears. "I shall reply."

⚓

Clarissa and the children would have a future. This change in their fortunes left Catherine with a sense of satisfaction. The nagging obligation she had felt to Charles's memory and to his family was discharged at last; better, she had frustrated her father in an issue of loyalty and responsibility to kin. She had stepped up where he would not. The act confirmed not her own selfless virtue, for she had no pretences to such, but Joshua Weatherhead's selfish vice. She took malicious pleasure from the thought, and was unashamed.

The news from Whitechapel had not improved, though.

Eden Mallick managed to get Catherine into the first day of the inquest on Catherine Eddowes. Rows of grave faces inside, an uneasy crowd without. They had stood at the back long enough to hear the City Solicitor, a Mr Crawford, questioning Frederick Brown, surgeon for the police. At least five minutes to make the wounds and cut out an organ, said Dr Brown. A kidney was missing. Death first, from a slashed throat, and then mutilation. She felt herself strangely detached from the reports; the violence of her visions was surely burrowing into her, becoming a part of what she knew.

Only later, as she and Mallick were heading back to the police station, did she lean against some railings and try to keep her breakfast down. It was not horror of the deeds described that turned her stomach, but the fact that the people who thronged the street immediately outside the inquest had shown such eagerness for gore. She saw no sign of care for the dead woman, only an almost savage curiosity as to the bloody details of the case.

More distressing was a shadow from the past that returned a few days later, a shadow which came in the form of a badly-written piece of correspondence from the old woman she had met at Christ Church, Mrs Hollis. Catherine had forgotten that the woman had something to ask of her.

The letter was a jumble of mismatched words which took time to decipher, but in the end held only one central question.

Mrs Hollis wished to know if Catherine Weatherhead had been the one who hired the killer at the Victualling Yard, the man who murdered Frederick Caille. If she were, wrote Hollis, then God bless her and keep her, for she had done a fine thing.

The question alone was a shock; that Hollis then explained that she was asking on behalf of a woman named Ginger made matters no better. How had that idea ever entered their heads? Catherine recoiled at the thought that another woman, a stranger, might know something of her involvement in that affair.

She wanted to tear up the letter and forget it, but a half-formed recollection troubled her. The woman Catherine had encountered with Jennie on Brantridge Street, the prostitute, had been introduced as Ginger.

Worse, Hollis wrote that her acquaintance enquired because she had fallen in with a certain man, a most unusual one, who was asking questions in Whitechapel. Ginger believed that this man was the Deptford Assassin. There was a description as well, enough to make Catherine sure that it was Edwin Dry.

Was it not enough that he was in her visions? Now he trailed blood through her correspondence.

Catherine lay on her bed that evening, reading and re-reading the letter. There was something she could not quite catch, a truth which eluded her until she woke from sleep with a start, around four in the morning. The room was cold, as cold as her tight belly.

No coincidence, no idle chance.

The Deptford Victualling Yard is sizeable, and has many shadows. He blends, dances in darkness, noting small details as he leaves. On Windmill Lane he sights a female figure clutching her shawl as she hastens to be elsewhere. She would be the one assigned to distract the night rounders...

First at Deptford, and then in Stepney...

The woman before him—Mary Jane Kelly—picks at her lace sleeves and tries not to meet his gaze. She has already been more useful than most, and he remembers her from Deptford, though she never saw him that night.

That face from outside Jennie's home, and the one in the vision—they blended so easily into each other now she had the link.

'Ginger' and Kelly were the same person.

And for two years Mary Jane Kelly and Catherine Weatherhead had circled the slender blade of Edwin Dry, knowing nothing of each other...

She plucked at her pillow, held it tight to her as if she were a child again.

All was connected, from her vision of Dry as he murdered a man in Islington, to the height of the Deptford Assassin's hunt through the squalor of Whitechapel; from the moment she first stepped into the house in Brantridge Street, perhaps, and became entangled in an affair of vengeance which should have been long forgotten.

She was a pawn in a great mechanism she could never hope to understand.

Later that morning she sat with Mrs Bessovitch and let her landlady read the letter from Mrs Hollis.

"It is too much," said Catherine. "What should I do? Should I write back—deny any knowledge of this?"

Mrs B brewed coffee, fortified with a spirit whose taste Catherine did not recognise—a fruit brandy of some type.

"Is hard," said Mrs Bessovitch eventually. "Here is old lady who hurts, and other woman who is not in good place. Somewhere is your bowler-hatted man, always watching."

"I know that." Catherine felt peevish. "Should I admit—in writing—what I have done? Is that not a dreadful risk?"

The landlady squinted at her. "Maybe I write with your words, and you do not put name. Then hand is different, and no one can prove it is you who says this or that."

It was a bearable compromise. She would go to Christ Church that week or next, speak as briefly as possible to Mrs Hollis and, if satisfied, hand over a reply which she had neither penned nor signed.

What "Ginger" made of it would be out of her hands.

The cab-man's hut by Borough High Street again—mugs of scalding tea, too much sugar and the milk on the turn. The occasional odd look from a hansom driver as the tall Russian woman spoke earnestly to the police inspector.

"Will you do it?" asked Catherine, for the third time.

Eden Mallick twitched and frowned, his face a map of indecision.

"He's mobbed, you know? Scrawny women holding up drawings of the Whitechapel Murderer, wives demanding their husbands be taken into custody. Bully boys who have nabbed a Jewish costermonger who once gave them the wrong change for a bag of oranges; letter after letter of useless information. Never seems to end."

For she had asked if he would assist her in seeing Chief Inspector Donald Swanson.

"It is a matter of great importance," she pressed.

"Not seen the murderer in one of your rum sessions, have you?" Mallick spat out a lump of milk, apologised. "Like half the table-knockers in London—and a few beyond."

"No. I have nothing to offer on the nature of the killer. But I do have something which may be of use to your friend."

"If you could tell me at least a little of what you intend..."

But she could not. She had seen Mrs Hollis, and satisfied herself that it was safe to leave the letter for Ginger with her. She had stayed through most of two sittings of the Eddowes inquest, and she had grown uneasy listening to the exchanges of men—some worried, some complacent.

As she heard yet another officer of the law admit that the investigation had made no progress, she became angry. She was not constrained by the thick, leather-bound books of medical and legal nonsense at the coroner's side, or by the tight collars of clerks, solicitors and officers of the law.

If Catherine Weatherhead was to be caught up in this dark game, whatever she chose, she would not be a pawn, she would be a queen. She would try, at least, to take a hand in what was to come, instead of waiting to be assailed by visions and hear of yet more terrible things beyond her ability to change.

A queen could order that dark things must be done, for the good of others.

"I beg that you trust me," she said to the inspector.

Mallick hummed and hawed, twitched, and gave in.

"I'll speak to him, if he has time."

"Thank you. I...I would appreciate it if you do not mention the matter to anyone else."

The inspector gave a sharp laugh. "Who would I tell, Madame? Hard enough that I must work with you, on rare occasion; harder if the lads at the station did say that I was all for tambourines and floating faces. Spirits should only come from bottles."

"It might be easier for us if that were so."

Mallick looked upon her thoughtfully, his eyelid stilled for once.

By Smithfield market, faced with Dry in the flesh, she had been consumed by fear and doubt. She had seen no option but to have her presence misunderstood, to commission him for murder before he grew wary of her, and left her bleeding in those alleys. In one sense, Frederick Caille died because at the height of her meeting with the assassin, Catherine Weatherhead wished to live.

Dry was the key. He was surely more lethal than any Whitechapel Murderer, meticulous, and, to the best of her knowledge, unstoppable. Not a vicious amateur with a hatred of street women, but one who was perhaps a master of his terrible trade.

A man who understood what was happening in Whitechapel; a man who might interest Chief Inspector Swanson greatly...

The summons to Scotland Yard came, at last.

At precisely eleven o'clock on Wednesday the seventeenth of October, Madame Rostov was ushered into an office inside the maze of the Central Police buildings. She walked from stark corridors into a room which was a monument to the investigation. Great maps of the east side of London were pinned to the walls, along with newspaper cuttings and handbills. Shelves bent under the weight of gazetteers and ledgers, propped against cardboard evidence boxes, and by the windows stood a large oak desk on which lay a single piece of blank paper.

Donald Swanson, the man behind the desk, rose to his feet. He had a long, heavy face with a prominent nose and a thick, drooping moustache. The eyes were sad, pre-occupied.

"Madame Rostov." He gestured that her uniformed guide could leave, and the door was closed on them. "I'll see ye for Eden Mallick's sake—the laddie and I go well back. We've shared a case or twa. But yuir pardon, Madame, I have nae time for fancy theories and spirit talk. A dozen letters from women claiming the Sight this day already, ay, all saying they know our Whitechapel man—"

"Deptford Victualling Yard," said Catherine, standing before the desk. "November 1886. A fire deliberately set in the rail sidings nearby, and four men dead."

He stroked his moustache.

"Sit ye down," he said, and took his own place as she did.

"A single man killed Mr Frederick Caille and his thugs. A single man who left no trace. Scotland Yard has no more idea now of that man's identity than they did almost two years ago."

"Ay, many have said the same. What do ye bring to me that's so new?" He squinted at her. "Is it yuir thought that the Deptford Assassin is this so-called 'Jack'?"

"Quite the opposite, Chief Inspector. My belief is that the Deptford Assassin may be your only chance of halting the Whitechapel Murderer."

"He has something useful tae me, this mystery man?"

"Yes."

They stared at each other.

"Ye're no a Russian," he said.

"You're not an Englishman. Does it matter? I can ask you, sir—do you seek an end to what is happening in the East End?"

He eased his large frame back onto the chair. "Frederick Caille is long gone, and scarcely mourned. Does this fellow of yuirs—if he exists—ken the name of the Whitechapel killer, and where he abides, for example?"

Catherine took a deep breath, clutched her bag across her lap.

"No. But he will, soon."

"Yuir spirits tell ye this?"

She stared. "Ask Eden Mallick again if I'm given to wild and vague statements. The Deptford Assassin is…I find it hard to explain. He is Death, when he wants to be. When he is paid to be, and he likes the coin."

Swanson tilted his head, his eyes narrowing. She was surprised, despite her bravado, that he had let her get this far.

"What is the blank piece of paper that you have on your desk, Mr Swanson?"

He looked puzzled.

"Not that it's yuir business, but it is from Sir Charles Warren. I am tae write tae him upon it when the Whitechapel Murderer is taken. A reminder of my duty."

"The man of whom I speak knows the streets as well as this 'Jack', and I do not believe he has ever failed to see a commission through."

He spread his fingers out on the desk top, almost touching the sheet of paper, and drew them together again.

"I have yuir general drift. Ye would set a hound on a hound, that's what ye're saying. But I dinna ken why ye're here before me with the tale, what Madame Rostov has to do wi' it. Last I heard, ye'd found a missing lassie in Southwark. Quite a step tae this."

It was. An insane, ludicrous step. But if it were taken, if the bowler-hatted man were all he seemed, then there would be no more women like Jennie killed, at least at the hands of the man sought by the police.

"Nor do I ken what you're bringing me that changes anything. I could offer bounty, as they say, but there are rewards on the air already. I'll wait, shall I, until yuir man decides if he's interested? Tell Inspectors Abberline, Reid and the rest tae wait a while?"

She was losing Swanson. She could see it. He was beginning to place her amongst the wild schemers and dreamers with just another fancy plan, people wanting to show that the authorities lacked skill and imagination. And the Deptford affair had been described again and again in newspapers and journals. Anyone could know if it.

She could walk away...

"You cannot wait." she said. "There are...rules. He needs his commission, and his coin. He needs to be asked."

A cough, a laugh, troubled Swanson for a moment.

"And ye'll be the one tae ask him?"

"I have done it before."

A definite laugh this time, deep in the policeman's throat.

"Lassie, I think we're done—"

"Deptford. Police Constable Retton was shot in the middle of the chest, with a bullet from Frederick Caille's gun. He fell next to Caille's desk. There was little blood there, because Retton was already dead. A long slender dagger had been thrust up under his jaw and into his brain."

Swanson bulked forward, his elbows on the desk.

"We didnae—"

"A single strike, and I saw it done. You did not publish all the details. If you wish, I can describe each move that was taken, each angle of thrust and fire. I can tell you which of the men in the outer office died first. These things are burned into my sight."

"How is that so?"

"It is so because whilst I work as Madame Rostov, I am also Catherine Weatherhead. I am the one who paid a man, a terrible man, to remove Caille from this earth, for what he had done to my family, for what he did to all those he touched. You will never prove it, Chief Inspector, because the man I hired does not make mistakes. He does not leave evidence. He has no personal interest in, or connection to, any that he has killed."

It was more than she had meant to say. It was more than she should have said.

His eyes widened in recognition.

"I did see ye afore, yes! I knew it. In Stepney, by God, where the Weatherheads lived, ay, when we sought motive for Deptford. You came to the door. I kenned there was something about yuir face when I met ye with Mallick, but could not settle on it."

"I told you. I am Catherine Weatherhead. I had good reason, very good reason, to do what I did, and you yourself know that is true. Not that anything said in this office could convict me—words from a hysterical young woman, the courts would say."

"I dinna..." He trailed away, his gaze drawn to the blank sheet on his desk. Catherine took her chance.

"I can help you lift your pen, Mr Swanson, and write upon that paper there. I can set the Deptford Assassin upon the Whitechapel Murderer."

An hour passed, with many turned away from Swanson's office. The two of them argued, and she managed to return as good as the Scotsman gave. She came close to being taken in charge, and close to being ejected from Scotland Yard as a hysteric who wasted police time. But he could not shake her—and he could not let go of what she brought to him.

Ye would set a hound on a hound.

Oh, she would, if she could manage it. Dry was almost there—a specific request and a decent purse would surely net him.

And he would net the killer of women.

She left Whitehall with more threats than promises behind her. But not only threats. Swanson and his colleagues were under intense pressure since the deaths of Catherine Eddowes and Elizabeth Stride. He could not hide the fact. He did not consider it impossible that he might petition for a 'fighting fund', to be used as it must be, without the usual accounting.

Most unsettling for her, most unsettling of everything which happened in his office that morning, Swanson mistrusted Madame Rostov—but was close to believing Catherine Weatherhead.

Four descriptions left, four men who appear to have the qualities and habits he seeks. A changeable way with women, from callousness to wheedling compliance; moments of brutal action or obvious intent; long hours spent in the East End where they cannot be located, and glimpses of a knife close to hand. The killer will likely cover inadequacy with arrogance. Other matters of physique and manner will be evident.

One of these men will fit the bill.

Mary Jane Kelly has done her work with commendable efficiency. So many incidents of violence, gathered from the women of the streets—incidents from the petty to the almost murderous. Almost. Someone has stepped across that thinnest of lines, and has not stepped back.

Dry will soon understand.

And there is the Gorse woman. He has agreed to remove her, to settle his informant's fears. Business is business, however small the coin. The woman who must die has no apparent value; had it mattered to him, he would have described Gabriella Gorse as an unpleasant individual. But then, so are a number of his clients. Morality is rarely relevant when craft is required.

The journeyman who works only for the virtuous has few customers.

CHAPTER TWENTY SIX

Clerkenwell, October 1888

By chance, Dry sees one of his informant's enemies die—an unimportant, red-headed thug by the name of Brevard, who had been following her. Kelly had clearly hoped that the Deptford Assassin might step in to rid her of the man. He might have; he might not. It would have depended on how useful she was— otherwise, it was her own affair.

In the end, there is no need for blade, gun or garotte. The day is overcast, and Brevard steps out into the road too quickly, without looking. He is taken by the hooves and wheels of a hansom cab; those or the cobbles beneath make swift work of him. The man's eye had been on Kelly crossing the street, and for that he died.

Appropriate, perhaps.

Dry is watching over his interests, as always. He slips between the gawking and trilling pedestrians. He murmurs the single word "Doctor," and makes a quick examination of the body. The head is crushed. As the cab driver protests his innocence, two drunks try to unhitch the horse, and further arguments ensue, drawing in the onlookers. In the moment afforded by this, Dry retrieves a wallet and a sheaf of small posters. They appear to be a duplicated drawing of Kelly, a sketched portrait that Brevard must have distributed as he tried to track her down. It is a reasonable, though not perfect likeness. "Andriette" is the name below the picture—one name amongst the several that his informant has used.

He pockets one of these, already seeing a use for it, and he is gone, before any can question his actions or his true profession. This incident has done no harm.

No harm at all.

October tore at Catherine, pushed her from one imposture to another. Revealed to Swanson by her own hand, she feared the consequences. She spent as little time as possible at the Southwark police station, wondering if Swanson would tell what he knew to Eden Mallick. And there had been snide comments from some of the officers at the station. If she were so good a psychic, why had she not yet identified the Whitechapel Murderer? They too had seen the newspaper reports of everyone and their spirit guide coming forward with wild theories.

Superintendent Neylan was less perturbed.

"The Lord will guide us, Madame Rostov," he said. "Only He can provide us with the Instrument we need."

The Instrument we need. Much the sentiment she had used with Chief Inspector Swanson, although she doubted that the bowler-hatted man came from the Lord.

As Catherine Weatherhead she brooded, steeling herself for what she must attempt; as Madame Rostov, she kept such appointments as would meet her living costs, nothing more. Her sittings were turbulent, broken in on by impressions of the East End, meaningless flares of dirt-floored rooms and filthy alleys, unexplained passage through rookeries, as if Dry were shedding images as he went, and only she were there to pick them up.

The nights were worse, for she was more open and vulnerable in sleep. Her fortune was that most of these fever-dreams were forgotten on awakening—most, but not all...

One man speaks to another, a joke which does not please. This is hardly a public house, more a ground-floor room with the back wall knocked through, a couple of casks raised on a broken table. The drink is cheap, taken illicitly from a brewer's dray between deliveries.

The men separate in ill temper, and Dry follows the one who did not laugh. A circuit of Flower and Dean Street, Thrawl Street and Angel Alley, then up towards Christ Church, and east.

His quarry has the look, the way of moving. It may be him. Eyes hooded, noticing each woman on the streets, a minute pause when a prostitute stands alone beneath a gas-lamp. Tall enough, strong enough. It would fit those copies of the autopsy reports which were so easy bought. Such a frame could have managed the tasks easily. Long, flexible fingers. The stranger has clothes that any man might wear at night around here, too anonymous to place his profession, neither so fine as to catch attention nor rags to elicit pity.

The description also fits well with that of an unknown client who could not stiffen his wand or spill his seed during two separate encounters with Kelly's prostitutes, back in June. Both women had been kicked in crotch and belly afterwards, though not fatally.

Most telling of all, Dry loses him. Somewhere in the maze by the Hanbury Street baths, his man is gone. Not because the stranger knew he was being observed—no one has yet seen Edwin Dry if he was truly not willing to be seen—but because it is a habit, a way of being. This man, this beast, slinks quiet and cunning by nature. He does not want his passing to be noted, even if there is no one to note it.

It is sufficient. Now Dry has a true feel of the man.

A note for Madame Rostov waited at the Holborn post office, unsigned:

Anderson has returned, but he has nothing. The hound from Deptford may be needed. By any means necessary, one far above me says, such is the pressure upon us. There are funds.

Chief Inspector Swanson had come to a decision, then. More, he had written to Madame Rostov. He had not named Catherine, which implied he might keep her deception between them.

It was to happen. Should she have the ability to find Dry, the courage to face him…and should he be able to isolate the Whitechapel Murderer. Her nights, her unwished-for moments in other places—these suggested that he was close to doing so.

He knew nothing of her mind, of that she remained sure, but she knew something of his. She also knew that he had places of business, not often used but always available.

~✢~

At six o'clock on a Tuesday morning she was settled in an alcove off the main room of the Crown and Sceptre, not far from Smithfield Market. A repetition of the time when she had, almost by accident, commissioned the murder of Frederick Caille.

She read the papers, and sipped at a chipped mug full of tea—the latter provided unwillingly by the landlord. She drew attention, a respectable-looking woman alone in a working men's haven, and she drew visitors. Each visitor to her table, from the awkward young apprentice butchers to the lurching porters with a glint in their eyes, received the same response. She would lift up an unread newspaper, and expose the barrel of a small revolver which lay beneath. A loan from Mrs B.

"Is from Belgium," her landlady said. "Has six shots, only three bullets."

"I hope to use none of them," Catherine reassured her.

The sight of the pocket revolver, and her hard stare, kept her from molestation. It also protected the fifty pounds that Swanson had sent her, a token of his seriousness.

When the patrons accepted that she had no intention of being chaperoned or providing them with entertainment, her presence brought talk, most of it on the edge of her hearing, and that was satisfactory. Necessary, in fact, for her purposes. Two hours later she folded up her newspapers, slipped the gun into her purse and departed.

She did the same the next day, with no result except braver chatter around her, gossip as to who she might be.

On the third morning, he was there when she arrived, his bowler hat placed in the very centre of the small table. This time he had round, tinted glasses and a short moustache. His suit was dark blue, with a narrow navy stripe in the trousers, and his boots gleamed.

"You wanted to speak to me," said Edwin Dry, and he rose slightly from his seat.

She sat down opposite him.

He was silent, motionless; she tapped her fingers nervously against her leg, an echo of Evelyn Caille. Catherine tried to look at him properly, struck by the lack of anything extraordinary, threatening or even interesting about his appearance. A bank teller, an accountant's clerk, secretary to a solicitor. A man of no importance in the greater schemes of those who thought they mattered. He smelled of...nothing. No cologne, no hair oil or other preparation.

She began to understand why he slipped so easily unnoticed, un-witnessed, across the capital. He was no one's concept of anything except a modest, quiet middle-aged man. Nor was he even middle-aged. Under thirty, she would have said now she was paying attention, but easily passing for almost fifty if he wanted.

"The moustache was not there before." It was an inane thing to say.

"It did not exist yesterday; it may not exist tomorrow. You require something of me."

She started to turn her head, to look around the tavern and he flicked one finger against the beaten copper of the table top. She stopped at the sound of his fingernail against the metal.

"The cautious, sidelong glance," he said. "The habit of those who feel vulnerable, feel they might be observed. It is one of the ways that others realise you *are* vulnerable."

"Yes, I...I suppose so."

"Preparation is key. I have already looked, already seen. The others in here are noted, filed for reference. None will interfere." He examined the finger he had flicked against the table, seemed to find it to his satisfaction.

"If you do not require my services again, then you have information for me. There is a matter which presses, that you feel you must bring to my attention."

"No, I have…I do have another commission." She had to haul that out, to make her lips form the words. That she could say "another" seemed ridiculous at that moment, however determined she had been when she planned this.

Pale eyes regarded her. Irises that were a watery, washed-out blue, with wide pupils. Wide black pupils, like the eye-sockets of the dead. Beneath those smoothly shaven cheeks were bones, hard white bones. He wears a skull, she thought. And he lets me see it.

"I am somewhat engaged at this moment. You have encountered another Frederick Caille?" The enquiry seemed perfunctory, without great interest. "I may be available, later in the year."

She felt over-heated; she perspired, and her hands were helpless things, fluttering from her wrists, unsure what to do with themselves. She must be more Madame Rostov, less Catherine. She had managed it with Swanson. Everything that came to mind was away from the point.

"Do many…do many clients come back to you, a second time?"

"No."

"Why not?"

"Because seeing me reminds them of what they have done, and their own vulnerability." The left corner of his mouth lifted, almost unnoticeable. "I am not owned, indentured or beholden to anyone. Thus anyone may purchase my services. This makes them uncomfortable. As it should."

"I do not fear you." Which was almost true, to her surprise. She feared the situation, the madness of what she had conceived, and she feared failure in her endeavours. What she felt about Dry himself she could not grasp.

"That is why I am still here. You interest me. To a point."

To a point. Her belly strained against her undergarments; her collar was choking her, and her throat was so dry. In the background, men laughed and sank their pints of dark ale, jostled and argued. Lived.

Say it. Say it. Strike to the heart of it.

"There is a murderer, in Whitechapel," she said, nearly a gasp. "You must know this. He has slaughtered four women at least."

"You assume that it is a man behind the recent killings."

"I..." Catherine laced her fingers before her. It was no assumption—it was taken from her visions, a matter she must not let slip. "Yes. I mean, surely—"

"Women should not be underestimated in these times."

Was this his humour, at her expense?

"But it is a man?"

"It is," agreed Dry. "A flawed one, but persistent. Weak, as far as temperament goes. He will continue, in a fruitless attempt to avoid his own failures."

"You know this already?"

"I do. He will not stop, because he can not."

"Unless the Deptford Assassin tracks him down and kills him."

His pupils widened slightly, a black stare that pinned her, examined her. As with their previous meeting in Clerkenwell, he was silent for some time, and then she saw that single, studied blink of his eyelids.

"That is your commission?"

"It is." There, she had said it. "I have access to funds from... certain authorities. I should say no more than that. If you need some proof, I may be able to bring clearer details of—"

"That will not be necessary."

"But do you not wish—"

"I take my clients at their word. If their word turns out to be false, then I remind them of their mistake."

You kill them. She wet her lips. "I would not deceive you. But I must know, can you stop him? The police would have him taken, and face justice."

"The police would have many things, but will receive few of them. I can put an end to him. That is my trade. You should know that better than most, after Deptford."

She had expected that response, even though she knew that Swanson would prefer the Whitechapel Murderer alive, in chains.

"You are sure that you can do this?" A remark she regretted immediately, for fear he would take offence.

He did not seem bothered. He took off his glasses and wiped the lenses with a small white linen handkerchief. "You speak of the constabulary—the source of your funds, I imagine. They are well-advised to have used you so. It caught my attention. And no doubt you have some personal stake in the matter."

"I want him dead."

She had not expected to speak with such vehemence. Yes, she wanted it, and for so many reasons that she could not sort them for herself. Sense did not apply. Because her brother Josiah would be waking now, and wondering at the cramps in his fingers from last night's book-keeping. Because Uncle Jack had taken so long to die of the rot within him. Because she had never been to Jennie's common grave...

Because Mrs Bessovitch was out of cocoa, and Catherine had forgotten to fetch more.

She drew a leather purse from her bag and placed in on the table.

"An advance for your efforts, a token, but better than a single sovereign this time"

He pocketed the purse with an economy of movement, slipping it inside his jacket.

"There will be one more death," he said. "Someone who is inconvenient, who is no loss."

And there is the Gorse woman. He has agreed to remove her, to settle his informant's fears. Business is business, however small the coin.

She remembered that, from her dreams. Something to do with the prostitute called Mary Jane Kelly. Again, Catherine was not supposed to know of such things.

"Surely that can be avoided?"

"No. She will die, whatever you say next. This way she will

die and might be of use. An end to 'Jack,' and all well again in London Town." He turned the hat before him, first to the left, then to the right, until it was exactly where it been. "Tell me, I am interested. We sit here in polite discourse, early on a fine—if brisk—morning. You are a young woman who tells her clients she can converse with the dead. I, on the other hand, tell my clients the truth."

"I do not understand your point."

"But you do. You wrestle and agonise over morality, ethics. I imagine that you have deceived parents, friends, acquaintances. You have done what was necessary. I make no judgement, but it is clear that you do. You judge me, and you judge yourself. Are such exercises a good use of your time?"

"You kill people!" she protested.

"Everyone does." He smiled, and took up his hat. "Good day, Miss Weatherhead. I have work to do."

She did not look up to watch him leave the tavern.

She merely sat, and wondered what she had done. *Good day, Miss Weatherhead.* She realised he had told her, without any particular emphasis, that he was aware of both of her identities.

He knew all that she was.

"Your tea," said the landlord, setting the mug down on the table and spilling some of it. He eyed the open door, then Catherine, almost crouched in her corner. "The gentleman paid. Yesterday."

CHAPTER TWENTY SEVEN

Southwark, November 1888

Dry has been commissioned, which means there is no longer need to ponder or make judgements on what he should do concerning the Whitechapel Murderer.

The decision has been made.

He watches, hat pulled low, overcoat tightly buttoned to the neck. High on the roof of an abandoned tenement, inches from a chimney stack of prodigious height and dubious integrity, the soles of his boots flat and firm against the few reliable tiles. Good boots make all the difference in his line of work. Double-stitching and supple leather; support for the ankle and enough iron in the toecap to disable with one kick. Laces which, if needs be, can be threaded free and twisted around a vulnerable throat.

Of late, he makes his own footwear.

Perched there, four stories above the streets, the sad world of human endeavour is spread out before him. He has often marked how rarely people look upwards.

A sly rain falls on Spitalfields, finding its way under every door, through every crack in every window. People talk of weather as a gift or curse, which should dictate their habits and their moods; they are close to obsessed with how it drives them.

To him it is merely one factor amidst a hundred others.

He faces an interesting challenge. The man is quick and handy with the knife, a beast as cunning as the rain—and fast. He has the measure of the area, and is watchful for interference—no one has yet been able to say they have seen him at his bloody work. Near every description Dry has seen contains a fragment of the man's appearance, but none are correct.

Are you sure you can do this?

That is what she said, the woman with ice grey eyes, her hair disordered, her jaw jutting out to hide her own doubts.

How would he be Edwin Dry if he was not sure?

As with Deptford, this will be a demonstration piece, the work of a journeyman who advances in his trade. Once again this curious woman, Catherine Weatherhead, brings him something of interest, something which offers to extend his abilities.

And there is the issue of his informant—Kelly—who wants her rival dead. Some matter of street gangs and prostitution which scarcely interests him, but she has been useful. The police and Weatherhead require this "Jack" removed; Kelly requires Gabriella Gorse removed. He sees no need to separate the two commissions.

He will conceive a single plan.

An elegant plan.

Eden Mallick was shot on a wet Thursday evening, not far from the Compass Rose. Around the same time that East End dockers broke into the house of a Polish family in Stepney and said they would haul the husband away as Jack the Ripper. The man had "looked queer" as he passed down Flower and Dean Street, on his way back from work as a cobbler. Cobblers used knives, said the dockers.

In Stepney, two constables managed to restore order. Called out to the uproar, one Inspector Reid of H Division swiftly concluded that the Pole had no part in the Whitechapel murders, and lost his temper with the crowd. On the arrival of more constables, five men were arrested for affray and disorder.

In Southwark, no one witnessed Inspector Mallick fall. He dragged himself to the door of the Compass Rose, and a doctor was called. The inspector would live, but there were doubts if he would regain the use of his left arm. The bullet had shattered the shoulder.

Superintendent Neylan had the entirety of the Compass Rose Bravos gang arrested. None would admit to having fired the shot. More distraught than she had expected at the news, Catherine visited Mallick in the infirmary the next day. He was conscious, his twelve year-old daughter out of school, presumably, to sit at his side. The girl had the same mournful look as her father habitually wore, but she had justification at the moment,

"This is Madame Rostov, Sally." He patted his daughter's knee with his free hand. The surgeon had told Catherine that they could not yet decide if amputation of the damaged arm would be required. When they were sure that he had escaped serious infection, more fragments of bone might have to be removed to see the state of the shoulder joint.

Unsure, the girl bowed. "Madame."

"You have heard me speak of her, Sal. She is the lady who sees things."

His face seemed more drawn than ever, his cheekbones prominent and his brow discoloured, pale. The surgeons said the policeman was in considerable pain. He was receiving morphine, but the doctors here were of a modern mind. They did not want to induce addiction to the drug, and were sparing in its use.

His eyelid had stopped twitching.

"We will find them, Mallick," said Catherine.

"We?" He managed a hoarse chuckle. "Have they given you rank now?"

She tried to smile.

"Sal," he said, "Fetch Papa a fresh jug of water, there's a girl."

When his daughter left, Mallick gestured Catherine closer.

"What did you say to Donald Swanson?"

She frowned. "Don't concern yourself, Inspector. You need to rest, recover."

Mallick's feverish gaze searched the small side-room, came back to her.

"He contacted me…Swanson. Said he might be about to make a grievous error, and was…was troubled in himself. Whitechapel. What did I think of you, he asked, and pressed me."

"What did you say?"

"That I had questions about the nature of your abilities, and much besides. That you are a strong-minded woman who could easily cause problems, and your solutions might not be much better."

"I—"

"And I told Donald that your word is as good as mine, if it's trust that worries him. He should listen to you. If you have gone this far and dared the heart of Scotland Yard, there will be sense there somewhere." He managed to smile. "I'm not deep, Madame, nor one for God and religion such as Mr Neylan is. But there are fellow officers who've not called on me, nor on the wife, yet here you are, and not that much of a surprise to me that you came. That says something, also."

"Get better," said Catherine. Mallick's daughter was in the doorway with a jug of water, watching them. "Try to keep both arms, and get better, Inspector. Good day to you, Miss Sally."

She swept out before anything else could pass between the three of them, before a tear came to her eye, and she had to work out what it meant.

Dry came to her that night, when she was sat alone in the front room of her lodgings, half-awake over a book on the travel of spirits through the Aether. She had warning this time, a pulse at her temples, but now she could only bear it and hope...

He approaches the Whitechapel Murderer in a nondescript tavern off Brick Lane. Stands next to him, breathes in the faint camphor of the jacket, the polish recently applied, shoddily, on the boots. And he speaks to him, soft-voiced.

"There is one who knows what you are. What burdens you."

The other man does not turn his head. "Are you some canting preacher, about to tell me of where my soul is bound?"

"Hardly. I bear a message which you should hear. Do you know of the Deptford Assassin?"

This time the neck—muscle and sinew—twists. The man's eyes are dull, a muddied brown. Dry knows what they see. They see an unimportant figure of barely middling height; round glasses of the type cheaply had from any maker of spectacles or travelling man. A Derby hat and a clean collar. A nonentity.

"Yes. I know the name," says the other. "A fine fellow, I hear. Happy to carve, but always gone by meal's end."

Dry can tell by the man's tone that, as intended, he has been dismissed as posing no immediate danger.

"He is interested in the way you take your birds, and slice them for the plate," Dry says.

"I would not—"

"He knows who you are—do not play. Do you think he has not marked your progress?"

The brown eyes swivel, looking to every exit from the drinking den, measuring distance and the nature of the other patrons. He may yet run, thinks Dry. Will he take such directness as a compliment? Another touch must be added.

"He knows of some pretty ducks for you, if you have a hunger."

The man hesitates. "Meet me behind this place, in five minutes."

The alley is little more than a trail of mud between pitted brick walls. Night-soil and a large dead rat are its only decoration. Dry allows the sudden punch to his abdomen, and the thick-haired arm which pins him to the wall. They would have been easy to evade.

"What is this talk, then?" says the man. "Talk of business that does not concern others."

"It concerns him. You may have talent."

"Threatened, is he?" The forearm lies hard across Dry's chest.

"Interested, I said. Else why would I have been sent here?"

The pressure eases. "An errand boy. Well, speak on."

"He has been watching for some time, the one of whom I speak. Did you think to work his fields and not be noticed?"

The man's lips curls, relaxes. He appears unsure of what response he should make.

"Your master wants something of me, does he?" Truculent,

guarded. "A piece of those I cut, maybe? These sluts can spare a kidney or two. Get to your point."

"Not now. The Deptford Assassin will not be rushed—he had to be sure he had the right man. I will be here Wednesday, in this very place, by ten."

The other man smiles.

"So might I be, errand boy. So might I."

Catherine awoke, cramped in the armchair, but could not trust herself to move. The book had fallen to the floor; her heart was pounding. She had seen the face of the Whitechapel Murderer. Seen it, and pushed it away, out of her thoughts. She would forget that sight. There was nothing that she, the police or the vigilante mobs could do, now that Edwin Dry was in play.

Nothing that he could not do better than any and all of them.

At the police station the next day she saw the Compass Rose Bravos in their cells, but she had little to offer. Some of the young men were bloody-cheeked and bruised, as was one of the girls also swept up by the local force. Either they had not come easy, or the constables had vented their displeasure as they pushed the youths into police wagons.

"It will get worse," she said to one of the oldest boys as he pressed forward to the cell bars and tried to complain to her. "You have given a grievous wound to a good man."

"The Lord knows that they have grown up in a rough nest, with few kindnesses," said Mr Neylan, pacing behind her. He was more agitated than usual. She suspected that Christian charity and the near-murder of one of his inspectors were at war within him. Her own charity was close to breaking point.

"Then let them go back to shooting their own." She could sense nothing from the sullen crowd incarcerated before her. These days her gift brought her little more than Whitechapel.

"Madame!" Neylan spoke in awkward reproach. "We must

trust in His Justice prevailing."

"Yes, Superintendent." Said hollow, and signalling her retreat. Alienating Neylan would serve no purpose.

"Is the inspector mending, Madame Rostov?" asked the elderly desk sergeant, a man who had once sniffed at her presence at the station.

"We must hope so, Cubbins. The surgeons are positive as to his life, and possibly his arm."

Assuming they did not lose him if they had to operate.

Alone on Borough High Street, uncertain where to go next, this was her small hell. She could not help Eden Mallick, nor conjure any sudden evidence to identify his assailant. And for the second time in two years she had sat with Edwin Dry and set death in motion—that was out of her hands, as it had been with Deptford.

Back at her lodgings, she cursed instead of weeping. Mrs Bessovitch baked and watched her, saying little at first. She had heard the tale of Inspector Mallick.

"I will ask." The landlady eased a large meat pie from the oven, and set the golden pastry, pooled in its own gravy, down by the sink.

"Ask?"

"Henrik Kaars, he knows men who know men. And women who know women. He is fence, moves things that may not be his. Lotte Kaars is friend of mine."

Catherine ran one fingernail along the grain of kitchen table.

"What would you ask him?"

"Southwark is not so big. I ask where is gun from? Where is gun now? Who had gun that shoots your police friend?"

"And he would be able to find out? I can't imagine him wanting to get involved in police business."

"Is not police business. Is Katerina business. And so is mine. Henrik does not speak to police, no. He speak to Lotte, and Lotte speak to fat old Mrs Bessovitch."

They face each other, in the alley where they stood before. The Whitechapel Murderer looms, his coat open. Dry knows where the other's knife is—slid into the belt at the back. One of the man's hands is always close to his hip, ready to reach behind him and slip it free.

It is tempting to end matters here, but Dry has purpose. The greater satisfaction would come from seeing this through to a more subtle conclusion than a mere back-street stabbing.

The other man is waiting. Dry begins.

"A woman—a cheap whore—has been gathering word from others of her kind. They talk of you, and would name you to the police if they could be sure. Jack, she says, I think I may know Bloody Jack."

"They have all been wrong, the poxed birds. She does not know me." The other man pulls his arm back, steps left and then right, watching the alley ends.

"This one is closer than you believe." Dry reaches slowly inside his jacket, so as not to alarm, and pulls out a handbill with the picture of a woman printed upon it. The man takes it.

"I am not sure I recognise that face," he says.

"The one who sends me knows it well. She has had many names—Andriette is one. She spreads her legs cheaply."

Catherine turned in troubled sleep, her memories and visions blurring, confused. She needed to urinate, but could not seem to rise, to pull away from what invaded her night…

The Whitechapel Murderer spits. "And she has wind of me, you say? This is your master's warning?"

Dry is satisfied to see the first trace of agitation.

"A courtesy, between two who know the value of a sharp knife. And an opportunity."

The man's face betrays his need for acclaim. A compliment, passed on from the Deptford Assassin. Respect, recognition, for his actions. He is close to being hooked.

A fox or cat shrieks some streets away. Men stumble and laugh as they pass the alley, not looking in.

"It is true I have not carved for some time," says the man. "Not since the two who offered themselves up in one night."

"The woman will be alone this Friday morning, between three and five of the clock. It has been carefully arranged. Before that time, her legs will be spread, and you would be seen by whatever man that uses her; after five of the clock, the world awakes and there are no guarantees."

"Little more than a day away. Why?"

"To determine if you are one who merits attention. Besides, if it is to be done, better now than when the woman squeals at the nearest police station. She is a cunning vixen, and may soon be sure enough to risk it, perhaps next week."

"And if I ignore your master's word? What if I leave this whore to her fleas and fluxes, or slice her when I please—tonight, or in a week's time?"

"Then you are not Jack," says Dry. "The Deptford Assassin has seen such as you come and go, cocksure in their prowess and dedication at first. They do not last. They relent, repent; they blunder. Or they are given up by mothers, sisters, wives and Andriettes, betrayed to dance the hangman's jig."

Dry feels that last touch appropriate. The man wears prejudice on his arm.

"A test, and one not on my terms," mutters the other.

"Each kill is a test. You know that better than most."

A grunt of assent. "Alone, you said. Where?"

"At her room. Thirteen Miller's Court, off Dorset Street. I have seen it—a dismal, quiet place, not visible from the street. Though if you are afraid…"

The other man kicks out at the dead rat, almost splitting it with his boot. A flare of anger in the gloom of the alley.

"Afraid? What need have I of fear? That's what I give them,

before I open their bellies. But if I find this Miller's Court lined with bluejackets and pistols…"

"You do not have to fear the police," says Dry. "That I guarantee."

On the Thursday morning, two days after she visited the inspector in the infirmary, Catherine was handed a name and an address, scrawled on the back of a butcher's account slip. From a cousin of a woman who once worked with a friend of Henrik Kaars's daughter, said the landlady.

"No one knows where name is from," said Mrs Bessovitch, and gave a slow, solemn wink. "Is mystery."

The details, rewritten neatly on a sheet of notepaper, was in Superintendent Neylan's hands within the half hour. He peered at it, turned it over a few times.

"This comes from your Sight, Madame Rostov?"

"A Guardian Spirit heard me, superintendent."

He nodded, smiling faintly. "Mrs Neylan…often wishes she had the Gift."

"It is a burden, also. Not to be asked for lightly, or used lightly either. I do not think that she would welcome the troubles it would bring."

Stronger nods, of approval this time.

"Indeed, indeed. I do feel the same. I am, as ever, pleased to note that you understand these matters, Madame. I shall have the men out instantly, and to this place. Let us pray for Justice."

Being Neylan, he meant that quite literally, and Catherine had to stand with him in the corridor for a long minute, head lowered.

"Good," he said at last. "Sergeant Cubbins, rouse a patrol. Two inspectors, and six of our most experienced constables."

"Should I perhaps—" Catherine began.

"Your part is done, Madame. Now we men must do the Lords' work."

The Superintendent was not someone with whom you argued, however dubious his statements. Though to his credit, she thought, he was actually going to lead the raid on the address in question. For the injury done to Eden Mallick, or for the principle of the matter, she did not know.

This time she kept her nerve and waited. She had one of Charlotte Chambers's more lurid novels in her bag, started the previous week, and she read it without seeing the words—at the end, she could not have given a single clue as to the plot, or the names of the major characters. Excepting that too many of the men in it were called George.

One hour, then a half hour more, and another quarter…

Superintendent Neylan strode into the station, his jacket askew and a rip in his right sleeve.

"Taken, Madame Rostov!" It was the most cheerful she had seen him. "Taken, praise the Lord, and the crime confessed, before all."

It would not have done to shake his hand, but she would have liked to. The officers who followed him were of equal good cheer, muted only by their superintendent's presence. One had his arm in a makeshift sling, another a bruised eye.

"The brothers of Ned Ginny, the butcher's apprentice," said Neylan, restoring some order to his uniform. "Hard, powerful men. We were Davids to their Goliaths, but we had Right on our side."

"Ginny? The boy who fired on that other gang near the Compass Rose tavern, months past?"

"The very same. His older brothers have apparently held grievance against Inspector Mallick ever since Ned Ginny went down for his crimes. Another gun came into their hands; a sudden opportunity taken, the cowards."

One of the other inspectors, Jentry, could not restrain a chuckle. "We took them in their lair, three of them, with the weapon and a fair few other goods which weren't rightfully theirs as well. And Mr Neylan was at them, bless me, he was."

Justice, at least, for Eden Mallick. If she could trust the surgeons, then one small corner of her world might yet be in order. She must go and see Mallick again, take him fruit. It was admitting that he was practically a friend, but she had few enough of those. There would be a reason for that, but what it was she did not know.

She had a slow, strange walk home, her head filled with so many thoughts. Exhausted and footsore, Catherine stretched out on her bed.

Turning on her mattress, she hoped she would not dream. And she doubted that her wish would be granted. Friday morning was only hours away.

Today was the eighth day of November, 1888.

CHAPTER TWENTY EIGHT

Whitechapel, November 1888

The second act is easier than the first. He has sent a note that day to the prostitute Gabriella Gorse, writ in a fair copy of his informant's weak hand, easy done.

> I must speak to you urgent. There is something you do not know about the gang with which you run, a threat. Though we are not friends, we are both women who must trust the street, and you are at risk. Come to Thirteen Miller's Court between two and three in the morning, when I pledge none will see. Ginger.

This to set his other target in motion.

Show them what they desire, what they fear. They do not understand the craft, will not sit and wait as he will. They will rush to heed the call. Gorse will go to Miller's Court either to learn, or to punish Mary Jane Kelly. Nor is the Whitechapel Murderer likely to resist his role in the intrigue.

And if, by some unlikely stroke, neither arrives and none of this can come about, then there are a dozen other ways to achieve the end he requires, all waiting to be played upon the stage.

They do not understand how Time is their servant, not their master.

They are not Edwin Dry.

Catherine woke, relieved herself in the pot. Her head held lightning from temple to temple, and she could tell that it would not matter if she slept that night. From the house next door to the lodgings came the strains of Mr and Mrs Gowing, the retired couple once more at their hymns. They sang late each night in their parlour, accompanied, Mrs Bessovitch said, by a small glass of whisky to end the day.

"Doubts are abroad: make Thou these doubts
to cease;
"Fears are within: set Thou these fears at rest!
"Strife is among us: melt that strife to peace!
"Change marches onward: may all change be
blest!"

She put a shawl around her shoulders, and brought out the last of the brandy from the wardrobe. It was Deptford again, and the night would unfurl inside her head regardless.

Edwin Dry haunted her, possessed her.

Strife is among us.

Midnight has long gone, and the deep dark of the small hours clings to the streets around Miller's Court. Dry attends to those streets, keeps them under his eye from the heights.

Two figures move through the thin fog. The woman called Gorse has not come alone, which is no surprise to Dry. She heads for Dorset Street with a man trailing her at a distance, a member of the local gang she serves. She and Kelly are near enough alike to the eye for his purposes, but her escort must be removed. This is not a time for complications.

When Gorse is about to turn off Bell Lane, Dry moves, slipping down from his vantage point. A hand goes over the man's mouth and a slender blade pierces one kidney, then the other. Less bloody than the throat. He slides the body into shadows to be dealt with later, whips free the man's long coat and puts it over his own shoulders, purloining the battered, wide-brimmed felt hat as well. A moment later, the woman's supposed protector is on the corner of the street, half-obscured by brickwork.

"I 'as to check a matter," says Dry, a low whisper which could come from any man. "I'll be behind yer."

The woman hesitates, but heads down Dorset Street all the same, to enter Miller's Court.

This is not a coat suited for what is to come—it constricts his shoulders and flaps at his thighs. He bundles it into a doorway near the body, retrieving his own hat as well.

Gorse will find the room in Miller's Court—Mary Jane Kelly's room—open and empty. A low fire burns. There are papers on the bed, copies of the information which Kelly collected on difficult and dangerous clients, on men who held some peculiarity in their stance or in their eyes. The route to the Whitechapel Murderer, when placed next to Dry's own observations. The woman will pry, will look at these papers, pondering their significance. Her attention will be distracted...

She will bear a different name by the time the night is done, and Kelly herself will achieve that other goal, to flee this place, supposed dead—free of debts, enemies and history. The small fears which have plagued her for so long.

Mr Edwin Dry is a fair man, and keeps all fair bargains.

Through the passage Gorse goes, under the damp brick arch. A candle burns in Number Thirteen, a single shabby room with a broken window-pane, directly off the courtyard. The door is half open, and she goes inside.

He waits a minute, and follows.

In, and across the room to where she stands by the table, her back to him. His hand goes over her mouth; his blade comes round from behind and pierces her heart in a single thrust, stilling it forever. This is his act of mercy. If the woman must die—and she must—he will not leave her alive to satisfy the perversions of the one who comes.

He props the body on the bed, face to the wall, as if asleep. It will do, and he must be away, to a perch already prepared. If "Jack" comes to Miller's Court, all will fall into place.

The houses clustered around the court are of mixed substance, crumbling in parts. Dry has been here twice recently, testing for loose tiles and stonework too weak to bear much weight. He has rope ready, to ascend and descend, and the drainpipe by Number Thirteen is just sufficient to bear him up and to the side. Only just—the brackets set into the wall give slightly as he climbs.

Crouched by a chimney stack, he lets the night hold him quiet.

By his pocket watch it is twenty minutes until four when another shadow falls in the passage. A figure slides along by the brickwork, glances around the empty courtyard and is presumably satisfied. The single gas-lamp on the wall below is enough to show Dry that this is no passing stranger or drunken seeker of a woman's pleasures. It is the one.

No doubt the killer has already quartered the area, assuring himself that the constabulary do not lurk in wait. Satisfied, his vanity has led him to the heart of the affair. It is as Dry expected.

The candle is guttering as the man enters Number Thirteen. Gorse's body will still be warm. Unless the Whitechapel Murderer suspects intrigue against him, he will follow his pattern and slice the woman's throat first, thinking he guarantees silence. If he realises that he deals with a corpse, he may run.

Or he may still carve, believing that an offering has been left for him.

There is no sudden exit, but a scuffle of activity inside. Dry can smell the opening of the body, even from where he is. He remains motionless for almost ten minutes, knowing that butchery is underway, and then his rope, slender but strong, goes over the edge of the wall. He slides down it to the paving stones, blade in hand. It would not do to fire a shot this night.

He approaches Kelly's room, the door still slightly ajar. Through the dirty window next to it he can make out the killer standing over the bed. Carving. If the man thought the woman dead, unconscious from drink, or deep in the grip of laudanum, it did not make him pause. The huffing of excited breath as he cuts is distasteful.

Dry kicks the door full open and lunges...

And the man has moved. An eight inch knife is in his hand, blocking Dry's thrust. The edge is dark with blood. He has speed, this one, and animal senses. Dry spins on his heel and ducks low so that the riposte goes above his head.

A bare half inch above it.

Dry's blade is reversed, driven down into the man's right boot, piercing the leather and the arch of the foot. A hiss from the other.

Recover and away, ready. Dry has his back to the hearth; the killer to the wall opposite, by the bed. The body upon the bed is a shambles of ripped and mutilated flesh. Gorse's face has gone, and much of the belly.

"What is this?" The tall man twists his lip up at one side. "Sent his apprentice, has he, the guv'nor from Deptford? His messenger boy means to test my mettle. Or do you have your own ambitions— maybe to steal Jackie's glory?"

Dry does not speak. Speech uses breath, concentration. He calculates, judging the man's next move. He might seek to use height and weight on the smaller man, or...

The open door. The Whitechapel Murderer is planning to escape. He does not care to fight an armed man, it appears.

He will not be given the choice tonight.

Dry leaps and slashes at the first twitch of movement, a cut to the other's knife-arm as the man charges for the door, but both are in motion and the cut is too shallow. Cloth and a sliver of skin. The killer is away into the courtyard, but not towards the passage to Dorset Street. Tenements line both sides of the short courtyard until it ends in a blank wall and the rear of taller buildings on Brushfield Street, to the north. Only the rooftops offer escape that way...

So Dry's quarry also has a head for heights.

A drainpipe creaks but holds, propelling the pursued man to the angle between the wall of another building and the Miller's Court roofs; Dry takes to the rope that he left in place, climbing up the side of the courtyard wall and along the tiles. The soles of his boots, painted with latex for this purpose, are almost silent.

Seven, eight paces between them.

Dry gains as the other man struggles by a rusting gutter pipe, heading high and east towards Christ Church, but the footing in this corner is uneven, uncertain—missing tiles and crudely patched gaps; lead unseated or stripped away by local entrepreneurs. With a glance behind him, the man drops down into the next courtyard, staggering as he lands. He has begun to favour the foot pierced by Dry's knife.

Dry is down after him, knees bent to take the shock, springing up to follow.

Six paces.

This yard leads through another arch and onto Commercial Street, an open stretch of tramlines and occasional traffic. The delivery men will be about their rounds soon.

The hands of the Christ Church clock, not so far away, stand at almost four in the morning.

In her Southwark lodgings, Catherine Weatherhead had lost her sight.

She could feel the crumpled linen of the bed beneath her, but she could not see the bed, her hands, her room. Her nostrils pricked to the smell of the Whitechapel streets—night-soil and horse dung, urine in the alleys, damp clothes hung across narrow streets. Cheap beer spilled in doorways, long with vomit.

She was possessed by the sight of two men, two monsters.

Let bishops debate whilst the workman does his job.

London town must provide...

The moon is near its first quarter, a bright crescent barely clouded now. The silver wound of it illuminates Commercial Street and the ways beyond. Almshouses and chapels, slum tenements and public houses, some showing a faint light. Mile End in the distance; breweries and rookeries around.

Dry's quarry slows, twists into Wood Street and Princes Street, past the synagogue and the old Yiddish Theatre. Four storeys of red brick and blank windows—no way to the roof ridges here. Brick Lane and back on himself, back towards the church. The man clearly knows the habits of the local police—he is dodging between routes where the constables trudge.

It is a strange pursuit.

Neither man wishes to be seen by others, and they move in silence. The pursued slows as two drunks stagger down the road and gape around, then speeds forward once the drunks have passed; the pursuer follows in the same fashion, but always closer.

Four paces.

Christ Church ahead once more, the white spire etched against the thick sliver of the moon. His man is tiring; there are occasional spots of blood on the pavement from his foot. Dry sees him vault into the churchyard, perhaps meaning to slip behind the rectangular bulk of the church and lose his pursuer. Great porch and Tuscan columns gleam ahead, but are not reached.

Two paces between them, and Dry is the faster.

He slides low on the damp grass, right arm outstretched, and his blade slices across the back of the man's left knee, cutting into the tendons. The man staggers, curses—the first sound he has made since the room in Miller's Court.

Dry has said no word since his misdirection to the prostitute, Gorse.

A limping turn by the Whitechapel Murderer. Left leg weak, right foot bleeding.

"Your guts, then, errand boy" says the man, steadying himself and raising his own knife.

Wet turf, the faint humps of old burials, a broken bottle or two and discarded protections from trysts behind the walls. The lawn of the churchyard is more treacherous than the cobbles of Commercial Street.

Dry has danced before; will dance again. Feint and thrust, the recover, the sudden break to one side, and turn. Never be still, when the opponent has strength and reach. His mind trusts his hands; his hands trust the blade.

The tall man has no formal skill in the fight, but he brings long, powerful arms and the will to survive. He brings growing anger, enough that in the next moment of their dance, he manages to slash Dry along the shoulder, the blow not so deep, but painful.

He does not remember when an opponent last cut him, but memory—and pain—must wait.

The killer takes a ragged breath. "Your master knew his business when he took you on. But you'll see that I am worthy. Concede, and we'll finish splitting the bitch together."

Dry gives no answer as they engage again; another wild blow comes close to his gut, but he pivots and is elsewhere. The killer is so very unschooled that he cannot easily be predicted, and Dry takes measure of that. The energy which drives his opponent is the same loathing that fuelled the deaths of five women. He knows, however, that he can outlast this brute.

Blades clash once more, without result. Both men step back, and in the heartbeat that they pull apart, an owl, of all things, calls across the churchyard.

For reasons which will never be known, the other man looks up.

"Enough, I believe," says Dry, and slashes deep across the tall man's wrist, making his opponent drop his knife. Before the other man can react, he leaps high and slams the weighted pommel of his weapon into the centre of the man's forehead, dropping him to his knees.

Dry lands steady and poised.

It is interesting. He has used such a blow before, and taken a man's consciousness with it. This one is dazed, but still aware.

"You," the other gasps. "You are no messenger. You are The Tradesman, the Deptford Assassin."

"The newspapers call me so."

Dry kicks the fallen knife far from reach, and shifts his own blade to the other hand, the undamaged arm.

"But I have…I have admired your work."

"I am indifferent to your admiration. You yourself are…" He pauses, considering the words. "An inconvenience."

The man on his knees looks confused, unsure.

"You wanted them, the whores? I said, we could share—"

"I want for nothing."

A dazed half-movement to rise; an iron-toed boot cracks the man's undamaged knee. He moans and sinks again.

They are silent statues in the moonlight, facing each other. The Whitechapel Murderer coughs, and lifts his head. His look is sly, a last search for some form of control.

"So, you have the advantage of Jackie boy, but who is Jack?"

Blood trickles down his forehead, the skin broken where the pommel struck. "All London wishes to know who I truly am, my story. Am I judge or Jew, doctor or docker?" The man laughs. "All London seeks me. And my name will be remembered, for—"

The exquisite blade seeks its target. Up through throat, tongue and palate, deep into the brain of one who liked to be called "Jack."

"All London seeks a clean privy," says the Deptford Assassin to the body which slumps before him. "Hardly a recommendation. As for your true name, I have no interest in the matter. It is dust, and will stay there."

He slides the blade free, wipes it on the man's coat and inspects the edges. Sharp as ever, and un-notched. Only now does he notice that his breath is tight with exertion. A rare occurrence. His hat is askew, and his jacket will have to be replaced. The slash in the cloth at the shoulder would make an ugly mend, even for a tailor of some talent.

But he is satisfied.

If he were a beast, a primordial force of nature, he would raise his face to the moon and howl his triumph. And the world would shake, that such as he walked this sorry Earth and held dominion over it. When he chose to.

He is, however, Edwin Dry. He brushes down his lapels, and makes sure that the encounter has caused no damage to his hat.

He has standards.

In the shadow of Christ Church, he drags the corpse upright and gets one arm around it. Cumbersome, but not impossible to transport. If any other should be walking the streets, they will see a drunk being escorted home by his friend.

He could leave the body here in plain view, a mystery for the police to consider, but why give the killer that grace? The man, even dead, offends him. A common murderer at heart, an amateur with an unpleasant weakness. Not even fit to be called an apprentice.

Not so far from here is a pig-yard, much like the one where someone once practised on a sow's carcass. The animals will be hungry.

The coarse teeth of pigs will rend the body—tainted meat, but they will not care. They will not wonder who he was.

By dawn the Whitechapel Murderer will be ordure in their sty.

CHAPTER TWENTY NINE

Southwark, November 1888

She was bleeding, her stomach hot and cramped. The moon's gift, a few days early, the same night she saw Edwin Dry at his work and the death of the Whitechapel Murderer—as if blood could bring blood. Confused, she managed to find a sanitary bandage in the drawer of her night-stand and press it between her legs. Some part of her was still in Whitechapel, a lantern show of fading images…

The pigs are fed, and mighty pleased they were with an early break to the night's fast.

Small tasks remain to be completed.

Dry must return to Miller's Court without delay, and ensure that the scarlet scene of another's butchery serves its second purpose, one which completes the commission. If Kelly wishes to be presumed dead, the body in Number Thirteen must not be identifiable. Gorse the understudy will step forward into a final leading role.

The Whitechapel Murderer has already conducted a frenzied mutilation—a savage progression from his earlier work. No one would know this woman, apart from hair and height. Little more will need be done with the bloody corpse. A few errant items can be disposed of on the low fire which still crackles in the grate, and the room arranged to suit those who will discover the scene— neighbours, creditors or constables. The details always matter.

Better if he could have put an end to the killer nearer Dorset Street—the chase has eaten into the time allotted. Each minute lost increases the chance that someone will look in through the cracked window of Thirteen Miller's Court before he wishes it.

He will retrieve his rope, and remove any other sign that he himself has been in the vicinity, leaving by the rooftops once more. The stage, when Dry has gone, will show only that a man entered, killed, and cut the woman who lived there.

For the newspapers and their readers, their "Jack" will have struck again. A select few, when he has reported his main commission done, will comfort themselves that the killer who so vexed them is gone.

"Mary Jane Kelly" will be the last victim of the Whitechapel Murderer.

Catherine gulped down water, and wondered if she should call out for Mrs Bessovitch. Her legs were shaking, and she had no more brandy in her room…

He is satisfied. All trace of Edwin Dry has gone from Miller's Court and Dorset Street. No one has marked his passage between the crooked chimney pots. He eases the body of Gorse's escort—a detail delayed but not forgotten—into a ruined cellar a few streets away, even as wagons stacked with milk churns begin to clatter on the streets. The tenement above is uninhabitable, even by East End standards, and will be demolished in the next few days, bringing all down upon the anonymous corpse; the November weather will keep it until then.

One single and signal item remains, some streets away. The knife of the Whitechapel Murderer lies in Christ Church yard, worthless now in the long grass which covers so many dead.

This he will leave for others.

Warm arms held her; the lullaby sang in her ears, a little cracked and tuneless but so welcome. Her lap felt damp, and when she looked down, she saw that Mrs B had removed her under-garments and wiped her clean, wrapping an old petticoat around her waist.

"You say things," murmured the landlady. "You dream, and say 'Christ Church.' It is vision, da?"

"Da. Yes." Catherine swallowed. "He has…I cannot say it.

Yes, another vision, a terrible one."

"This man in bowler hat—he does bad thing?"

"Bad? I no longer know. A wicked thing or a marvellous one. A necessary one, I pray."

"This is world. Some times, is many years later when we know which is which."

Catherine eased herself free of her landlady's arms. "I must wash, dress. I will have to send word to someone. What time is it?"

"Almost eleven in morning. Can I take message for you, Katerina?"

"You are a dear, but it is my responsibility. I have passed coin to the Devil, and bought what I had to."

Had she wanted to eat, there would have been no time. Before she had finished dressing and bound back her hair, someone was at the door. Catherine heard low, guarded speech from her landlady, then Mrs Bessovitch was on the stair.

"I think you come, Katerina."

The visitor was a slim, middle-aged man with a long brown coat. "Mr Swanson would see you. At the infirmary."

Catherine gripped the balustrade.

"Inspector Mallick—"

"Will you come with me, miss? The Chief Inspector is waiting." Crisp, but not unfriendly.

"This is not arrest?" Mrs Bessovitch stood close, formidable.

"No. An urgent, quiet word, that is all."

She was helped into the cab, to be followed by the slim man.

"You are with the police?"

"I am with Mr Swanson." He would say no more.

The cab driver took a fair pace through the morning traffic, depositing them at the main infirmary doors. Swanson's man gestured to her.

"Inspector Mallick is well. Mr Swanson has been sitting with him, but would speak to you alone. There is a room, to your left, a former porter's office. You should wait there."

The night had left her confused, unsure. She went where she was told, and for want of anything else to do, sat down on a linen box in the corner of the room. Shelves were piled with bed-linen in crisp white order and folded uniforms—nurses' garb, perhaps.

Swanson arrived soon after, turning and using his weight to slam the door shut behind him.

"I might apologise, lassie, but time is short. If we meet here, then none will ask—all do ken that I visit Eden Mallick, ay, to check his progress. The one who brought you will nae talk." He paced, his boots coming down heavily on worn floorboards, deep furrows above the bridge of his nose. "When is it to be done, for God's sake? Yuir man…there's been anither, a rare cutting-up that will give the newspapers joy and bring down more talk on oor poor necks, as though—"

"It is over, Chief Inspector."

He had not seen her face as he rushed in. Now he looked, and looked again. She knew from her wash-stand mirror that the night had left its marks. Her eyes were shadowed, bloodshot; her lips were pale.

"Over? What dae ye mean? A woman has been murdered, off Dorset Street."

"That was the last, I swear. The Whitechapel Murderer is dead."

"At the hands of…yuir hound from Deptford?"

"Yes."

He gritted his teeth, lost for a moment in unknown thoughts. "The guid Lord knows, I had my doubts on all o' this. Ye swear he's gone, this Jack?"

She could not tell him how she had seen it, felt it, but she must convince him. Men like Swanson were fond of facts…

"The killer was taken straight after his deed at Miller's Court. Yes, I know what has happened, and where. But I assure you he was served justice. One knee—the left one—slashed, the other shattered. A long blade thrust into his wicked head, and the end swift after. Dead, Mr Swanson." Fragments of that other place spun behind her eyes. "Do you know Christ Church, in Spitalfields?"

"Aye, I ken it well enough."

"Send your man outside to that place. Or an officer you trust. In the churchyard, ten paces from the oldest yew to the east, and half-hidden where the grass has not been cut. You will find a knife there. If you have a police surgeon with tight lips, let him examine it. It is the one used at Miller's Court, and on most, if not all, the other women. It will not be used again."

Swanson let out a breath which sounded as if it had been held for weeks.

"Ye swear? No, I cannae keep asking that." He leaned against the shelving, fingers pressed to one temple. "Ye tell me that we have grand victory, and few will know."

"They will know eventually, when no more mutilated women are found on your streets."

"Aye. True enough. I'll ha' the body, then? Many will wish to know who he was."

"That is also gone, and the name with it." She looked up at him. "Better this way, Mr Swanson."

"How so? Am I to be swindled?" An angry, petulant touch to his voice.

It was something which had weighed on her, had grown as she read yet one more newspaper's speculations, or seen yet another supposed identification of the murderer in the spiritualist journals. Dry had also influenced her feelings on the matter, she supposed. The man they called Jack was nothing, and worth no one's time. Any care, any consideration or debate, should be saved for the poor women he had slaughtered.

But perhaps there was another, practical argument she could use on Swanson.

"What is your Scots saying, Chief Inspector? Wheesht a moment, and think about what you say. His identity died with him, and so did what might have followed."

"What might have followed?"

"Yes. Consider it. Were he to prove a Jew, a Pole or German, there would be demonstrations, even riots. Mobs would seek out others of his kind. Prejudice would feed, and innocents would suffer."

His frown brought thick eyebrows so close together they might have been one.

"And were he to turn out to be of high station or rank," she continued, "Then you would face worse, in other ways. Deceptions and concealments would be in order—or scandal. Would the women be less dead for that? Would your job be easier?"

Swanson's scowl remained. "Ye have a point, lassie. But—"

"It is done. Let us be thankful."

They stared at each other, challenge or assessment. Catherine could not tell. He was the first to look away, though.

"I will arrange to send you the remainder o' the fee. If the knife is where you say, and all else tallies."

"It will. And the man will find me to receive his due, I have no doubt." She clutched her arms around herself. "I wonder though—I cannot help but wonder…we have done something, set a hound on a hound, as you would have it. Are we the better for using such a dreadful device?"

He looked away from her.

"There are two or three folk above me," he said. "High above me, ye ken, not those at Scotland Yard. They approved when I told them what I might do—yuir name was not mentioned, if ye feared that. But lassie, they approved so quick that I have ma doubts as to their games. This man, the Deptford Assassin, as the papers call him. I asked once, should we no be hot on his heels?"

"I would question as to whether or not he could be taken."

"Aye, there's that, but listen tae me. I was told, and didnae like it, that I should look elsewhere. Why, I asked? Because there are times, they said. Because there are times."

"Such as now?" Catherine rose from the linen box. "We shall never know who has called on him before, Chief Inspector. How many villains or innocents he has claimed."

"It galls me, lassie."

"Then you are a decent man. I have summoned the monster twice, and must live with it. You have only done your duty. What will you do next?"

Swanson sighed. "There are names I can throw around, to please others. It will dae nay harm. And there will be false claimants, and those who would copy what has been done. We cannae be so sure that all were by the same hand. Those above will hear the truth; the rest o' us will carry on oor work. We will speculate and cast blame aroond, pretending I had never met ye. Oor single comfort is yuir certainty."

"My word is good."

She did not want to see Eden Mallick as unkempt as she was, She would come another day. All Swanson could tell her was that the inspector might yet keep his arm—the surgeons were more hopeful than before.

The Chief Inspector's man outside still had the hansom close by, and offered it to her. She accepted. It was early in the afternoon, but she needed to sleep—and prayed that it would be dreamless.

Two men, two wicked men, had died—Frederick Caille and the Whitechapel Murderer—and it was Mardy Cath Weatherhead of Fell Lane, Keighley, who had done for them. Not by her own hand, but by her word. Which was not always good, but surely held purpose.

As the hansom took her back to Mrs Bessovitch and safety, with a clatter of wheels on cobbles and the annoyed cries of the cab-man, Catherine sat back, her mind elsewhere. She had revulsion, doubt, and satisfaction at war within her.

And perhaps—in dark and solitary moments to come—there would be a touch of fear in there as well.

He has her scent.

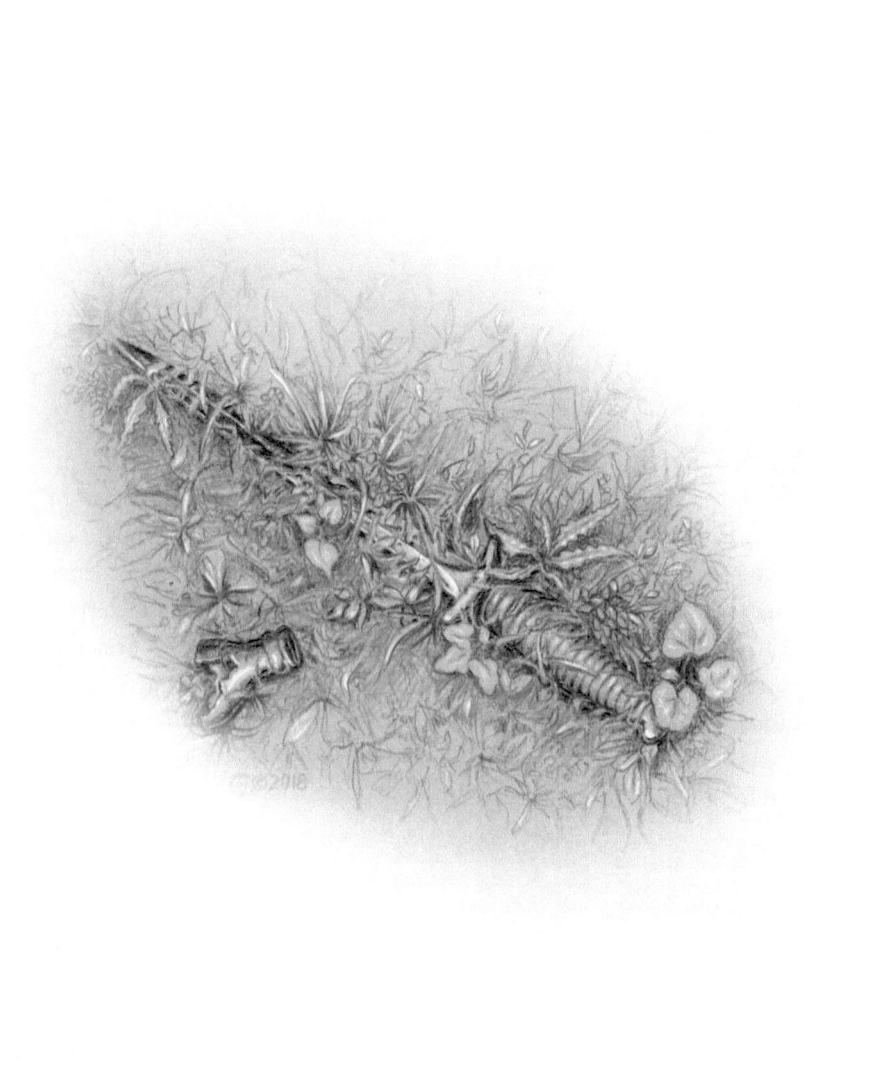

To understand more fully events hidden from the point-of-view character, Catherine Weatherhead, in this story, please read the companion novel, *The Prostitute's Price*, by Alan M. Clark, also available from IFD Publishing.

About the Author

John Linwood Grant is a professional writer/editor who lives in Yorkshire with a pack of lurchers and a beard. Widely published in magazines and anthologies, he writes strange period fiction, including the Mamma Lucy tales of 1920s hoodoo, the Last Edwardian series and contemporary weird stories. He is also editor of Occult Detective Quarterly, plus forthcoming anthologies, including 'ODQ Presents' and 'Hell's Empire', the incursion of the Prince of Darkness's forces into Victorian Britain. News of his projects can be found on his popular website greydogtales.com, which explores weird fiction and weird art. And lurchers.

IFD Publishing Paperbacks

Novels:

Of Thimble and Threat, by Alan M. Clark
Baggage Check, by Elizabeth Engstrom
Bull's Labyrinth, by Eric Witchey
The Surgeon's Mate: A Dismemoir, by Alan M. Clark
Siren Promised, by Jeremy Robert Johnson and Alan M. Clark
Say Anything but Your Prayers, by Alan M. Clark
Candyland, by Elizabeth Engstrom
Apologies to the Cat's Meat Man, by Alan M. Clark
Lizzie Borden, by Elizabeth Engstrom
A Parliament of Crows, by Alan M. Clark
Lizard Wine, by Elizabeth Engstrom
The Door that Faced West, by Alan M. Clark
The Northwoods Chronicles, by Elizabeth Engstrom
The Prostitute's Price, by Alan M. Clark
The Assassin's Coin, by John Linwood Grant
13 Miller's Court, by Alan M. Clark and John Linwood Grant
Guys Named Bob, by Elizabeth Engstrom

Collections:
Professor Witchey's Miracle Mood Cure, by Eric Witchey

Nonfiction:
How to Write a Sizzling Sex Scene, by Elizabeth Engstrom

IFD Publishing EBooks

(You can find the following titles at most distribution points for all ereading platforms.)

Novels:

The Prostitute's Price, by Alan M. Clark
The Assassin's Coin, by John Linwood Grant
13 Miller's Court, by Alan M. Clark and John Linwood Grant
Guys Named Bob, by Elizabeth Engstrom

Apologies to the Cat's Meat Man, by Alan M. Clark
Bull's Labyrinth, by Eric Witchey
The Surgeon's Mate: A Dismemoir, by Alan M. Clark
York's Moon, by Elizabeth Engstrom
Beyond the Serpent's Heart, by Eric Witchey
Lizzie Borden, by Elizabeth Engstrom
A Parliament of Crows, by Alan M. Clark
Lizard Wine, by Elizabeth Engstrom
Northwoods Chronicles, by Elizabeth Engstrom
Siren Promised, by Alan M. Clark and Jeremy Robert Johnson
To Kill a Common Loon, by Mitch Luckett
The Man in the Loon, by Mitch Luckett
Jack the Ripper Victim Series: Of Thimble and Threat by Alan M. Clark
Jack the Ripper Victim Series: The Double Event (includes two novels from the series: *Of Thimble and Threat* and *Say Anything But Your Prayers*) by Alan M. Clark
Candyland, by Elizabeth Engstrom
The Blood of Father Time: Book 1, The New Cut, by Alan M. Clark, Stephen C. Merritt & Lorelei Shannon
The Blood of Father Time: Book 2, The Mystic Clan's Grand Plot, by Alan M. Clark, Stephen C. Merritt & Lorelei Shannon
How I Met My Alien Bitch Lover: Book 1 from the Sunny World Inquisition Daily Letter Archives, by Eric Witchey
Baggage Check, by Elizabeth Engstrom
D. D. Murphry, Secret Policeman, by Alan M. Clark and Elizabeth Massie
Black Leather, by Elizabeth Engstrom

Novelettes:
The Tao of Flynn, by Eric Witchey
To Build a Boat, Listen to Trees, by Eric Witchey

Children's Illustrated:
The Christmas Thingy, by F. Paul Wilson. Illustrated by Alan M. Clark

Collections:
Suspicions, by Elizabeth Engstrom
Professor Witchey's Miracle Mood Cure, by Eric Witchey

Short Fiction:
"Brittle Bones and Old Rope," by Alan M. Clark
"Crosley," by Elizabeth Engstrom
"The Apple Sniper," by Eric Witchey

Nonfiction:
How to Write a Sizzling Sex Scene, by Elizabeth Engstrom

IFD Publishing Audio Books

Novels:
The Door That Faced West by Alan M. Clark, read by Charles Hinckley
Jack the Ripper Victim Series: Of Thimble and Threat, by Alan M. Clark, read by Alicia Rose
Jack the Ripper Victim Series: Say Anything But Your Prayers, by Alan M. Clark, read by Alicia Rose
Jack the Ripper Victim Series: The Double Event by Alan M. Clark, read by Alicia Rose (includes two novels from the series: *Of Thimble and Threat* and *Say Anything But Your Prayers*)
A Parliament of Crows by Alan M. Clark, read by Laura Jennings
A Brutal Chill in August by Alan M. Clark, read by Alicia Rose
The Surgeon's Mate: A Dismemoir, by Alan M. Clark, read by Alan M. Clark
Apologies to the Cat's Meat Man, by Alan M. Clark, read by Alicia Rose
The Prostitute's Price, by Alan M. Clark, read by Alicia Rose